MW01671208

going
going
gone

going
going
gone

A JOURNEY
INTO THE HEREAFTER

D. D. Lanz

Two Harbors Press
322 First Avenue N, 5th floor
Minneapolis, MN 55401
612.455.2293
www.TwoHarborsPress.com

ISBN-13: 978-1-62652-782-9
LCCN: 2014905160

Distributed by Itasca Books

Cover Design by Alan Pranke
Typeset by Jenni Wheeler

Printed in the United States of America

Dedicated to the atheists, agnostics, and Christians

looking for answers to this life and the one beyond

CHAPTER ONE

Sentenced to Death

"I have bad news for you, Mr. Janne," Dr. Davis says as he enters his office and sits down.

I'd prepared myself for bad news, but his tone and the look on his face are much worse than I'd expected. My shoulders slump, my stomach falls, and my head drops to my chest. We sit in silence until I finally raise my head.

He stands up and places a scan in the light box, and we look at it for a few moments. "You have lung cancer, and it has spread." Pointing to several spots on the scan, he says, "It is a very aggressive cancer, and it's already advanced a great deal—you have stage four cancer." There is more silence as he gives me a minute to fully understand what he is saying.

"What are my options?" I ask.

"As I see it, you have two options. The first is an aggressive regimen of chemotherapy. The other would be to accept the diagnosis, in which case I would prescribe pain medication to comfort you."

"So this is terminal if left untreated?"

"Yes," he says. "You would have maybe six or seven months. The first two you would see a slow deterioration and the last month would be rapid deterioration. The cancer cells have invaded your lungs deeply, and they will induce pneumonia. Your lungs will no longer absorb oxygen, and breathing will become labored and eventually shut down."

"And what about chemo?"

"That would start as soon as possible and would last indefinitely."

"And what are the chances of success?"

"The cure ratio is one in ten."

"By that you mean nine out of ten will die anyway," I say.

"Yes."

I realize "one in ten" is his way of giving me some measure of hope, when there really is none. Doctors always want to leave the patient with some measure of hope.

As the doctor continues to speak, I'm overcome with fear. The chemo treatment, which would likely be of no use, would make my final days even worse. I wouldn't be able to eat, my taste buds would die, and I'd lose my hair. Nausea and fatigue would be my future. I know that if I choose to live out my last days this way, I'll become bitter and irrational, making my wife's life a living hell, not to mention my own.

"Now you have my considered opinion, but you may want to seek a second opinion."

Right, I think. *This is the Mayo Clinic.*

We sit in silence for a while. When he finally stands up, he says I should speak with my family and decide what to do within the next few days. He puts his hand on my back, and we walk out to the nurse's station, where he writes prescriptions for several medications, including one for pain. "Will you be all right driving back to Minneapolis?" he asks.

"Yes," I reply, scanning the slips of paper he hands to me.

"Stop at the pharmacy and have these prescriptions filled on your way out," he says.

When I approach the pharmacy, the woman at the counter looks closely at the prescription and then gives me a knowing look as she fills it. She smiles and hands it to me, asking if I need assistance.

"No, I'm fine."

As I walk across the street to the parking ramp, I hear a car screech and a horn honk, but I don't even raise my head. My mind is racing, trying to cover everything at once. I find my beloved twenty-two-year-old sports car in the ramp and get in, but I just sit there with my head on my chest, my mind going blank. I cannot process what I just heard. My mind just shuts down. I sit there until someone notices me and taps on the window.

"Are you okay?" It's a nurse from the clinic. "Do you need assistance?"

"No, I'm just waiting for someone," I say. After she leaves, I finally shift into reverse and pull out.

I hand the parking attendant a ten-dollar bill, but I don't wait for him to count out the bills from his register. After I speed away, he yells after me, "You forgot your change!"

Driving down the street, my chest begins to hurt, and I think, *Well, I won't have to put up with that much longer.* At the first stoplight, I open a bottle and take two of the antidepressant pills. I don't care what the bottle says I should take. *Those damn cigarettes; they've killed me. What am I talking about? I've killed myself. I'm a murderer.*

My name is John Janne, and on July 12, 1997, I was diagnosed with inoperable cancer. I am fifty-five years old, a lawyer, and married with two children. It has been a month since I first realized I was in trouble. I had been coughing up phlegm for a few months, but when I saw blood, started having chest pains, and my eyes became jaundiced, I finally called the Mayo Clinic to schedule an appointment.

It is hard to get into the clinic, but I had been there before for a hernia surgery, so they had me in their records. "There's a five-month wait for a physical," the woman on the phone had said.

"I don't think I can wait that long," I replied.

"What's the problem?"

When I described my symptoms, she said she would book me as soon as possible. Two days later, I received a call from the clinic, and my fateful appointment with Dr. Davis was scheduled. I didn't tell anyone I was going to the clinic, because I was so apprehensive about what was happening to me.

One week later, I had an all-out physical, where I met Dr. Davis for the first time. When he came into the examination room, he was wearing a white lab coat. With his bald head, he looked like a ghost floating in. While I sat there in a flowered smock, he asked his first question.

"Do you smoke?"

"Yes," I replied. "I started smoking in college."

"How much do you smoke?"

"Well, I used to smoke a pack a day until my office went smokeless a few years ago. Now I only smoke outside or in my garage."

He said nothing.

He started probing my body and stopped at my neck. "Do you know you have a nodule on your neck?" he asked.

"No," I said. "I didn't notice I had a lump."

He looked into my eyes but said nothing, even though I knew he could see they were yellow. He asked me to spit up some phlegm so he could take a sample to the lab. Dr. Davis was not big on small talk.

"I'm going to schedule you for a complete physical while you're here. I want you to wait here until you're called. At that point, you'll be given a series of departments to visit." Everything about Dr. Davis was right to the point. Then he left the room, and I didn't see him again until I was finished running through several departments. They took a blood sample in the lab first, and then I had the test that doomed me: the CT scan. Dr. Davis scheduled the following week for a full review of the tests, and that is when I got the bad news.

It starts to rain as I leave town. Between the rain and my tears, I can barely see the road. After an hour and a half, I'm finally home, but I just sit in the car in front of the house. I can't go into the house in this condition. I don't want my wife to see me this way. How could I explain that I have cancer? How could

I *ever* tell her? Everyone has been after me to quit smoking for years. *No,* I say to myself. *They can never know.* Rather than go inside, I call my wife.

"Dear, I have to go to Chicago for a client meeting early tomorrow morning." This is the first of many lies, but I can't go in to the house I have no explanation for her.

"Are you all right?"

"Yes," I say. "I'm just tired, and I'd rather not go to Chicago, but I have to go."

"Don't you have to come home and pack?" she asks.

"I don't have time. The plane leaves in an hour. I have underwear and a clean shirt in the office; I'll just put them in my briefcase. See you tomorrow."

I drive around until I find a dreary motel that suits my mood, and I check in. When I collapse on the bed, everything crashes in on me. "Why me?" I actually say this out loud. I'm only fifty-five years old, and I don't smoke that much. I need something more than painkillers, so I drive to a liquor store and buy a fifth of whiskey and two big bottles of Diet Coke. I laugh at the Diet Coke—I won't have to watch my weight anymore.

Back at the motel, I drink until I don't feel so bad. *I feel fine,* I think. *The diagnosis can't be right. Dr. Davis isn't perfect and neither is the Mayo Clinic. Maybe they got it wrong.*

And yes, I light a cigarette but soon cough up crap again, and yes, there's blood in it. I become so angry that I throw the pack of cigarettes into the wastebasket. But it only takes me an hour to convince myself that it doesn't make a difference whether I smoke anymore, and I retrieve them. Reading the warning on the back of the package, I curse them and light up.

Oh, my God, why have you forsaken me? If only I'd gone to the clinic sooner. If only I'd listened to my family and friends who warned me to quit smoking. Oh, God. I haven't been a bad person. Please give me time. Please tell me what I can do. My mind goes out of control.

I think of my family and begin to cry. *I've let them down. How many times have my children told me to quit smoking? At least a hundred times, and yes, I knew better.* I turn on the

TV with the volume off and watch in a daze. A thick depression washes over me. *Everyone's*

going to be angry with me for throwing my life away.

Here I am, with great blood pressure, good cholesterol, strong muscles, and a low glucose level, and I'm dying because of those damn cigarettes.

Anger comes over me when I think about the free cigarettes that were handed out like candy in the fraternities during the college years. Every weekend, tobacco companies hired students to hand them out. Everyone smoked. When we played bridge after class, the air would be blue from smoke—and, being college, boys' farts.

Those executives at the tobacco companies should be the ones with cancer. They're the ones to blame. They knew then that those freebies would hook us. They knew about cancer; they just didn't care. Yes, they eventually warned me, and it was my fault after that, but they didn't warn me before they hooked me. Sure, I could have quit. But I didn't, and I've killed myself.

I'm going to sue their asses in the morning.

I have a few more drinks, but the Coke doesn't taste good anymore, so I use less of it.

God, I'll do anything for a few more years of life. Then take me. You know it's not fair that I go so young. My mother is eighty-two, and even my dad lived to be seventy-two. Why me? I haven't been bad—stupid maybe, but never a bad person. I know we all will die, but why now? Tell me what I can do.

But there's no escaping it. I'm a dead man. I'm staring the Grim Reaper in the face.

Depression overtakes me and there seems to be no point in going on. I am crying again.

I should end it right now. What more is there to do when you know you have no future?

I drink half the bottle of whiskey.

When the wave of sadness finally subsides, I review my life. I've been productive, earned a very good income, and am a successful professional. I have a loving wife and wonderful children. I wasn't the greatest churchgoer after my children were raised, but I contributed generously.

I decide that if I can't fight death, I'll prepare for it. I only have few months, and I have to use my time wisely.

After a few more drinks, my pain is gone. Somehow numbing myself into oblivion gives me the clarity to pull myself together and create a plan. Now is the time to get it together. I don't want to subject my family to that kind of end. They don't deserve to go through that. The labor of a long death would be agonizing. I can't subject them to that because of my own stupidity with cigarettes.

I will not die in a hospital with tubes in my chest and my eyes sunken into my skull, horrifying my family.

Nor do I want people draped over my coffin, telling my wife how peaceful I look. A strange relief comes over me when I realize I will never have Alzheimer's, like my mother, or suffer being medicated in a nursing home. But then again, it would have been nice to die of old age at home.

I pour myself another drink, and just as the glass touches my lips, the solution comes to me. *Suicide.*

Sociologist Karl Menninger espoused that there's a little suicide inside everyone's heart. Suicide does run in my family. Two of my uncles used guns, but the pain they left behind for their families was heartbreaking. I can't let that happen. I can't accept the confusion and guilt I would put my widow, children, and friends through.

I'm already doubting myself. The problem with suicide is that my family would suffer just as much with wondering what had gone wrong. They would think that *they* were the reason I found life unlivable. They'd ask themselves questions like, "What did I say? What didn't I say? What did I do? What didn't I do?" My death would haunt them for the rest of their lives. They might even grow to hate me for leaving them.

But how else could I manage to die in a few months? *My dying must be a work of art,* I think. *How shall I do it?* I was given six or seven months, but I'll deteriorate rapidly during the last few months, so I really only have a couple months to reconcile myself and prepare for the end. I have to get over my fear quickly and get on with the planning.

But how can it end in two months if I don't end it myself? Ending it myself would be suicide.

I pour another drink, and just as before, the answer comes to me with the first sip: *It can't look like suicide—it has to look like an accident. But how can I pull that off?*

Whatever I do, I know it has to be final. Ending up in an emergency room would be the worst possible outcome.

How do other people do it? They use guns.

I could stage an accident with a gun. It could go off when I drop it. But that isn't going to work. What if I don't hit myself? What if I only wound myself? Besides, I don't have a gun; buying one now would look suspicious. I would look like an idiot. *He buys a gun and then proceeds to shoot himself.* My family would see right through it, eventually, because I haven't been hunting in thirty years.

There's asphyxiation, when people shut the garage door and run the car. I could die in my beloved antique sports car. The car and I could go out together, because I'm sure they'd get rid of it if it killed me. I'd heard that it's a pleasant way to go; a person just falls asleep without pain. But it could take up to three hours, and there's no guarantee someone wouldn't discover me and call an ambulance. Not only that, I have told my wife many times not to start the car before opening the garage door. I just can't figure a way to stage this as an accident. My family would eventually figure out it was suicide.

Jumping off a building would do it. It would have to be at least five stories high, or I might survive and only injure myself. But what would I be doing on the roof of a tall building? How would I even get up there? They always lock the roof access at the building where I work.

I could con a maintenance man into letting me up on the roof. I could tell him I'm a lawyer, looking into a possible lawsuit. But jumping isn't going to work; it would be questionable as to why I would be up there. Both the building owners and my firm would figure out there's no lawsuit. They would know it was suicide the moment they realized the parapets are so high that a person would have to jump over them.

I could step in front of a bus. People who send text messages while walking often step in front of buses, but I don't use text messaging. Lawyers don't text, at least not the older ones. Anyway, what if it doesn't kill me, and I just spend my last days in the hospital, still dying of cancer? I can just hear my law partners snide comments. "The dope didn't even know enough to look both ways at the intersection. He always thought he was so smart." Whatever way I pick, I can't let them talk about me that way.

Poison is another possibility, if I could get my hands on some. I could research and maybe even buy it over the Internet. Somehow, this doesn't appeal to me. There would be a record of the purchase, and I know experts are able to go through a person's computer to find everything the person has ever done. There would most certainly be an autopsy, and they would discover the poison and most likely my cancer. It would be an obvious suicide. Whatever I decide to do, it can't result in an autopsy. Maybe they would think one of my law partners poisoned me. The thought actually makes me laugh, but when it comes down to it, that isn't what I want either.

What about a drug overdose? I quickly throw away this idea, because it would be obvious to everyone. I don't do drugs—I would never have been able to function at such a high level in my profession if I did. And I can't see myself dickering with some dealer on the corner. I would probably get caught and end up in jail with a lot of explaining to do. And again, there would be an autopsy.

I think back to an old movie I saw in which the main character was hopeless for some reason that I can't recall. He wanted to leave his insurance money to his family, so he decided to hire a hit man. *I could hire a hit man,* I think. There would be several advantages to going this way. It would be fast and painless, and I could pick the time and location, and the money would not be a problem. But then I remember that the movie didn't turn out well for him, so I discard this idea too. How in the hell would I hire a hit man anyway? Anyone who would risk murdering someone for a few thousand dollars had to be an idiot, and idiots get caught, and then what? I don't want to imagine the crap that would come out in the news.

Many people slash their wrists and bleed out in warm water. I've read that this is actually another pleasant way to go, even though it doesn't seem like it would be. But this is suicide, and I see no way to accidently slash my wrists or cut my throat. I could cut my throat in an alley in a seedy part of town. There are many killings in north Minneapolis every year. But then, what would I be doing in that part of town, especially when I've never even been there before?

I could roll my car. I could have easily rolled it over driving back from the Mayo Clinic in the rain, considering the distress I was in. Or I could simply drive it into a bridge pier. There would be no autopsy. But there's no guarantee I'll be killed, and worse yet, I could kill someone else. Ending up in an emergency room isn't an option. My accident has to be fatal. Everyone would wonder why I was driving so fast. ("He never drove that fast before.") Demolishing my car also doesn't sit well. It would be messy, not the artful end I am looking for. I pour a drink in honor of my beloved sports car and the twenty-two years we've spent together.

I think about the Golden Gate Bridge and remember that it's the most popular suicide site in the world. *Drowning does have an appeal, and filling my rotten lungs with water would serve them right.* My lake cabin in northern Minnesota would be doable. But there would be problems there too. There were usually several boats on the lake, and it's a small lake. Most often, there's someone nearby who would probably call for help, and help would arrive quickly. I also don't know how my family would feel about spending time at the lake in the future if it was the cause of my death. They would likely sell the property, dumping it with bad memories. I have told my wife many times to pour my ashes on the shoreline. I hope she remembers to do that. It's my favorite place on earth. But there are many lakes in Minnesota. Who says I have to drown in *my* lake. There's also whitewater canoeing, which can be dangerous.

And then it comes to me: the Boundary Waters in northern Minnesota. I always see stories in the newspaper about accidental deaths in the Boundary Waters, and most of them are drownings.

I've found the answer. This is as artful as it is going to get.

My mind finally stops racing and I fall asleep.

CHAPTER TWO

Getting It Together

When I wake up the next morning, I feel so awful that I can hardly look at myself in the mirror. When I do, I see I look like hell! I had thrown my pants, shirt, and coat in a pile on the floor the night before, and they're all wrinkled.

What am I going to do? I can't go home, and I have to go into the office sooner or later. I can't find my shoes and look all around the room for them. Sitting down on the small worn-out sofa, I start to cry again. I remember that I threw my shoes at the wall in disgust the night before, and there they are, behind the sofa on the floor. I continue to cry as I lace my shoes. *I've let everyone down, and those damn cigarettes have killed me*

I have no razor or toothbrush, just an almost-empty bottle of whiskey. I can't go into work looking like this. My mouth is dry, and I feel like I could spit dust, so I drink the rest of the whiskey and then check out of the motel. The guy at the desk looks at me like I'm just another drunk. My breath must really be bad.

I drive to the mall, but it's only a quarter to nine, so I sit and wait for it to open. But allowing myself to wait is not a good idea. My mind begins to race over everything again.

When the mall finally opens, I buy a shirt at Brooks Brothers and put it on in their dressing room. On my way out, I throw the old shirt into the wastebasket. At the pharmacy, I buy a disposable razor and a toothbrush and then go into the restroom to get ready for work. A clean-cut businessman comes in and gives me a look like I'm a homeless man who shouldn't be in here. I'm more than thankful he doesn't know who I am. He's close to being right—I *feel* homeless. But I am not homeless; I have a wonderful home.

After cleaning up, I stop at the coffee shop to order a big cup with a scone, which settles me down a little and wipes the lingering taste of whisky and fermented sugar out of my mouth. But I'm not completely rid of the taste, so I buy a pack of gum and chew a few pieces at once. I finally start to feel better and head for the office.

When I walk into the office, my secretary, Anne, says I look tired. I can tell she really thinks I look much worse than tired.

"You're right, Anne. Actually, I think I need to take a couple days off." I call my assistant, Terry, into the office and tell him I'll be taking time off over the next few days. I need time to work things out. "Terry, I want you to file a Motion to Dismiss on the Ellis case," I say.

"Do you think that that will work?" he asks.

"No," I say, "but I know the judge. He feels overworked right now and might not want to increase his caseload. The case is thin, and he just might go for it."

"Will you be here to review the motion?" he asks.

"No, you can do it. I know you can handle it. I want you to also watch over my other cases for the next few days."

As he leaves, I hear him say to Anne, "I think he needs more than a few days."

"Yes," she says, "he looks like someone beat him up."

Anne and Terry are the backbones of my practice. They take care of all the busy work, while I work directly with the clients. We are going to miss each other.

My specialty is construction law. It's a very lucrative specialty because it involves three parties (rather than just two parties) suing each other: architects, contractors, and owners. When anything doesn't turn out to their satisfaction, there's always another lawsuit or further negotiations that take forever to resolve. On every building project, there is always someone unhappy with something. Each party has fingers pointing at the other two, forming a loop that never seems to end. They all have insurance, and the insurance companies don't care who's at fault; they just want it resolved without running up exorbitant legal fees. This seldom works, however, and we seem to schedule endless meetings on each issue.

Owners have issues with cost overruns, which are never their fault of course, even though they continued to add to the project after the bids were finalized. Contractors maintain that the architects aren't providing enough information and that they need more money to cover something that was not shown or was inaccurate on the architect's documents. And the architects demand more money from the owners who continue to make changes after their documents are complete. Then it always comes back around to the owners, who, in turn, feel that the architect should pay for everything the contractor said was missing, because they should have somehow known the owner needed it. Around and around they go as they drive up the fees.

My reputation in the firm is that of a smart-ass who should never be crossed. Indeed, I almost always have the largest, most lucrative caseload. This gives me immense influence and control in the firm, not to mention one of the largest bonuses. My partners are always on guard around me, as most of them have felt the sting of my sarcasm at some point. I know I'm smart. I guess that's what makes me a smart-ass, but that's my personality. I won't be missed, except as someone who brings the big-buck clients to the firm. The managing partner, Wayne, is a friend, and between the two of us, we set the agenda.

At the board of directors meetings, the partners always look at me after a proposal is made, because if I go after it with my usual sarcasm, it almost always will be the end of it. If I'm calm, whoever made the proposal lets out a sigh of relief. The smart ones bounce their ideas off me long before our meetings.

I *know* that when I slip out of those boring meetings for a cigarette my partners snicker as soon as I'm out the door. They use my smoking habit to deride me behind my back. But I don't care.

I can hear it now. "How smart was he really to die so young from cigarettes? He was a dumb-ass after all." I can't give them the satisfaction of knowing my habit killed me. *I won't do it.*

Telling my secretary I'm taking a few days off is an easy sell, because I do look like hell.

Later that evening I tell my wife, Betty, that I don't feel well, as if she can't tell. I go to bed early, but before long, I have to get up to take a few painkillers and sleeping pills. Nietzsche once said, "The thought of suicide can get one through many a long night." The thought is not helping me tonight, however.

Wish I could talk to Nietzsche about it. Somehow, I need to find a way to get through these nights.

The next morning I decide to go to the library. I tell Betty I'll be at the library doing research, because I don't want her calling the office and finding out I'm taking time off without an explanation.

"You have a library at work. Why aren't you using that one?" she asks.

I have to think quickly. "There's a noisy team working in there, and they're disruptive. I need some space."

"You have people to do that for you. Why are you digging through precedents?"

"Well, they're busy, and this is a complex case. I have the time, so I'm doing it myself."

All lies.

At the library, I log on to the Internet to look for cancer cures and find everything from Mexican charlatans to the most bizarre cures I could ever have imagined. I look at a site for holistic cures. Then another for omega-3 fats. And another for Tibetan medicine, with a list of natural supplements.

Santalum album—white sandalwood for hotness disorders of the lungs.

Bambusa arundinacea—bamboo, for God's sake, for all kinds of things.

Crocus sativus—saffron for inflammation.

Adhatoda vasica—from the malagar nut tree for inflammation and stress.

Picrorhiza kurroa—from grass used for epistaxis, whatever that is?

Hippophae rhamnoides—buckthorn for lung diseases. I have that crap in my backyard.

Vitis vinifera—from the grape plants used for pneumonia.

Glycyrrhiza glabra—licorice. I don't think candy's going to help me now.

All of these could be taken in one pill. The instructions say to take two pills a day to see benefits within a week. "You will be balanced in three months," they say. "There are no known side effects with this regimen." *Right,* I think. *There are no effects. Period.*

I come across a Mexican clinic that seems interesting. Located just over the border from San Diego, for your convenience, they will pick you up at the airport and provide free housing during your stay. They also advertise their book online for less than twenty dollars. Looks to me like they're just over the border to escape regulation. These people prey on the desperately ill, like me. I spend another four hours searching until I realize I'm wasting time I don't have.

I search "Boundary Waters Canoe Area Wilderness," and a ton of information comes up—so much so that it's obvious a lot of planning will be necessary. The BWCAW is part of the Superior National Forest in northern Minnesota. There are 1,500 miles of canoe routes and 2,200 campsites. One needs a permit, and the fee is sixteen dollars per trip per adult. I see the town of Ely is a major entry point. This wouldn't be too hard to figure out, as there are over twenty outfitters listed.

On one of the sites, I find Sigurd Olson, a conservationist who wrote about the North Woods. He is credited with being largely responsible for putting both the Boundary Waters and Quetico Park on the map. He wrote about the romance of retracing the path the voyageurs took. I decide I need to have his book, and when I search for it, I learn he's written several. I decide to buy his first book. I think that all authors use up their best ideas in the first book.

I immediately call one of the outfitters in Ely, and a man named Alan picks up the phone. After I ask him to recommend a spot that would be isolated, he tells me about the Quetico Park area. "You know, in the summer there are hundreds of canoeists in the Boundary Waters, and by noon they've taken all the good campsites. You're also required to only camp at designated sites, or you'll be fined. In Quetico Provincial Park, though, you can camp anywhere you can pull up a canoe. Quetico and the Boundary Waters are about the same size, but there are almost ten times as many canoeists in the Boundary Waters."

I ask him to send me a map and brochure, and I give him my credit card number.

"Can I schedule the trip for you?" he asks.

"No, we don't have a date set yet. There isn't much I can do until I find out when my friend's available." I don't know why I said "we," but then it occurs to me that an imaginary friend will be useful.

While in the library, I decide to look into the afterlife. *Why not see what's in store for me?* I quickly see that I'm not the only one concerned about what's ahead—there are tons of books on this subject. It's overwhelming.

I figure the fear of dying or becoming nothing is a natural human fear and the primary motivation for believing in an afterlife. When death approaches, we are so stunned, we're unprepared. *I need a cigarette.*

Lord, how I crave a cigarette. Mark Twain once said, "If there are no cigars in heaven, I shall not go there." I hope he's up, there puffing away. I wonder what Twain died from.

I decide to start at the beginning; I go to ancient Egypt to see what I can find. I learn that at first, it was only the pharaoh who could ascend eternally, launched up from the pyramids to join the sun god, Re. But later, they decided to let everyone in if they could pass the Anubis test. Anubis was a man figure with the head of a jackal. He's one scary-looking dude, and he appears on all of their tombs. He would place the heart on a scale and weigh it against a feather. If your heart was heavier than the feather, you were burdened with sin and consigned to the underworld. If Anubis were still around, I'd be toast; I don't think any of us lawyers could pass that test. My mind conjures up an image of Anubis placing my heart on the scale, and it sinks like a rock. He bends over me, licking his chops. *Stop it. I can't let my mind run wild like this.*

The Egyptians hated the thought of extinction at death—hence all the ornaments and tools in their tombs for the afterlife. And it had to be gold or it wouldn't last, and boy, did it last. There has to be something in human nature that can't accept complete death. I'm sure I won't need any tools where I'm going. *Well, maybe a pitchfork.* I move on to the next stack of books.

I start to realize that the notion of the afterlife has been around almost as long as man himself. The caves of Stone Age man, tens of thousands of years old, indicate that their dead were sent away, who knows where, with provisions and tools. It seems the human race has always believed in an afterlife of some sort. Many religions espouse a hereafter, where the body is resurrected into heaven. I just can't buy this, though. In the first place, why would we need a body in heaven, and second, why turn us into dust only to then reconstruct us?

The Mesopotamians were scary. The only thing I can find on them is something called *The Epic of Gilgamesh.* He was a king somewhere in Iraq. They believed that two feet underground was the underworld, where it was dark and silent. You would spend eternity in this darkness under two feet of dirt. I wonder whether they made good fertilizer. Is this why they call it the Fertile Crescent? This epic seems to convey that hopes for immortality only get in the way of living a happy existence on this earth because there is no immortality. *Now's one hell of a time to tell me.* If this is true, there's no hope for me. I become depressed, and my chest starts to ache again.

I wonder if the concept of immortality does make this life unnecessarily difficult—or at least more difficult than it should be. The book of Job in the Bible clearly conveys the ancient Israelite belief that there is no resurrection or afterlife. God, or YHWH, would reward or punish us in *this* life, but that's it. Resurrection was left out until the book of Daniel. Personal immortality didn't become the norm until the time of Christ. Not a moment too soon.

I'm amazed how religious dogma changes over time. *Who the hell has it right?* Then I correct myself: *All thoughts of hell must be banished from my mind.* After all this revisionism I am reading, why can't I write my own version, like the ancients did, and have everything turn out the way I want?

The ancient Greeks came up with a new one: we survive only through fame or by being remembered forever. Maybe they were right, because we still honor their philosophers. I guess all the other Greeks who weren't famous are just plain dead. The early Greeks believed that this life was it, so they lived it to its fullest. One of their tombstone epitaphs expresses it clearly, "I was not; I was; I am not; I don't care." I hope this guy is wrong, because I'm about to become "I am not, and I *do* care."

The Romans were not much different from the Greeks. They believed that the gods (I don't know how many they had, but it was a lot) were so into themselves that they didn't care about mere mortal humans. Why should the gods be bothered when they were kept busy with one another?

Cicero said the act of dying is momentary, after which there is "a pleasant sensation or no sensation at all." *Just how would he know that?* Socrates said in 399 BC that "one must face death with a good hope and know for certain that no evil can happen to a good man, either in life or after death." I take a moment to think about my life, and it has basically been good. I don't know about the good hope thing, though. I need to develop some good hope fast.

The Greek, Plato, was one of the first to raise the hope of life after death, when good and evil would be recognized. Plato believed that all human souls were immortal and ascended into heaven. Later, the Christians jumped on this one with both feet; heaven and hell were fully developed. From John the Baptist came, "Repent ye, for the kingdom of heaven is a hand." The message was, time is short and the Last Judgment is at hand. The more than two thousand years that have passed since are apparently meant to be considered short. Those evangelical Christians who are waiting for the Last Judgment have to be the most patient in all of history.

I leaf through the book some more until I find something else that interests me. The Greeks believed that when a person dies, the psyche is the last breath that leaves the body. hence the term, "breath of life." The psyche then becomes an image, like a phantom or a shade. This phantom has the power to enter the dreams of the living. In *The Iliad,* Patroclus is killed and his psyche hovers above his friend Achilles. He wants Achilles to hurry up and bury him so that he may pass through to Hades, where his psyche can find rest. *It might be nice to be a phantom.* It could be fun to hover over my partners in the office and torment them. Then I remember that Hades is another name for hell. One has to admire the Greeks. They're the basis of our civilization. They excelled in politics, law, art, architecture, engineering, science, and mathematics. I am, however, not going to go along with anything that mentions Hades.

The following morning, the first thing I see at the library is the Book of Mormon. I begin to explore the religion, or cult, or whatever it is. While in the woods, Joseph Smith received a visit from a messenger, an angel sent by God, telling him that all religions are false and corrupt. On a second visit, Smith was told where to find gold plates buried in a hill. These plates were supposedly written in Egyptian and told God's true story, as it was presented to the ancients. Everyone since the ancient Egyptians had apparently corrupted the original story. After finding the plates and digging them up, Smith translated them for his first disciple, who transcribed them, and *voilà*, we have the Book of Mormon. Not bad for a man who was barely literate but claimed to have studied Egyptian. And what happened to the gold plates? *Gee, no one seems to know.* Apparently, God took them back. In 1838, Mormons fled the state of Missouri to escape the governor's threat of execution. Religious tolerance wasn't too prevalent back then. They eventually fled to Utah, where Smith was later jailed for treason and shot dead by a gang while still in jail.

His wife denies that he practiced polygamy, but there's a photograph of him in the book with several women and a ton of children. There are no pictures of a wife with several husbands. I've always had great admiration for the Mormons and the way they raise their children with such discipline. But really, what is it with all the wives? The book says Smith had one wife as young as fourteen among his eighty-seven. Brigham Young, the prophet who followed Smith, had seventy wives. I wonder where they got all the women; some men had to have been left out. It seems to me to be just another religion that holds women in servitude.

Mormons are taught that heaven is a beautiful shiny celestial city—a shining city on a hill. *I didn't know Reagan was a closet Mormon.* Mormons believe that God himself was once a human being and that we can also become gods if we follow his example and that this "Eternal Progression" extends into the afterlife. Lorenzo Snow, an early leader in the church, said, "As man is now, God once was, as God is now, man may become." *So I could become a god? Never going to happen.* I know the evangelicals consider Mormonism to be a cult, but then again, I'm still not sure just what a cult is.

During dinner that night, I receive a call from a cemetery salesman. While I stand there, stunned, with the receiver in my hand, he goes on and on with his pitch.

"It's much better to do this now, before the need arises. You don't want to be a burden to your family, do you? Our counselor will be happy to come to your home and meet with you."

Before I start to cry, I get angry. "No," I said, "I don't want to be a burden, and it's none of your business."

It's been years since my wife and I filled out the forms from the Cremation Society. I wonder whether anyone will remember that I want to be cremated. I will put the form at the top of my deskat home. *Oh no, there can be no tip off. I'm sure they'll remember.*

After my long pause, the caller asks, "Are you still on the line?"

I just hang up.

CHAPTER THREE

Planning

The next morning at work, Terry comes rushing in, very excited. "The judge threw out the case," he laughs. "You were right."

"Good work on the motion," I say as he beams with pride. We go through the remaining active cases together, but as my mind begins to wander, I cut the meeting short. Annie comes in with the mail, and there's my information on the Boundary Waters Canoe Area. My heart almost jumps out of my chest. My plan is about to come together. I tell her I'm meeting with a prospective client and leave the office at 11:00 a.m. for the library. *More lies.*

I open the package and am stunned by how much information there is. The options are endless, as are the requirements. It says that Quetico is a protected, pristine wilderness retreat of international acclaim, west of Lake Superior on the Canada/US border. The park's tangled network of lakes once formed water routes traveled by the Ojibwe Indians and French fur traders. Now, it is primarily the destination of experienced canoeists seeking solitude, rare glimpses of wildlife, cascading waterfalls, glassy lakes, and expansive forests. It doesn't advertise that it's a good place to die, but it sounds good to me.

The first problem I find is that Quetico is in Canada and not Minnesota. This means I have to get permits and go through customs. My plan of simply shoving a canoe off the shore is now laughable. After going through many different route options, I become enamored with the Maligne River. Seems this river's been a highway all throughout history, used by the Sioux and then the Ojibwe, the French and English fur traders, and then by loggers. To navigate the Maligne River, I would enter the park at the western end from Lac La Croix. Ojibwe legend has it that Quetico is a kind spirit whose presence can be felt throughout the park. I hope to find that spirit, and I think I will. I decide to book my access at the Lac La Croix Ranger Station.

The second problem I run into is the park schedule. I had planned on the first part of September, but the entry stations close on September 2. I adjust my trip to the last week in August. My next surprise is that I can't get there from here. There are no good roads into the ranger station. I have only four options: 1) have an outfitter tow me in from Crane Lake; 2) paddle in from Crane Lake, adding at least two days to the trip; 3) drive all over Canada and then over fifty miles of bad road; or 4) fly in. I decide, *What the hell. I'll fly in from Ely.* After all, this must be a work of art. First class all the way.

I need to make all my arrangements with Canadian Immigration and Customs, as well as US Customs, at least a month ahead of time. Better get on that ASAP. Online, I order an application for something called a Remote Area Border Crossing Permit. Once I have that and a copy of my passport, driver's license, and thirty bucks, I'll be ready for a remote area. The more I get into this, the more remote I start to feel.

I soon realize I also need something called a Wilderness Camping Permit. I reconsider my initial idea of just launching a canoe and ignoring any requirements. But I decide it wouldn't look good in the newspaper. A lawyer dies while breaking the law? I think the public would cheer.

The brochure has many warnings, designed, I suppose, to make you think twice. In July, there are swarms of mosquitoes and black flies that eat you alive if you're not completely covered. They go right through thin clothing. Forget about wearing shorts or a swimsuit. Those insects abate in August, but I see I'll still need a lot of repellent, as I don't want to die that way. Abate is not good enough for me.

More warnings: If you can't paddle and portage a canoe, you should not go. If you can't build a fire with wet wood, you should not go. *Crap, who the hell can start a fire with wet wood?* If you can't read a map, you should not go. If you can't carry your packs and canoe across a portage in no more than two trips, you should not go. If it's windy, but you can't allow for extra days, you should not go. It was obviously not a promotional brochure.

It says I should paddle next to the shoreline, like the Indians did, to protect against high winds and waves. I should never leave my food unattended; too many campers have watched the rear end of a bear running off into the woods with their food supply for the week. *Isn't that better than watching them run the other way?* There can be several days of rain in a row, leaving no dry wood for a fire.

"Some portages are killers." That's not what I wanted to read. "*He lay dead under his canoe on the portage trail*" would not read well in the paper. "The park is hard on novices; it is isolated and unfriendly to the inexperienced camper or canoeist. They are best off with a guide." It's beginning to sound like this trip could kill me even if I didn't want to die. I've made the right decision to come here. Damn, I *am* smart.

The brochure has a lengthy section on how to make your campsite "bear-able." They contend that the bears in the park are not the ferocious man-killers one reads about in the newspapers. *Ha, I'm not sold on that one.* They're rarely bigger than six feet and three hundred pounds, and they are timid. They feed on plants, berries, fish, and some large animals. *Good Lord, am I not a large animal?* Then here it comes: "They may be dangerous when wounded, cornered, teased, or protecting their young." It says to never take food into your tent. *Am* I *not food in my tent?* Quetico is a good choice to complete my plan. But damn, I might not be so smart after all.

The warnings continue: You are to keep a clean campsite and never cook aromatic foods like bacon—bears can smell bacon a mile away. Well, who the hell doesn't like bacon? To chase bears away, you are to bang pots and pans together. I was going to take one pot—who knew it would be a one-pot mistake? Here is what you are supposed to do: "Climb ten feet up a tree and tie a rope around the trunk. Then loop it over a branch about eighteen feet above the ground and tie the packsack with the food on the end of the rope." Then I see I have it backwards. First, you should tie your packsack to the rope, then loop the rope over a branch eighteen feet off the ground, and then climb the tree and tie the rope ten feet up. I wonder if it wouldn't be easier just to feed the damn bear. I'm too old to climb ten feet up a tree.

The brochure says not to worry about nighttime noises. "The noise you hear will most likely be mice, chipmunks, or squirrels." Bears are almost always quiet, so you will not hear them anyway. I expect to be knocked out on painkillers, so this will not be a problem for me.

The average high temperature at the end of August is 72.8 degrees, and the average low is 53.3. The average rainfall is 3.91 inches. Finally, something that doesn't sound like it will kill me.

The park regulations are as follows: "Group size may not exceed nine." I am relieved to see there is no regulation against a single traveler, as I thought there might be if it's dangerous. "Each person must carry the Wilderness Camping Permit with him." I guess so they can identify the bodies. "All food and containers must be burnable. Separate groups cannot camp together. Molesting wildlife is prohibited." Damn, I'd wanted to molest the wildlife. "No guns allowed. Fires must be on bare rock or soil. Latrines should be dug on a flat surface in deep soil one hundred feet from the water and covered with soil before leaving. Garbage that can't be burned must be carried out of the park." That has to be a problem for the beer drinkers. "Damaging any vegetation is prohibited." Just how are you going to dig a hole one hundred feet away from the water without walking over some ferns?

Again, they try to discourage you: "Sometimes people die in the park. They die by drowning, being hit by lightning, and from hypothermia. And many more are hurt." They hack their legs with an ax, they sprain their ankles on the portages and can't continue … and the list goes on. This is confirmation that I've made the right decision to go to Quetico and that my plan is workable. But what is it with these Canadians? I wonder if they really want anyone to come to the park.

"Never go anywhere without a compass, and never leave it behind on a portage. Believe in your map."

That's right; I have to get a map.

"When a thunderstorm is approaching, get off the water and seek shelter." Sounds to me like a good fast way to go—we'll see. "When the waves are running high, ride it out on the shore. Shooting rapids is to be discouraged unless you are a skilled canoeist. Check out the water level first." Sounds like another piece of advice I may ignore. "When portaging with a canoe on your shoulders, a high wind can blow you over." I'm going to love these portages. "Don't stand up in the canoe." Well, really, if you don't even know that much, you shouldn't go. "Don't over exert yourself," as you are not as young as you used to be. Tell me about it. "If the canoe tips over, grab it, as it will float. Do not climb steep cliffs. Leave your itinerary with someone. To avoid getting sick, boil your drinking water." I'll drink from the lake. "Take an extra paddle. Know how to swim." Unfortunately, I do know how. "If you do have trouble and need help, send up a smoke signal." What? I read that one again and start laughing in the library. "Three puffs are a distress signal." What happens then? Does someone return a smoke signal in response? Do the Indians arrive? There are no instructions on how to make smoke signals.

"You need to closely follow the map when looking for the portage locations. Detailed maps are a necessity. They can be ordered online from Fisher Maps once you decide your route. The bays and islands can easily confuse when you are never sure how far you have come or how fast you are going. Portages most often start at a low spot on the shore and will look somewhat worn, as they have been used for several hundred years. There are, however, no signs anywhere." I think they could put out signs. For God's sake, even the Indians had methods of signage.

"When alone, you will most likely have to make two trips to move your gear." I will die on a portage for sure. "Carry the canoe on your shoulder on the first run; then you can rest when you go back for the packs. But you must always have the food pack with you." Why? So the bear can run you down? "Wearing your life jacket will make the canoe ride easier." No way, I have never found that wearing a life jacket makes paddling a canoe easier. I will not be wearing one anyway. "A portage may show that it is thirty rods on your map, but could be longer in overly dry or wet weather." What the hell is a rod? I look it up: six and one half feet.

Then it tells me to have a great trip. I like the way this is coming together.

Later, on the drive home, I cough up blood and have to stop at a gas station restroom to clean up. I am terrified that I will spit up blood in front of my wife or at the office. That will ruin my plan. I have to move this along faster.

The next morning in the shower, I spit up blood again. I must be careful not to get any on my shirt or tie. At the office, I spend my time going over the routes for the Maligne River. When Anne brings me some coffee, I mention to her that I am considering a canoe trip in the Boundary Waters.

"Oh," she says. "Al in corporate did that a few years ago. You might want to talk to him."

"Sure," I reply. "Can you mention to him that I want to talk to him?" After she leaves, I gobble a few pills with my coffee.

There are only two routes I see to choose from. The river flows into the northwest corner of Lac La Croix. Crap, that means canoeing upstream. The decision between them is easy, however, as the other route says that in low-water periods, canoeing may be difficult, and early fall is a low-water period. I also note that there are more portages on the low-water route. I suppose it makes sense that if the water's low, you would have more portages. So it will be entry point number 42, route number 17 (the Maligne-Jean Route), to and from the Lac La Croix Ranger Station. This route is said to be unaffected by fluctuations of the water levels, so the decision is easy. The route goes up the Maligne River to Sturgeon Lake, up Jean Creek, through Rouge Lake, Burntside Lake, Jean Lake, Conk Lake, Quetico Lake, Beaverhouse Lake, down the Quetico River, up the Namakan River, and back home at Lac La Croix. This is a winner—no way will I make it. I wonder how anyone ever makes it. This route is noted as a fisherman's dream with trout, walleye, bass, and northern pike. They recommend adding a day or two for fishing. I'll have to sell this adventure as also being a fishing trip. The more credibility the better. I order the waterproof maps online.

Al knocks on my door, and I wave him in. He looks nervous as he enters my office. Junior partners usually do. When I tell him I'm interested in a Boundary Waters canoe trip, he brightens up immediately.

"Oh yes," he replies. "We went two years ago."

"Tell me about your trip," I say to him. "I'm considering going with a friend of mine whom I met in Chicago."

"Well, we had a good time. Did some fishing—the place is just stunning. The portages aren't bad if they're short, but we had a couple that were backbreakers. Canoeing was fun. There were four of us with two canoes, so that went well."

"What about the wind?"

"We didn't have anything but a gentle breeze, but I hear it can be bad. They warned us to get off the big water if it was windy."

"Would you go again?"

"Maybe in a few years. It's not something I would do every year. I'd also advise going with a large group, because it helps to share the cooking and the portage load."

"Did you see much in the way of wildlife, like bears?"

"Yes, we saw just about everything. Moose—they're magnificent animals—beaver, wolves, and yes, there are bears. Many of the bears we saw were with cubs. For someone who's never been there and loves nature, it's a must."

"Well, I think we're going to go," I say.

As he leaves, he says, "We'll have to get together for lunch when you get back. I'd be interested to hear how it goes for you."

"Okay," I say and smirk at the thought.

All that was left to do now was schedule the trip. When he shuts the door behind him, I call the outfitter Alan again to book a plane to fly me and "my friend" into the Lac La Croix Ranger Station to start our trip up the Maligne River.

"We don't fly into the ranger station anymore. What we do is fly you to a resort on Lac La Croix and then tow you to Twin Falls, where you start your trip up the Maligne River. You can pick up your Quetico Park permit at the resort, and you can pay for it there. You can also purchase your Ontario fishing licenses there. At the resort, they'll load your gear and canoe onto a boat and take you to Twin Falls to begin your trip."

"Great," I reply. "I start my trip right off with a portage around the falls."

He laughs and says, "I guess that's right. You could canoe over to the falls if you wish, but that would take another day, I think."

"How much is it?"

"The plane would be $475, but the price of fuel has gone up so much, I'm not sure they will hold that price. Hold on, and I'll call them now. When do you want to go?" he asked.

"On the twenty-fourth of August."

"No problem. Most of the pilots are eager for business that late in the season. How many will there be?"

"Two of us. How long is the flight?"

"As the crow flies, you'll be there in less than an hour. And when do you want to return?"

His question stops me cold. The realization that I won't return hits me hard. "Just a second," I say as I try to compose myself. "Ten days."

"Okay, that would be on the second of September. Is that right?"

"Yes."

After a short wait—I think the pilot must have been in the store—he says they will honor that price, but they want a credit card, and there will be a 15 percent cancellation charge. There's also a charge of one hundred dollars for the tow from the resort to the falls."

"We'll be driving up from the cities through Duluth. By the time we arrive, get outfitted, and fly into the resort, that'll take the whole day, won't it?"

"What I would recommend is that you stay overnight at the resort and start out early the next morning after a good breakfast."

"That sounds better, because my partner is coming in from Chicago and may be late."

"Do you want me to make the arrangements at the resort?" he asks. "Can I use your card?"

"Yes, and what other costs are there?"

"Well, the Kevlar package, which includes the canoe and all the supplies and food you will need, is eighty dollars a day per person, and a nonresident fishing license is twenty dollars a day, but you can take care of these when you two get here."

"Twenty dollars a day?"

"Yes, it's expensive."

"Do they guarantee that you catch fish?"

He laughs, but I don't think it's funny. In my head, I figure the whole thing will cost a little over two thousand dollars. But I realize it's a hell of a lot less than a long stay in the hospital.

"Are we all set then, or am I forgetting anything?" I ask.

"No, I think you're set better than most of the groups we see come up. At least you know what it is you want to do and where you want to go. Do you have any more questions?"

"Yes, can we fly over the course I want to take?"

"No, it's not allowed."

"Do you fly the canoe in on the plane?"

"No," he replies, "that takes a bigger plane that we use for larger parties. You'll be taking a Cessna 185, and there will be a canoe for you two at the resort. Late August, early September is a good time to go. The bugs and kids are both down."

"One last question. From what I can tell, the Maligne River flows out of Sturgeon Lake, so I'll be canoeing upstream. Is that right?"

"Yes, but it is a manageable flow, and if you stay in the middle, you'll hardly notice the current."

Great, I think. *The book says to hug the shore.* But I remember I shouldn't worry. What have I got to lose?

"Singles don't seem to have trouble with the current, so two of you shouldn't either," he says.

I'm relieved to hear him say that, because I didn't want to go on record asking if a single was allowed to go out.

"Will that be all, Mr. Janne?"

"Yes."

"We will call you if there are any problems."

I'm all set then; everything's in place. I have one month, twelve days, and twelve hours to go. I hope my body holds out long enough to pull this off with my wife. Would I quit smoking in the meantime? No, there was no way I could hold it together without smoking, but I would cut back. Besides, if I quit now it would be suspicious. When dying, Macbeth proclaimed, "Life is nothing but a tale told by an idiot, full of sound and fury, signifying nothing." I still haven't figured out what that means, but I've lost my fear of death. This will be my last and greatest adventure.

I pass Anne on the way out to tell her I'm leaving the office to make a marketing call and will not be back until noon the next day. Then I head to the library again. The thought of the afterlife has taken me over.

The corruption of the Catholic Church during medieval times is unbelievable. The clergy began selling indulgences, which were "get into heaven for a price cards." The pope went so far as to issue a price list for each sin, including adultery and murder. The Protestant Reformation was a reaction to the practice of selling these indulgences, as well as selling clerical positions. The church became fabulously rich and, with their wealth, controlled everything. On a trip to Rome, Martin Luther was shocked to find that the pope was licensing brothels. The next pope was no better, fathering seven children by two mistresses. The church acknowledges 263 popes since its founding. I guess they can't all be above reproach. It's not surprising that the nuns never brought this up at my Catholic grade school.

The Protestant Reformation, led by Luther and John Calvin, was countered by the Catholics with their own Counter-Reformation. Both Luther and Calvin considered life on earth to be nothing but poverty and pain, which would be absolved in heaven. It must have been a terrible time to have lived. Luther and Calvin agreed in general on almost everything but soon had a falling out.

Frederick the Wise was a collector of religious items, and every year before All Saints Day he displayed them for the public. There was straw from the manger, myrrh given by the wise men, bread from the Last Supper, a branch from the burning bush, a thorn from Jesus's crown, and a nail from the cross. I think that Frederick was more gullible than wise. If you visited this display, the pope would grant you an indulgence good for a suspension of 1,902,202 years and 270 days in purgatory. Martin Luther had the audacity to point out that this was not covered in the Scriptures.

The Vatican was desperate to get their hands on Martin Luther. Frederick the Wise, who was harboring Luther, received the following letter from the pope:

"We have you to thank that the Churches are without people, the people without priests, the priests without honor, and Christians without Christ. The veil of the temple is rent. Separate yourself from Martin Luther and put a muzzle on his blasphemous tongue in the name of God and Jesus our Lord, whom we alone represent on this earth, you will not escape punishment on this earth or in the hereafter. Repent before you feel the swords." Frederick would not give up Martin, so the war began and lasted for thirty years.

One thing that confuses me is that when under pressure from the landowners who funded Luther's church and fought his war, Luther stated that if the peasants did not obey their masters then the landowners were allowed to kill them. I wonder if this is true. Apparently, the Lutherans knew, just as well as the Catholics, where the gold was. Definitely a tough time to have lived.

I also don't understand why the Lutherans and the Catholics don't get back together. My daughter and her husband are Lutherans, and I've been to several of their services. It's impossible for me to tell the difference between the two. If the Catholics would just admit that those indulgences where wrong, maybe they could work it out. Well, I don't care anymore.

I'm struck by the treatment of women in almost all religions. I'm glad I wasn't born a woman; I couldn't have handled it. I've always tried to promote women's issues, especially in our firm. They were among my biggest supporters at work. Look at women in the Christian Church: in its beginning, women were treated as vassals who required a man to control them and protect them. They were suspect as temptresses, so they could not have a major role in the hierarchy. Jesus said nothing about the role that women should have in his church, not a single word. Paul was the first to dictate that women should not speak in church but remain silent and that they should keep their heads covered. Paul stated in First Corinthians that marriage is an antidote for sexual immorality but that celibacy was preferable. Paul was not married.

From what I'm reading, the reason women are secondary to the male in patriarchal society is because God created Adam first, and Eve was the temptress. Celibacy was established in 1139 to separate the holy men from the laity. Or was it to separate them from women? It was thought that priests should stand above the average man. So I say to the clergy, *how did that work out for you?*

I think about the meaning of life. Here I am, about to die and I still don't know. I think it should be about happiness. Am I happy? I think so. I made a lot of money, and I think that helps. But there were hard years getting there—twenty years on airplanes before I could send the junior partners on the planes instead. Who are the happiest people? What makes them happy? Fame? Princess Diana was famous. Was she happy? Does God make people happy? TV makes us all want to be young, beautiful, and thin. In other words, to be someone else.

I see that the afterlife is an overwhelming subject. There's just too much to go through, and I'm so tired. I start to feel ill, so I leave the library and drive home.

CHAPTER FOUR

Lies, All Lies

Later that night over dinner, I tell my wife I got a call from an attorney I met in Chicago. "We happened to run into each other in the courthouse cafeteria. Since the case was resolved, we had lunch together and talked about it. When he found out I was from Minnesota, he started telling me that he had always wanted to canoe the Boundary Waters. He had it all set up to go last year, but his son was in college and couldn't go at the last minute. I told him I've always wanted to go too. We hit it off really well, and we had a lot in common. I agreed to call him next time I was in Chicago. Well, today he calls me, out of the blue, and asks if I would like to go with him. And maybe his son . . . but he is not sure about his son."

"What's his name?" she asks.

"Jerry Peterson," I reply. "Well, I'm not sure if it's Peterson with an *o* or Petersen with an *e*."

Smart, I think to myself. If anyone tries to trace a Peterson or Petersen in Chicago, they'll have a hell of a time. Oh, the lies I must tell to pull this off. Who was it that said, "Oh what a tangled web we weave when first we practice to deceive"? I had become an accomplished liar. But what the hell? I was a lawyer.

"What did you tell him?"

"I told him I would love to, but I don't know how we could ever pull our schedules together. It would have to happen sometime within the next month or so, or the weather would be unpredictable. He said if I can pick a time within the next month, he could adjust."

"Do you think you can get away?" she asks.

"Yes. I think I need some time off, and the exercise would be good."

"Well, I don't know that you look well enough to go."

"Oh, I'm feeling better. I'm slowly working my way through this cold." Lies, all lies.

"You've never said you wanted to go to the Boundary Waters."

"Well, there are a lot of things I've never said before."

"Like what?"

"Well, like I've always wanted Marilyn Monroe the way the Kennedys and Frank Sinatra wanted her."

"Men," she says. "You're all pigs."

The next morning, as I browse through the library, I realize just how little I know about religion, let alone the afterlife. But at the same time, I realize that no one I know knows any more than I do. I'm driven to explore the end because I'll soon be there.

The Quran was revealed by God to the prophet Muhammad through the angel Gabriel. Muslims believe Jesus was only another apostle of Allah, that Jesus was not the Son of God, because God is above having a mere mortal son. The Quran describes heaven as green gardens, palm trees, couches, castles, and bountiful food and drink, with females to serve your every wish. I think if this is what they want, they should just go to Vegas. Why wait until you're dead?

Muslims also believe in hell, especially for Christians and Jews. Muslim tradition sees hell as bodies burning in fire and snakes tearing at them. Wonder if this is how snakes got such a bad reputation. Heaven seems to be for men only. Mohammad said that almost all women who are . . . let's say, *dirty* cannot go there. But each man who gets there will have more than one beautiful wife. A sumptuous meal will await him, with naked females to serve his every wish. Muhammad died in 632. I wonder which of his wives killed him.

I can't believe how Muslim women are treated. They must walk behind the man, can't go anywhere without a male relative, can't drive, can't go to school, and must hide their faces. It seems to me that this whole religion has been designed to enslave women forever. It is no wonder that Muslim countries have not kept up economically. The Fertile Crescent was the birthplace of civilization. Bagdad was a major hub of commerce; they invented our system of numbers, but they went into decline after embracing Islam. It's no wonder, when their kids spend all their time memorizing the Quran rather than studying science and math.

The Quran states that if you kill just one innocent person, it's as if you've killed all of humanity. The extremists seem to have forgotten that point. Apparently, they didn't *all* get an A when it came to memorizing the Quran. Many Muslims who become Jihad suicide bombers have been convinced that if they die in Jihad, they will get seventy-two virgins. How crazy is that? Sex in heaven? Without a body, no less. In the heaven of St. Thomas Aquinas, there are no earthly pleasures and certainly no sex. Only adoration of God. No wonder the Muslims and the Christians can't get along.

Muslims believe in the Last Day of Judgment, but it runs counter to the fundamentalist Christian view of the Last Day. The concept of a judgment day seems to be adapted by both religions from the Persians. Muslims believe the Antichrist will come first, and they believe he is a Jew. Allah will destroy him and Israel, with any remaining Jews converted to Islam. The Last Day of Judgment for the Jews foresees the coming of the Messiah, who will save and fully restore the nation of Israel and punish its enemies. He will set the sheep—I read, Jews—and the goats—I read, Muslims—apart. What is with the farm animals? It seems to me that the Jews and the Muslims will never get along. Maybe the fundamentalists have it right: nuclear war might be the end of times. Muslims believe that anyone who believes that Jesus was God's son is doomed. Christians, on the other hand, believe you will burn in hell if you don't believe this. I wonder who is right; I am soon to find out. Jews and Muslims both abstain from eating pork, so they have more in common than they think. Wonder what pigs ever did to get this kind of a pass.

Next up are the Christians. The Christian Bible that I own is from St. John's University in Minnesota. It is a new version and is beautifully illustrated. I never intended to read it cover to cover. It was to be an investment. I tried to read it, but the script was difficult to read and gave me a headache, so I bought a cheap Bible at the bookstore and read the entire thing over the next six days. You can't read the Bible in six days, you say? Well, I did. I'm a lawyer, and I do know how to move the paper. We're all fast readers.

In the fourth century, Pope Damasus commissioned a new Bible in Latin, called the St. Jerome's Vulgate version. I wonder if anyone could read it, aside from Damasus.

Many scholars believe this Bible was never intended to be read by the people. It was how they were controlled. The people needed the newly established hierarchy to interpret it for them.

For centuries, the Vulgate version was the only Bible in existence, until Tyndale, a sixteenth-century Protestant scholar, translated his own version from Greek and Hebrew writings. And in 1536, the church hierarchy burned the unsuspecting Tyndale at the stake. Wouldn't you just know it? Seventy years later, King James of England called together a conference of his bishops to translate the Bible again into what is the most used version in the world today, the King James Bible. Tyndale's work wasn't wasted, however, as it was the basis of this new translation. So there you have it—the most popular Bible, the one that is in use today, is four hundred years old. But there is progress in religion; there have been more than 250 translations of the New Testament in the last four hundred years. Still, all of our current beliefs are based on two-thousand-year-old happenings.

After all this research, I think I'll write my own version. The John Janne Bible has a nice ring to it. I would get rid of all the fairy tales and the "begats" and the "knoweths."

I was educated by Catholic nuns in the Augustinian tradition, which goes back five centuries. The list of sins became more fully developed by St. Augustine. For example, gluttony became a sin. Hmm, so why are so many priests fat? Jesus proclaims, "Whosoever looketh on a woman to lust after her hath committed adultery with her already in his heart." All men are toast. It looks like all the Muslim women and Catholic men will have to get together somewhere other than heaven.

Here's a saint I can relate to: St. Francis of Assisi. I like his story, as opposed to that of St. Augustine, who wants to write his own rules and boss everyone around. After seeing his friends killed in war and spending time in prison, St. Francis renounced his inheritance and became a virtual beggar. He had been born to great wealth, so his parents were furious with him. His story was well known, and as he traveled and preached, many began to follow. Soon, the Order of St. Francis evolved. It is said that as he lay dying, he was offered a pillow for his head, and he declined. His example inspired many in the church to reform. He must have shamed them into it.

For St. Paul and St. Augustine, faith in God was essential for salvation. But I wonder, does that faith have to include the church itself? In the Old Testament, "heaven" was a synonym for the sky above. What, then, was hell—the center of the earth? In

Dante's *Inferno* the very center of hell is reserved for the fraudsters, the hypocrites, and lying cheaters. Wall Streeters and politicians beware.

I was taught in Catholic school that in heaven, I would sit at the right hand of God, forever enjoying his beatific vision. Forever sounds a little long and boring to me. It seems to me that all the interesting people are in hell, but that line of thinking is going to get me in trouble. The apostle Paul suggested that Christ will eventually abolish hell, and all will be saved. I like Paul.

The Christian tradition that stems from Paul sees death as an enemy who punishes all mankind for the original sin of Adam. In Paul's letter to the Romans, he says God, being all powerful, has predestined all of us for heaven or hell. *Well, this cannot be allowed to stand.* If we're all predestined, what's the point of being good or bad when it won't make any difference? I think this has been misinterpreted; God, if there is a God, doesn't predestine but instead, being all knowing, simply knows ahead of time how we will all turn out. But if he knows how we'll turn out, isn't he just playing with us down here? According to Matthew, Jesus will come on Judgment Day and separate the sheep from the goats. Here we go again with farm animals. I worry I might be a goat.

The Council of Trent convened in the sixteenth century to slap down Calvin and the Protestants. Calvin's doctrine was that man is depraved, and his place in heaven or hell is predestined by God. I see where it would be hard to build a congregation with that philosophy. The council decided that those who died could be assisted in purgatory and on into heaven by continual prayer and donations by the living. This further drove the Protestants up the wall, and those donations made the Catholic Church richer. Why does the Catholic Church never tell the faithful how much money it has?

In the early years, life was so hard, and the thought of a wonderful place called heaven led many to suicide. The high rate of suicide among fourth-century Christian martyrs was not only morbid, but it gave the religion a bad reputation. St. Augustine came to the rescue, and *voilà,* suicide became a sin. St. Thomas Aquinas considered the act of killing oneself the ultimate violation of God's property. Dante banished those who commit suicide to below murderers in the seventh circle of his Inferno. During the Renaissance, suicide was so vilified that the corpse was sometimes mutilated or his property confiscated. I don't think I have to worry about that. Okay, I get it. It's a sin, but I'm dying anyway, so I demand a pass. I am not doing this just to get into heaven.

The book of Daniel has a passage that states, "Many of those who rest in the earth shall awake, the good to everlasting life." Is this not a resurrection? So the idea of resurrection was around 165 years before Christ. The concept of heaven and hell is first noted in the writings of Zoroaster, a Persian prophet, about six hundred years before Christ. The storyteller Virgil tells of a virgin birth and a child who will save the world—this was in 40 BC. *I'm beginning to realize a shocking trend here. The concepts of a virgin birth, resurrection, heaven, and hell, all predate Jesus and the apostles.*

The resurrection of Jesus may be hard to believe, but belief in heaven requires you to be a believer in the resurrection. It seems to me that the resurrection of Christ is the linchpin of all forms of Christianity. But there was no one who saw it, only an empty tomb. It is interesting to note that Mary Magdalene and the women who found an angel in the empty tomb were taken seriously. Nowhere at that time was the testimony of women given any credence whatsoever in the Jewish community. His disciples do say that they later saw Jesus and talked to him, but no one else saw him. It takes a lot of faith, doesn't it? I am not sure where all this investigation is leading me. Is there a God, or isn't there? Is anything that I'm learning here helpful or trustworthy? Many historical scholars consider the story of the resurrection as just a religious myth, but I think that something big did happen that day. How else can you explain the inspired energy of his disciples as they spread his word? But could this be the greatest con job in history?

Then I see there is a disagreement over the Apostles' Creed. The phase "he descended into hell" is the subject of contention between various Christian faiths. Jesus was crucified on Friday and ascended into heaven on Sunday, but what did he do on Saturday? Some say he did not go to hell, but as in the Bible, according to Luke's Gospel, Jesus said to the thief on the next cross, "Today you will be with me in paradise." Others cite Peter: "Christ was put to death as a human, but made alive by the Spirit, and the Spirit went to preach to the spirits in prison." "Prison" is interpreted as hell. It is easy to see how those preachers who went after Jesus have mangled the whole thing.

The early testaments have many contradictions and, it seems to me, outright fairy tales. Jonah and the whale and Noah's ark, for example. In the Gilgamesh and the Babylonian myth, Atrahasis, a god, tells the hero to build a boat because an epic flood is coming. The hero brings animals aboard and survives the flood. This must be where God got the idea, since this story predates Noah by hundreds of years.

In Genesis, Eve disobeys the Lord and eats the forbidden fruit and then feeds it to Adam. The Lord then says to the woman, "Because you have disobeyed me, you will suffer in childbirth, and your husband shall rule over you." I don't think my wife knows this. The man is sentenced to toil in grounds cursed with thorns and thistles. Well, at least he rules. St. Augustine and St. Paul espoused the concept of original sin; that is, sin stemming from Adam and Eve's eating forbidden fruit. Because they disobeyed God, all babies are born with original sin, but babies born with handicaps, physical or mental, were conceived in sin. Can you believe that? When I read this, I laugh so hard that the librarian gives me a dirty look.

Adam and Eve conceived two sons, Cain and Abel. Cain killed Abel and then was banished by the Lord to wander the earth. Cain fled the presence of the Lord and settled in the land of Nod, east of Eden. Cain and his wife conceived a son, Enoch.

Exactly where did his wife come from? And how can all this happen without incest? There is no reference that I see of Adam and Eve having any girls. Enoch has a son, Jrad. Jrad has a son, Mehujael, and in turn Mehujael has Lamech. And on and on it goes. All of this is hard to believe. DNA shows us as springing from monkeys, so were Adam and Eve monkeys? Many scholars maintain that the Creation story wasn't intended to be an account documenting the origin of the universe but only religious statements to show God's greatness. But that's certainly not the way it was presented to us in grade school.

In the Gospel according to Mark, he describes the end of times. The sun will darken, the moon will not give its light, and the stars will fall from the heavens. They will see the Son of Man coming in clouds with great power and glory. He will send out his angels and gather his elect from the four ends of the earth to take them to heaven. Mark tells us this generation will not pass away until all these things have taken place. Wait a minute—"this generation"? We are way past the time of Mark's generation. He seems to have gotten ahead of himself.

"As to the time, no one knows, neither the angels in heaven, nor the Son, but only the Father. Beware; keep alert; for you do not know when the time will come. It is like a man going on a trip, when he leaves home and puts his slaves in charge, each with his work, and commands the doorkeeper to be on the watch. Therefore, keep awake for you do not know when the master of the house will come, in the evening, or at midnight, or at cockcrow, or at dawn, or else he may find you asleep when he comes suddenly."

This is obviously a metaphor—at least I hope it is, because what difference does it make if I'm asleep? It seems to me to be a metaphor for a metaphor. And why do these holy men condone slavery? Nowhere in the Bible have I seen a word spoken against slavery.

Then I come across a reference to lawyers in the Gospel according to Luke. *Crap, I hope it's good. Crap, it's not.*

Jesus says, "Woe to you Pharisees, for you neglect justice and the love of God. It is these you ought to have practiced." Then, one of the lawyers hearing this says, "Teacher, when you say these things you insult us." And Jesus replies, "Woe also to you lawyers for you load people with burdens hard to bear, and you yourselves do not lift a finger to ease them. You have taken away the key of knowledge; you did not enter yourselves, and you hindered those who were entering. Woe to you."

Crap, there must not be a single lawyer in heaven. I'm glad I'm not a criminal defense lawyer. Defending someone you know is guilty seems to be a ticket to hell.

In Paul's letter to the Romans, I see where he says that men committing shameless acts with men will receive the due penalty for their error. So I guess the Bible does condemn homosexuality. So why was the clergy allowed to protect all those pedophiles? I feel sorry for the good priests who have to endure the embarrassment. They do not have to be perfect, but committing homosexual acts while condemning others for it is a step too far.

In Paul's letter to the Romans, he also brings up circumcision again. "Circumcision indeed is of value if you obey the law.

But if you break the law, your circumcision has become uncircumcision." Right, tell the Jewish babies that if they break the law they get their foreskins back. What is this obsession with circumcision?

In Paul's letter to the Thessalonians, he boasts of the steadfastness of their faith while enduring their persecutions and afflictions. "This is evidence of the righteous judgment of God, and is intended to make you worthy of the kingdom of God, for which you are also suffering. For it is indeed just of God to repay with affliction those who afflict you when he is revealed from heaven." *What does this even mean?* Since I have not been blessed with affliction, I've not suffered and will have no chance at heaven? Since lawyers have been known to persecute others, will they go to hell?

He goes on to say that the "Lord is faithful and he will strengthen you and guard you from the evil ones." As a lawyer, I think this seems a contradiction. Which is it? Is he going to afflict me so I can suffer and get into heaven, or is he going to guard me from the evil that is afflicting me? He tells the Thessalonians that they will be fine with the Lord as long as they do the things that "we command." *We* command? Shouldn't it be God's command? Sounds like Paul is leaking a little bit of ego.

I had always assumed that Paul was one of the original apostles because he is so important in the history of the church, as his many letters form much of the New Testament. I see now how little I really know about the history of Christianity. Paul at first hated the Jesus movement and stood by while many were stoned to death. On a journey to Damascus, Jesus speaks to Paul and he is converted. He becomes a dedicated disciple of Jesus. He alone set out to spread the word through the Western world. He travels thousands of miles on foot along the Roman roads. He is driven by the conviction that the end of the world is close at hand. I think that Paul, more than anyone, is responsible for Christianity today—more so than any of the apostles. Without Paul, the story of Jesus might easily have died out in a small Jewish community.

And finally, there's the part of the Bible that interests me the most: the book of Revelation, where I'll see what's in store for me. The lead-in however gives me pause. In a dream, God gave John the revelation of Jesus Christ to show his servants on earth what would soon take place. He made it known by sending his angel to his servant John. John testified to the Word of God and to the testimony of Jesus Christ to all he saw. "Blessed is the one who reads aloud the words of the prophecy, and blessed are those who hear and who keep what is written in it, for the time is near." So here we are, all Christians trusting this one man, who just had a dream. I will give John the benefit of the doubt, but "the time is near"? It's been two thousand years!

John has an active vision of what happens at the end of time. It must have been a long dream, because John sees many things. He sees an angel coming down from heaven with a great chain. The angel seizes a dragon, which is Satan, and binds him with the chain for a thousand years and throws him (or her?) into a pit. After the thousand years are up, Satan is released and gathers up the nations of the earth, who march on the camp of the saints and the beloved city surrounding it. Then a fire descends from heaven and consumes them. Satan the dragon and the false prophets are dispatched into the lake of fire and sulfur, where they will be tormented forever. He then sees a throne where one stands in judgment with the book of life. Anyone whose name is not found in the book of life is also thrown into the lake of fire. This, he notes, is the second judgment. There's a long list of offenses that will keep you out of the book of life: cowardice, faithlessness, murder, fornication, sorcery, idolatry, and lying. I give myself an 85 percent on this test.

John then sees heaven and, from the throne on high, hears God. "God will live among the mortals and they will be his people. Their tears will be wiped away, mourning and pain will be gone and death will be no more." Don't know what to make of this. Would God have said that his people would live with him?

I start to wonder whether I should be talking to a priest. *No, that won't work.* No one can know I'm terminal.

Then an angel carries John away to a high mountain and is shown the holy city of Jerusalem. The angel has a ruler of gold and measures the city for Paul. Its width, length, and height are equal. (Apparently, it's a cube.) The angel then measures the city wall at 144 cubits (whatever that is). The wall is built of jasper, and the city is pure gold. The foundations of the city wall are adorned with many layers of jewels: first is jasper, followed by sapphire, agate, emerald, onyx, carnelian, chrysolite, beryl, topaz, chrysoprase, jacinth, and finally, the twelfth, amethyst. The streets are paved with gold. The gates to the city go through a hole in a single huge pearl and are always open during the day (but there's no night, so I would guess they're always open). That is where the saying, "You'll meet St. Peter at the pearly gates," comes from. Better St. Peter than Anibus.

All this raises a lot of questions in my mind. Why is the city on a mountain and not in the heavens? Why does it need walls when the gates are always open? Why does it use materials of this earth? Why is it a cube? One should be able to calculate the size of the city and determine how many people can fit in it. Then figure that only, say, one-third of the earth's population will go to heaven, thereby determining when the end of days is coming based on total population. I must be over thinking this. Or is John just hallucinating?

At the very end of Revelation is this warning:

"If anyone adds to what has been written, God will bring a plague upon that person. If anyone takes away from the words of the book of this prophecy, God will scratch his name off the book of life and he will be denied access to the holy city. Behold he is coming soon. Amen."

John, if you could be so specific on the construction of the foundation walls, why couldn't you be more specific about the date the world will end? But then I read that "it was common in ancient times to consider dreams as expressions of divine revelation if you were a priest or a prophet." *Well, there you have it.*

The Song of Solomon is a poem in the Bible about a man and a woman, and it is absolutely pornographic. It's explained or interpreted as being about Jesus's love for the church and Israel. *You're kidding, right?* Abraham had children with his servant as well as his wife. Jacob married two sisters. Husbands did, in fact, essentially own their wives and daughters. Good God, just like cattle. They could do whatever they wanted with them, including stoning them for adultery. No mention of male adultery. The sixth commandment says, "Thou shall not kill," followed in Exodus by descriptions of offenses whereby you can kill. So how is a guy to know if he can or can't kill the opposing lawyer? I think some of the offenses apply.

Many Christians take their guidance from the Old Testament, but my God, you can find references there that condone slavery, polygamy, and incest. For several centuries after the death of Jesus, Christians interpreted certain Scriptures to say that there was more than one god. Some thought that whoever created the world was really evil, and some denied that Jesus died at all and that he still lived. This led to the creation of the New Testament. As far as I can tell, the only difference between the Old and New Testaments is that the Old Testament contains problematic Scriptures the clergy felt needed revising. Thank goodness they revised it for all of us ignorant people. They maintain that the Old Testament is an analogy that only they can interpret for us. My, how we do need them. Thank goodness this mess was cleared up; after hundreds of years it was about time to rewrite history. Many consider the Bible to be nothing more than an irrelevant relic, and I see plenty of evidence that could lead one to that conclusion. The gospels of John, Mark, Matthew, and Luke do not claim that they personally witnessed the events they describe, nor do they note themselves as the authors of the Gospels. It's possible that I'm being too hard on the Bible. It is, after all, an attempt to describe a God who is not of this world by people many years ago, who were only human.

I find a survey online that says most Americans believe in angels and that they each have a guardian angel. Hitler's guardian angel must have been asleep. I don't think there are many lawyers with guardian angels either. It says that one-fifth of Christians believe in reincarnation. What nonsense. If you don't know you've been reincarnated, what's the point? It's meaningless. Like if a tree falls in the forest and there is no one to hear it, does it make a noise? Who cares? It might as well have never happened if you don't know about it.

I realize how tired and irritated I am, and as I leave, the librarian says, "I see you in here a lot. Are you getting a taste of religion?"

"That reminds me of an old joke. Do you know what happened to the cannibal when he ate the missionary?" I ask her.

"No," she says.

"He got a taste of religion."

She just smirks.

CHAPTER FIVE

Getting Ready to Go

The pain in my chest is beginning to affect my mind. I'm having trouble holding myself together. Fits of depression come and go, but somehow I am able to get through the days without anyone being suspicious—at least I think so; I can't be sure. I decide I need to be more vigilant. Going to work the next morning, I resolve to stick to my normal routine and spend less time at the library, even though I am now driven to explore the afterlife.

Right after I arrive, Anne comes in to say she's scheduled a meeting for this afternoon but that she couldn't confirm until she talked to me.

I told her it was all right. "Go ahead and confirm it in our office."

The worried look disappears from her face. I take a deep breath, and it hurts like hell.

Then my computer crashes. "Damn it! Anne, call the IT guys."

They come in, and of course, the problem is me. I yearn for the days when we just used pencils. We never had a pencil department with four overpaid guys to fix them.

When I finally get back to work, one of the senior partners comes into my office and exclaims, "I hear you are going up to the Boundary Waters."

"Yes, it's not set yet, but I am pretty sure I'm going with a friend of mine from Chicago."

"And here I thought you were strictly a four-star–resort guy," he says. "Are you sure you're up for sleeping on the ground and paddling your ass off?"

"Well, I've always wanted to do it, and I am not getting any younger. Do you want to go along?

"No," he says. "I'm a four-star–resort kind of guy."

As if I didn't know that.

Just as he walks out the door, Dick the accountant comes into my office. "Do you have a few minutes?"

"Yes. Sit down. What's on your mind?"

"Your billable hours are down," he says, "and I just wanted to check it out. Is there a problem I should know about?"

"No, I've been planning this trip to the Boundary Waters, and it's been more work getting it together than I anticipated, but I am on top of my cases and clients. Is there a problem?"

"Oh, no. I was just wondering what was going on, as you're one of our top revenue producers."

Damn right, I think as he leaves my office. *You have no idea how much you'll miss my billable hours, and then you'll have to cash out my share of the partnership.*

I'm unfortunately popular this morning. Wayne, the managing partner, comes into my office and says, "I hear you're going on vacation. Going canoeing in the Boundary Waters?"

"Yes."

"Cool," he says. "I've always wanted to do that. Who are you going with?"

"I'm going with an attorney from Chicago. I got to know him on the Norman case. He's an avid outdoorsman and has always wanted to do the Boundary Waters thing. I've always wanted to do it, too, so we were off and running to do it together."

"Is the Norman case all wrapped up?"

"Yes, the Chicago attorney was a consultant on the case for the plaintiff, and we resolved it out of court." The case had actually wrapped up a month ago.

"Are you set with your staff?"

"As much as I can be. Terry's been doing a good job, and he can handle anything that comes up."

The afternoon meeting is with a nearby school district I represent. They've just completed a major remodeling project on one of their high schools and are fighting with their architect and contractor over change orders that have increased their costs. We start with changes to a music suite that include adding costly cabinets. The architect wants additional money for his time after he completed the original project. As the owners' lawyer, I ask the architect if he's an expert in school design. I know right away I've got him, as his ego won't permit him to admit he's not an expert. He squirms in his chair—he knows full well that their marketing materials say they are experts and have done a boatload of schools.

"Then why were these changes necessary?" I ask. "Why wasn't it done right in the first place?"

"Well, we're willing to compromise," he replies.

I'm satisfied with a compromise. I know the school hired a new music teacher after the architect had worked closely with the previous teacher on the design of the suite. The new teacher simply had a different approach, and the architect was most likely not even at fault. I've found over the years that most architects are weenies with their clients and lawyers.

Contractors, however, are not. Especially in hard times, many contractors lowball their bids with the hope of making a profit on the back end with change orders, and there are always change orders. So here we go.

"Have you reviewed the costs of this change for accuracy?" I ask the contractor.

"Yes," he replies. "We have, and the costs are due."

My staff had reviewed the bid and found questionable items, so I go after him. "Why, then, when you gave credit for these twelve cabinets that were removed from your original bid, you gave the owner a credit of $7,170, but when the same twelve cabinets were used in a different way in the revised layout, you wanted $10,234?"

He is silent for a few seconds and then says, "They must have gone up in price."

We're way ahead of him. "We've checked the price with the manufacturer and know they've not gone up. In fact, two of the cabinets have gone down in price."

He now realizes we've also checked the price of the additional cabinets that were added in the revised layout, and they don't match his asking price. "I'll have to go back and check these out with my estimator," he replies sheepishly.

I know his price will come down. Estimators never want to deal with owners directly, and they have sent this poor guy in as a sacrificial lamb. *Sacrificial lamb.* I've never used that phrase before. My time in the library is working its way into my brain.

Next, Anne ushers in the mechanical contractor, who's run into an issue with a major ductwork run that had to be rerouted due to an unknown conflict with a water main. The contractor wants $25,200 for the work. Here we go again, round and round, where all the fingers point at each other while my meter runs.

While they are talking, I excuse myself to go to the restroom, spit up some gunk, and take a few pills.

When I return, the owner maintains that the engineer should have known about the water main conflict. The engineer says his design is based on the as-built drawings from the owner, and he has a right to rely on them when he does his designs. Furthermore, he should be paid for the additional work in the redesign. It's not his fault the as-built drawings were wrong. The owner squirms and doesn't reply.

This is where I jump in and pull out the drawings. The engineer points out the difference between the original design and the change. He says the change isn't major and shouldn't cost much. Now the contractor squirms and does not reply.

"How much do you think the work should cost?" I ask the engineer.

"No more than $12,000," he replies.

"Okay, here's what I want you all to consider. It's this, or you can call your lawyers. The owner is to pay the contractor $12,000, and the engineer is absolved."

They all give me pained looks. No one is happy, so I know I've got it right. They agree to go back to their offices and let us know if they can accept this arrangement.

When they're all gone, I sit down alone with the owner to discuss what needs to happen next. He's somewhat pleased with the way the meetings went, but he also squirms as I tell him he has to be fair with the architect. "You did hire a new music teacher, and you did instruct the architect to work with and satisfy the old music teacher. It's not his fault you hired a new teacher."

"Okay," he responds.

"While you shouldn't have to pay for those twelve reused cabinets, you should pay for the new ones that were added. You can't expect to get something additional without paying for it. You should also pay the $12,000 for the water main change."

"But I don't have the money," he replies.

But I know better. "Find it in your contingency fund."

"I was hoping to use that money for furniture."

"Sorry, but you know full well that the fund was established just for these reasons."

Meeting over. I go to the bathroom and spit up more gunk and blood.

People think that all lawyers are liars, but it's not true. Lawyers can get in deep trouble for lying. They can even lose their licenses. I, however, am getting good at it now. But I would never lie in court. People, and probably God included, don't realize that we're charged with defending the guilty, and that makes us look bad. I hope God realizes that it's the law. But I think it's possible that he doesn't care about our laws. My conscience tells me, *When you know they are guilty, you should just say so.*

I don't know what to do about all the blood and gunk I'm spitting up. I can't carry a box of tissues around with me. What would I do with a wastebasket full of bloody tissues? Someone would notice. Nor can I bring bloody handkerchiefs home to Betty. Finally, I decide to use handkerchiefs but throw them away in the wastebasket in the building's front lobby.

Over lunch, I visit JCPenney, where the salesclerk must have concluded that I'm starting my own hanky business. I've gone through as least three dozen so far. I realize I'll have to go to Sears next time.

That afternoon I make a to-do list—loose ends I need to tie up for the family. Must call my brother in Denver, have lunch with my sister in Minneapolis, and visit my mother in the nursing home. How am I going to find time for my children and grandchildren? How am I going to work them all in?

And a will—can you believe that I, a lawyer, never made a will? I don't have a will, and to create one now will raise suspicion. A living will shouldn't be necessary, as I won't need anyone to make medical decisions for me—if all goes well. My solution is to go on the in-house computer and find a standard form that looks like it'll work. After Anne leaves the office for the day, I type in the blanks myself, adding the names of my children and wife, and then backdate it three years. After spending an hour figuring out how to get the printer to work (Anne is more valuable than I thought), I make only one copy and sign it. It won't be a proper legal document, but it will look like I just never got to it. I know Betty will follow it anyway. I then erase the file from my computer. I crumple the paper, spray a little coffee on it, and take it home with me to bury in my personal files. I make a mental note that Anne must get a raise before I go. Anybody who can work that damn printer is worth big bucks.

To make sure I'll be cremated, I added it into the will. I want to be cremated immediately after death. I don't want to be remembered as a gray stiff, lying in a box. My ashes are to be spread over the shoreline by my lake cabin. People are to remember me as I was—alive. I'm not sure anyone in my family will remember my wish if it's not in the will.

Cremation was once viewed as the desecration of the human body and the ultimate insult to God. In 1977, the Catholic Church decided ashes were okay, but that bodies left to rot were still preferred. I wonder if maybe I am doing too much research for my own good. When I get to wherever it is I'm going, will they let me smoke, or will they *make* me smoke? Will they make me go outside to smoke, or will I be able to stay inside? I wonder if there will be an inside or outside. I sense that my life has gone by much too quickly. Yesterday, I was young; today, I'm old and dying. This doesn't qualify as aging gracefully. Those damn cigarettes have cheated me out of my retirement. It occurs to me that some marijuana would help. I would feel better, and I'm still smoking anyway. But I don't know how to get any.

I read in the newspaper that night that there's a preacher named Harold Camping who is predicting the cataclysmic end of the world the following Saturday. "God is coming and he is pissed off" or something like that. There will be rolling earthquakes across the world, and the good people, who are assumed to be his followers, will be taken to heaven. The rest of us will be left to perish. In preparation, many of his followers have sold their houses, quit their jobs, and cashed in their insurance policies. Guess they'll need the money in heaven. If Harold Camping is right, all this planning I am doing is a waste.

I recall reading about one of the televangelists in the newspaper. Seems this Texas preacher, Copland, who endlessly solicited donations from his television viewers, has oilfields, a power plant, huge cattle ranches, an airport, and several airplanes. When challenged about all this wealth, he said this is proof that God provides for those who are true believers. Just how dumb has this country become? And we let churches get by tax-free? I'd like to put *him* through the eye of a needle.

Here is a quotation attributed to the founder of the Church of Scientology: "If you really want to make a million, start your own religion." His followers insist that he didn't really say this and that it's just a rumor, but he should have said it, because it's true. All these televangelists are highly questionable, as far as I'm concerned. I remember Tammy Faye Bakker and her husband, Jim. She died, and I think Jim is still in prison. They were running a real-estate scam using donations from their television show. A popular evangelist once said he hoped to be driving a yellow Cadillac in heaven. I wonder just what his concept of heaven is. Why doesn't he just take one of his cars with him? Why does he not disclose his vast net worth? Why is it a secret? Maybe he doesn't want all those people who make donations to know he can't possibly need any more money. I've seen estimates that indicate over $500 billion is contributed to Christian churches and causes every year. Wouldn't it be refreshing if just once, one of these preachers would say, "Don't send in any money this week. We have enough for now"?

Even in these modern days, heaven still works as a motivator for death. David Koresh, the Waco, Texas, crazy, convinced his followers that if they fought and died with him, they would go to heaven with him.

Then there's Jerry Falwell, who died a few years ago. He was a real piece of work. His grandfather was an atheist, his father was an agnostic, and he was an evangelical. Guess it took the family a while to come around. He founded Liberty University, which has tens of thousands of students. He also started the Moral Majority, which was little more than a political lobby for evangelical Christians. He was an outspoken advocate for his ideas, and I think he even ran for president. Many in the evangelical community were critical of Jerry for pushing a political agenda that had no basis in religion.

Falwell's TV program, *The Old-Time Gospel Hour*, frequently featured segregationists. I wonder if any of the students at his Liberty University are black. They must not be, because he preached that blacks and whites should be schooled separately. He backed a video titled the *Clinton Chronicles,* which alleged that Bill Clinton was behind several murders. The video was later proven to be a fraud. This is funny: the atheist Christopher Hitchens said upon Falwell's death, "If he had been given an enema, he could have been buried in a matchbox."

CHAPTER SIX

Research

Today is Saturday, and I'm going to visit my mother in her nursing home. It will be for the last time. She is eighty-two years old and has Alzheimer's disease. My father died young.He grew up on a farm, and he and his brother both contracted rheumatic fever and had enlarged hearts. This condition kept them out of the war but later killed them. My mother lived on her own for twenty years after my dad died, and those years were not easy. She was often lonely, and then she developed Alzheimer's; it's been hard for us to watch her progressively go downhill. She was a teacher for over thirty years, and between her retirement pension and social security, she's never been a financial burden. But as she's grown older and her friends have died off, she's become increasingly depressed.

It's a difficult meeting for me because, as usual, she doesn't recognize me and over the course of our visit, she probably asks me ten times where I live. I hold her hand and cry, because I know she won't miss my visits; she never remembers them anyway. I'm convinced that when your brain is dead, you are, in fact, dead. A person without a functioning brain is not really alive. I know that's a terrible thing to say or even think, but it is absolutely true. Your brain is your essence and therefore must be your soul. I'm not proposing that we should treat them like the living dead. There could be something inside that's aware but just can't get out.

On my mom's dresser I find an unopened letter addressed to her from the Catholic Women's League, and I open it. It's their newsletter, which she can no longer read or understand, but I read it to her anyway. It lists two members who have passed on, with the following notation from John 11:25–36: "I am the resurrection and the life. Whoever believes in me, even if he dies, will live, and everyone who lives and believes in me will never die."

"May they rest in peace." I now see references to death in almost everything. It stuns me to think that I will die before my mother dies. It's not fair. After holding her hand, which she seems to like, I turn into a basket case. I kiss and hug her and leave after an hour, telling the nursing staff that I'm going on a trip and won't see them for awhile. On my way out, I'm reminded that it costs eighty thousand dollars a year to keep her here, and she's been a vegetable for three years. I'm not even sure she would want to live that way. I know I wouldn't, but then, I won't have to. There are residents here who are very much aware mentally but have severe physical problems. Several have told me that they don't know why they are still alive. They say they don't know why God has let them live this long.

As I leave, I see a pamphlet titled "Letting Go." It deals with the final days before death. I sit down to read it in the lobby.

"Each individual comes upon death in their own unique way. It's the last experience in life; it comes when the time is here. As a person reaches the understanding that they are dying they begin to withdraw. They withdraw from friends, then family, and become introverted." It says they begin to evaluate their lives and are oblivious to all that surrounds them. They quit eating and their bodies wither. There is constant sleep, and then death comes. Just what I needed to hear. *I have to get out of here.*

I know this is what would be in store for me if I were to let the cancer run its course and die in bed. I've made the right decision, but I won't withdraw before I go. I can't withdraw from my family, but I know I must to some degree, or I'll lose my mind. My withdrawal can't be obvious.

I drive to the library. The librarian really seems to wonder why I'm so interested in religion. Guess I don't look the type. My time here is occupying my mind and keeping me from going crazy.

The Vatican has, at best, a checkered history. I wonder when and how the first pope or bishop came to be. Where did all this hierarchy come from? And there were women in the early leadership. Where are they now? The Acts of the apostles notes sisters who were evangelists, so when—and why—were they cut out?

And then there are all those saints. Pope John Paul canonized more saints than all the 263 previous popes combined. That's a lot of miracles to come up with. It used to take three miracles to become a saint. I try to calculate it in my mind. There were 482 canonizations by Pope John Paul, so that would take 1,446 miracles. But that was too many, so he cut the required number of miracles to two. I wonder why I can't remember any of those miracles.

Before Cardinal Ratzinger became pope, he moved a pedophile priest into a new congregation, where he again abused children. Bishops obviously were instructed to keep such cases quiet. I guess you could say Ratzinger was fallible before he became infallible as Pope Benedict. The Catholic Church seems to protect itself over and above its own children. The Vatican's bureaucratic elite, the Curia, is proving to be history's first old boys club. Vatican City was created in 1929 in a deal between the fascist Benito Mussolini and the papacy. I wonder what the details of that deal with the devil were. I do know that the Jews suspect that the pope cut a deal to remain silent about the Holocaust in return for the Vatican land. I hope they're not right. St. Augustine preached that Jews could exist in the Christian Church but only with inferior status. His interpretation of Psalm 59:11 was, "*Do not slay them, just scatter them.*" The Jews were considered to be God-killers at that time. I am not sure how St. Augustine can justify this position, as Jesus himself was a Jew.

In the seventeenth century, the concept of hell began to be challenged. If God were merciful and good, how could he (or she) be so inhumane? But then, he's not human, is he? Francis de Sales was influential in softening the notion of hell. He espoused that sin could be forgiven rather than sending us straight to hell. I like St. Francis; he seems to want to give us a chance. Many other religions now think of hell as just the absence of heaven or separation from the glory of God. But I think there was a problem with this approach. How could the churches control the congregation and keep the alms flowing if they didn't scare the crap out of them? Purgatory was certainly taught to me in school, but it was never adopted as official doctrine. Pope Benedict seemed to be backing off the concept of purgatory as he took the church back to the Middle Ages.

In the seventeenth century, Pope Urban put Galileo on trial for heresy. It seems Galileo's findings that the earth revolves around the sun was a violation of Scripture. I didn't know Catholics were so concerned about astronomy to go so far as to actually try to hang someone. Pope Urban obviously felt very strongly that the sun revolved around the earth. He also must have thought he was infallible. I don't know if they ever updated the Scriptures, so the Catholic sun may still be revolving around the earth.

Galileo was the most famous victim of the Inquisition. The Inquisition was the Catholic Church's fight against heretics. Apparently, anyone who disagreed with the church about anything was considered a heretic. Inquisitions were started in the twelfth century and lasted until the nineteenth century. *Wow. Catholics do not give up easily.* The Protestant Reformation was, to say the least, heresy. In response, Pope Paul III established something called the Supreme Sacred Congregation of the Universal Inquisition. Crap, anything with a name like that would have scared me into line. Those suspected of heresy could be tortured, and those found guilty could be burned at the stake. Galileo narrowly escaped this fate. Most of the guilty were given penances, such as a public scourging or fines, but many were sentenced to life imprisonment.

In 1992, Pope John Paul II expressed regret for the church's handling of Galileo. He issued a declaration acknowledging that the church's tribunal, which judged Galileo, had committed errors. I notice that he did not say the pope made errors; it was the tribunal—they were the ones who screwed up. He declared that a statue of Galileo would be erected on the Vatican grounds in tribute to him. Pope Benedict also praised Galileo's contributions but suspended the statue. The only conclusion I can draw from this is that the clergy doesn't want to remind the faithful that they, the clergy, are less than perfect. Will they stop at nothing to protect their legacy?

In 1962, the Vatican Ecumenical Council was created to modernize the church through full-scale reform. It was to achieve social justice in all issues. It was intended to place equal emphasis on advocating for the poor and for peace, rather than just focusing on birth control and abortion. Pope John Paul and his right-hand man, Joseph Ratzinger, later changed all that right back. Nowadays, you hear much from the clergy about abortion and gay marriage but very little about the poor and the homeless.

Pope John Paul set up a commission to study birth control methods. The commission voted to allow oral contraception under certain circumstances. But again, this was reversed by the pope in 1968. American Catholics seem to have ignored him, as evidenced by the smaller number of children in Catholic families. Why would the church be so against birth control? I think they just want to populate the world with followers. I can think of no other reason.

After all the sex abuse cases in Ireland, the Vatican called for overhauling the training of priests. Makes one wonder just how they were trained in the first place. Why would they need any training at all? Shouldn't they know intrinsically what is right and what is wrong?

Monsignor John Tracy Ellis, who taught Catholic Church history, always started the school year by telling his students, "Ladies and gentlemen, be ready to find out that the mystical body of Christ has a lot of warts." I wish I could have taken his class, because I'm finding more warts than I can deal with.

In the eleventh century, the pope led the crusaders to believe they'd go to heaven in exchange for fighting to recapture Jerusalem. Looks like the Muslims and the Christians were killing each other so they could get into heaven together. This is interesting: it seems Jerusalem has been the cause of fighting forever. The Babylonians, Israelites, Jews, Philistines, Jebusites—don't ask me; I've never heard of that one either—the Assyrians, the Persians, the Greeks, the Macedonians, the Maccabees, and then the Romans have all fought over it. Whatever happened to peace-loving religions? And it still isn't resolved; we still have the Jews and the Muslims fighting over Jerusalem. I think we should own it; I think the money we have dumped into Israel and Palestine over the years is enough to have bought Jerusalem. It would be cheaper to make them our fifty-first state. Kick everyone out and start over.

The Cathars were a Christian sect that didn't follow the lead of the Vatican. They held that the Eucharist could not be the body of Christ; they claimed that the prelates of the church were living evil lives, that baptism was just a water wash, and that confessions to the church's priests were useless. They believed only in Jesus and the Bible, as taught by the apostles. This infuriated the Vatican until the year 1209, when the pope sent the abbot of Citeaux on a crusade against them. Losing the fight, the Cathars were forced to retreat into the city of Beziers in Spain. The abbot's crusader in charge of the siege was Simon de Montfort, who instructed his troops to gouge out the eyes of a hundred prisoners, cut off their noses and lips, and send them into the city as a warning that they should surrender. They did not surrender. When the crusaders finally took the city, Simon instructed the troops to kill them all. The troops asked, "What about the true Catholics among them?" Simon replied, "Kill them all. God will sort them out." The abbot wrote to Pope Innocent III, "Today twenty thousand heretics were put to the sword." Over the next fifty years, all of the remaining Cathars were executed. They do not exist today. Pope "Innocent." *Really!* Actually, I think there still might be one Cathar around: me.

If there is a loving God, how can all these religions rationalize the wars and killing that has gone down in his name over the centuries? In the fifteenth century, the Reformation led to a thirty-year war between the Catholics and the Protestants, during which a third of the people in Germany were killed. The war ended with a treaty, the Peace of Westphalia, which pissed off the pope, who promptly declared it null and void for all time. His verdict was ignored by everyone, including the Catholics, who were tired of fighting. They don't teach you this fascinating stuff in Catholic grade school. I wish I'd looked into it sooner.

Why are so many wars called holy wars? What is so holy about killing? Jesus did not espouse warfare; the Bible says to beat your swords into plowshares. So why are there so many Christians ready to go to war? The Crimean War, fought in the mid-nineteenth century, took the lives of three-quarters of a million people. Roman Catholic France and Anglican England, along with Caliph of Islam, were at war with Christian Russia over control of Constantinople. The west did not want the Russians to take over Constantinople. Since it's now Istanbul, it's obvious who won. The real story, however, is how the public and the soldiers were motivated and manipulated. They were told that Russian Christian orthodoxy was an impure version of Christianity and that it had to be stopped because it was heresy.

And we now seem to consider Islam to be the heresy! Go figure. How many have died in the name of religion? And how many more are to die? In the early 1800s, the Ursuline Catholic convent in Boston was burned to the ground by Protestants because they were practicing an evil religion. Soldiers on both sides of the Civil War believed God was on their side. Because the North won, did all the soldiers from the South go to hell?

There was an article in the paper about a guy who was captured by the Japanese in World War II and was a survivor of the

Bataan Death March. He credits his survival to his faith in God. After the horrific experience, his faith in God is unshaken. Well, okay, but what about the hundreds who didn't survive? Did none of them have faith in God? Did they pray for God to take them? I think not. Why did God allow almost all of them to die?

How is it that God, who has assured us everlasting life in a future world, would place us in a world of constant war and religious hatred? The Buddhist and Hindu people have been at war forever over boundaries and religion. Religion does bring a feeling of comfort and morality to many, but many others are inspired to terrorism by religion. They fly planes into buildings and blow up funerals. How again does religion make the world a better place? Then I see that there are those who believe the God of the Abrahamic Bible is more consistent with the devil. They find God to be divine, but he is a God who wreaks suffering, destruction, and death upon mankind, a God who leads us into war and genocide.

I am beginning to lose it; my interest is creating more questions than answers. Much of this is making me angry.

I have felt sorry for myself long enough. Who am I to feel sorry for myself when all those twenty-year-olds are dying in Iraq and Afghanistan? Many of them took their own lives. I have had a wonderful fifty-five years, and they've died violently in a foreign land. Religions deserve credit for their moral codes and their gods, which, through the fear of hell and the hope of heaven, have made the faithful more civil. To some extent, they have even fostered democracy. Religion seems to be at the center of most wars and a lot of politics, but what if there is no God? What if all religion is a fraud? How could all the people who've ever existed be so wrong? Wasn't America founded by people escaping religious persecution? *I'm confused.*

Countless men have gone to war, assured by their religion that heaven would be their reward if they died in battle. Their death would be for the glory of God. How does fighting to the death glorify God? It seems that only radical Islam gets by with this crazy notion now. Have the rest wised up? I think few are willing to buy this crap anymore.

After supper, Betty badgers me into taking a walk around the neighborhood with her. I'm not sure my lungs can take it, but I can't say no. We walk past a home where an older couple are having an auction. Rumor has it they're moving into an assisted living facility somewhere. A large crowd is gathered around furniture, clothes, and assorted junk lying all over the lawn. We dodge traffic for two blocks before we clear the parked cars and enter a wooded area.

Then, out of the woods comes a voice, "Going, going, gone."

My heart stops as Betty walks on in front on me. I know I'm going, going, but the thought of being gone overcomes me.

"What's wrong?" she says.

My mind is racing, unrelated thoughts colliding.

"Are you okay?"

I pause to collect myself. "Oh, I was just thinking about that rocking chair I saw. It could look good in our living room."

"No way," she replies.

After another block, I tell Betty I forgot there's a call I need to make and that she should go on without me. I'm breathing hard, and I spit blood in the grass on the way back.

On Sunday we go to church with my son and his family, and I have to sit through the songs and psalms. I can hardly bear it.

"Be not afraid; I go before you always. Come follow me, and I will give you rest."

"Then sings my soul, my savior God to thee. How great thou art, how great thou art."

"When through the woods and forest glades I wander and hear the birds sing sweetly in the trees, when I look down from lofty mountain grandeur, and hear the brook and feel the gentle breeze." (They must know I'm going to the Boundary Waters.) "And he will raise you up on eagle's wings, bear you on the breath of dawn, make you to shine like the sun, and hold you in the palm of his hand." This song is so powerful and inspiring that I actually feel uplifted.

The sense of "I," of "me," is disappearing. I can sense timelessness, infinity, and eternity, and my fear of death is vanishing. I wonder what I've done with my life. Did I do a good job? Did I add value to the world, or did I take from it? Who am I? What was I meant to do? Did I fulfill the promise everyone had for me? I think in great measure I did. Each human must have a purpose, and his or her life should be a search for that purpose. I've always been proud of my family. My wife, son, and daughter were all college graduates with multiple degrees. I will miss my children, who taught me more than I ever taught them. I'm very proud of them. I did well as a parent. I'm leaving behind a legacy to be proud of. Well, my wife, Betty, did most of the work. I feel a deep sense of joy and a new energy consuming me.

On Monday morning, I'm late for an early partners meeting, which I'd forgotten about. I'm well aware that I must appear as interested in the firm as I've always been; to appear disinterested could be a tipoff. So in the meeting I bring up our long-range marketing plan. I think it's particularly clever to be talking long-range in front on them. "We should be advertising," I say. "Other firms are. We're missing the boat here. Let's at least look at sponsoring something like *MacNeil/Lehrer NewsHour*—that's where the Democrats are. And *Fox News*, where the Republicans are. We need to reach the decision makers, the people who hire us." After listening to the older partners talk about how it used to be unprofessional to advertise, we agree to have Anne check into the costs of sponsoring these programs. The rest of the meeting, I tune out.

Afterward, I think of my partners who are all very well off, and I think of what Jesus said. You are either with me or against me. "It is easier for a camel to pass through the eye of a needle than for a rich man to enter heaven." Maybe I should be giving away all my money before I go. It's too late now. We all have just one life to live, and we can't take money with us. We only need so much to live comfortably; we can only drive one car at a time; and we only eat three meals a day. I do think, however, that Jesus was wrong when he said "the meek will inherit the earth."

Maybe he meant they'll inherit a place in heaven, because they sure haven't gotten anywhere on earth for two thousand years.

Why did I have to rush through my life? What was the hurry? All those meetings . . . in retrospect, I cannot think of a single one that was so important or anything that couldn't have waited. In fact, the more I was unavailable to my partners and even my clients, the more they seemed to appreciate me. It would have been nice to take a long walk at lunch or a day off just to read a good book. I think of all the classics I wanted to read but never did, and all those vacations, where we ran through Europe, taking no time to enjoy the culture. It seems I raced right through to the end of my life, and I always thought I was smart.

Well, there will be some advantages to my demise. I won't have to work with my stockbroker anymore. I won't be stuck in traffic in snowstorms anymore. There will be no more boring partner meetings where everyone needs to put in their two cents on every single issue, every single time it is brought up. No one will snicker at me for smoking anymore. I wonder how I'll be remembered. General MacArthur said, "You're remembered for the rules you break, not how you followed the herd." I was good at breaking rules. I like the feeling—most lawyers do.

Terry comes into my office and says, "You know Fred in accounting is leaving to join the Church of Scientology."

"What?" I ask. "Who's Fred?"

"You know, that weird guy in accounting with the earring and the ponytail."

"What's he going to do?"

"He's leaving to work for the Church of Scientology."

"Is that the bunch that short skinny actor that plays all the action heroes belongs to?"

"Yes, that's the one."

"Well, I never had much to do with Fred."

As soon as I'm alone, I check out this bunch online. From Wikipedia, I read, "Scientology teaches that we are beings, immortal beings, who have forgotten our true nature." Crap, I didn't even know I had a true nature to forget. "We are rehabilitated through some type of counseling known as 'auditing,' which is suppose to recall painful events in order to free ourselves." They believe that psychiatry is a destructive practice and should be abolished, but "auditing" sounds a lot like psychiatry to me. They believe our souls, which they call "thetans," are reincarnations, and that before living on Earth, we lived on other planets. Geezus, I wonder which planets I lived on. I have this rash that might have come from some place hot like Mars. I see that Scientology is a creation of Ron Hubbard, who is also a science fiction writer. Okay, now I get it. Then I see that they also do some social service work in antidrug programs and prison rehabilitation and have good moral guidelines.

Looking into Scientology on the Internet leads me to parapsychology, which is the study of reincarnation and out-of-body experiences. It maintains that people who have died and come back report experiencing peace and love as they float above their bodies and the surroundings. I'm not sure this is meaningful, because they didn't really die. Could just be a nice dream. Spiritualist mediums convinced many gullible individuals that they could communicate with the dead. All were later exposed as frauds. Studies by Ian Stevenson, a Canadian biochemist and psychiatry professor, are interesting, however. He conducted research on thousands of children who claimed to remember events from a past life. His research was most successful on children between the ages of three and seven, with memories fading as age advanced.

One case was a boy in Beirut who said he had been a mechanic who was thrown from a moving car and died. The boy could remember the names of his previous family members, the name of the driver of the car, and the exact location of the accident. This proved to match the life of a man who died several years before the boy was born, a man who had no connection to his new family.

Another case study was a three-year-old boy who started talking about his previous life in a different city in India. He claimed he had ownership of a medical company and said he lived in a large house with many others to serve him. His brother shot him in a quarrel over money. He remembered the name of the company, and indeed, there was such a company with such an incident involving two brothers. Upon hearing about the child, the family of the dead man invited the boy to visit. They were astonished when the child recognized places and people and knew details only the family knew.

While I find all this impressive, it's hard to believe in reincarnation. Even Stevenson did not claim that his work proved the existence of reincarnation. I also note that these two cases are from countries that have cultures that believe in reincarnation. But even if it is true, what difference does it make?

I call the doctor's office and ask for an extension of my prescriptions, notifying them that I've decided not to have any treatment and thanking them for their service. Then I leave the office for the day and go to the pharmacy and the sporting goods store.

Alan the outfitter had told me to get nylon pants, because they dry out within minutes. "Don't wear blue jeans; when they get wet they take forever to dry out, and you will be uncomfortable. No cotton," he said. "Among the backpacking folks there is a saying: 'Cotton kills.' It doesn't dry fast enough, so your sweat just stinks. Anything made of cotton is worthless. Wool or fleece is the way to go. It's cool as well as warm. Fleece also makes for a great pillow. Also, get rain gear, because storms come and go here every other day."

At the sporting goods store, when I tell them that I'm going canoeing in the Boundary Waters, they know exactly what I need and take me to the pants, shirts, and rain gear. I try them on, but I don't like them. They just don't feel right on my skin. They feel slimy and slippery, but I buy them anyway. I'll take blue jeans along, too. So what if I'm a stinky corpse? All corpses are stinky, aren't they? Then they try to sell me everything else under the sun that they think I need. But I remember the list of things included in the Ely outfitters package, so I tell them I need to check that out first before I buy anything more.

That night at dinner, I tell my wife that my canoe trip to the Boundary Waters is on. "I called him and asked if he was still interested, and he said yes."

"So when would you go?" she asks.

"I gave him my best date—leave on August 21 and return home on September 2. He checked his calendar and said that is just enough time to get his affairs in order. It's a go."

"So you'll be gone for . . , what? Twelve days?"

"Well, it depends somewhat on the weather. If it storms, we may have to lay up, so figure twelve to fourteen days."

"Is he going to come here?" she asks.

"No, he'll fly into Duluth, and I'll meet him at the airport. Then we will drive up together."

"What was his name again?"

"Jerry Peterson. Remember? He's the lawyer I met in Chicago."

"Okay, but I still don't know that you look good enough to go."

"I feel good. And I need a vacation." Of course I feel good. I just downed a few painkillers.

"You look like you've been losing weight. Are you sure you're okay?"

"Yes, I am fine. I'm trying to get in shape to go."

"Why are you trying to lose weight? Aren't you going to lose weight with all that paddling?"

"Damn, I think your right. I'd better quit dieting." Never-ending lies.

After that, I start eating a Big Mac, fries, and a malt every day for lunch. And they actually taste good. I spend the next few days taking care of work at the office and cutting out to the library as soon as I can. The thought of my afterlife has taken me over. I want to know what is in store for me.

In the Jewish Talmud, souls of the dead are judged. The good are led immediately to something called the "World to Come." The bad are schooled and then allowed into the World to Come. There's no concept of hell or eternal damnation. Sounds good to me. Maybe I should have converted to Judaism. I would have looked good in a beanie, and I could have changed my name to Jannish. It would have been good for business.

There are some odd ideas here, too. In the book of Ecclesiastes, Solomon finds that both men and animals are to be judged alike. I know some Jewish lawyers who are also jackals and are going to need a whole lot of that schooling. If it's true that all the animals are God's creatures, why does he allow us carnivores to eat them? Why is it not a sin to eat God's creatures?

Jewish family law has divided the Hasidic and Rabbinical Jews over something I don't understand. However, they both agree that a "foul odor" can be grounds for divorce. So can you hide some cheese under the bed and declare divorce? Orthodox Christians and Jews insist that if you believe the Bible is true, then you have to believe that Jesus's body, as well as yours, will be raised from the dead. Not only that, but we will be buff and beautiful. It must drive them nuts that many of their own people just don't buy it. The Pentateuch, or the Torah, is about the five books of Moses. In it, the Lord speaks to Moses almost every day, telling him what to do, what not to do, where to go, where not to go, and so forth. The Lord and Moses are very chatty. The Lord even gives Moses medical direction on what to do for a bad member. Yes, he is referring to *that* member. He talks a whole lot about what to do with "unclean members."

Then it hits me: is that why Jewish parents circumcise their babies? Oh, for heaven's sake! Don't they think hygiene has improved over two thousand years? In the book of Genesis, circumcision is, as God says, a sign of his covenant with Abraham and the descendants of Abraham. From Genesis 17:30—"This is my covenant, which you shall keep, between me and your descendants after you. Every male child among you shall be circumcised." I guess you could say that a lot of Jewish men have skin in the game. In Judaism, circumcision is performed by mohels. I have no idea who mohels are, but keep them away from me.

This whole segment in the Pentateuch about Moses and the Lord is never-ending—and not very believable. Tradition has it that Moses wrote the first five books, known as the Pentateuch, based on revelations from God. It seems unlikely, however, that he could have recorded his own death, as noted in Deuteronomy. Outside of the Bible, there is no evidence that a Moses ever existed on this earth. There is no evidence that his flight from Egypt, crossing the Red Sea, ever took place. Apparently, few other than the Jews buy into these Moses/Lord discussions, because no one really knows who wrote it. But I do believe in and have tried to follow Moses's Ten Commandments.

Peter and Paul had a huge argument over circumcision. Peter maintains that if the Gentiles wish to join the Jewish community of Christ, they must be circumcised. Paul disagrees, as he is preaching the Word of the Lord to the Greeks, and I assume circumcision was a tough sell. Looks like there were hard feelings between the two that lasted until death. If Peter had won this argument, I'm sure there would be a lot fewer Christians today. I wish I could ask my mother if they ever thought about circumcising me. It doesn't matter now.

Then I remember that the Catholic Church celebrated a Feast of the Circumcision when I went to school, it was on New Years day. But it is no longer celebrated, and the church never bothered to tell me why. I'm a Catholic, and I know so little about the Catholic Church. I don't think it's all my fault, though. Why didn't they teach more of this history in school? The more I find out, the more I think I can see why.

I recently watched a TV program about Israel's ultra-Orthodox Jews who have a lifestyle that is simply amazing in this day and age. The men dress in big black hats and long black jackets. They interest me, because I remember seeing a large group of them in the Chicago airport, going somewhere together, and did they ever stand out. They spend almost all of their lives studying the Torah, at the expense of other studies, like math and science. They do not have television or computers, and consequently are quite ignorant of anything going on in the world. The women are the real saints, though. They have to do everything, because the men do little to no work. The women have an average of six children to look after, they do the household chores, and then they are expected to work for a wage. I think that sucks.

I come across a chapter in a book about how the ancient Hebrews buried their family members beneath the floors of their houses—the better to keep and care for them. This reminds me of a newspaper article where Forest Lawn Cemetery in Los Angeles auctioned off the burial vault above Marilyn Monroe's. The high bidder wanted to be buried face down. But this memory is totally unrelated, and I feel guilty for thinking about it. I say a silent apology to the Jews.

Fundamentalist Christians take the Bible literally, even though it was written many hundreds of years ago by uneducated storytellers. They insist on the literal interpretation of every word. Are we not smarter than those who went before us? Why would we so blindly buy into fairy tales? These Christians take their guidance from the Old Testament, which condones slavery, polygamy, and incest. Then we have the Rapture, where Christ comes again and gathers the faithful to heaven and banishes the rest of us who are not fundamentalists. At this "end of times," the Jews will convert to Christianity. I'll bet that drives the Jews crazy.

For born-again Christians, hell seems to be embraced mainly as a place for all the rest of us. They seem to have pledged that their life on this earth is to have no joy whatsoever, and they're determined to see to it that no one else has any either. What a bunch of sweethearts. Christian conservatives contend that the average person cannot really understand what the Bible is saying without proper direction, that they—and only they—need to be there to interpret it for you. For their leading preacher, Hal Lindsey, the Revelation of St. John foretells that Armageddon is at hand. However, the literal interpretation of the Bible does not include the nuclear missiles that Lindsey mentions.

I become tired and disappointed with religion, so I decide to go home. I still don't know whether I believe in God. I still don't know much about heaven and hell or if they even exist. The more I learn, the more I'm convinced that no one, not even the clergy, knows anything. The deeper I dig, the more questions I have.

CHAPTER SEVEN

Back to the Library

The time is going by quickly. I'm down to my last week now, and my heart is so heavy that I can hardly hold myself together. It's all happened so fast that the reality of it all is only now sinking in. I am going to die. I've accepted my fate and am resolved to go through with my plan. So far, it's come together, and I'm still confident I can pull it off. The harder I work in the office, the more bearable the wait, but the time also goes by so much faster. I must review my plan now in detail and tie up a few loose ends. The last week is to be spent getting my family, clients, and staff in a position where they can continue without too many problems.

I call my son. "You want to meet somewhere for lunch? It's been awhile."

"Yeah, let's do it."

While we eat, I maneuver him into inviting Betty and me over to his house for dinner so I can see my grandchildren.

When I return to the office, I study my finances to see how secure I will leave Betty. The stocks look to be fine long-term investments, and Betty or my son, Ralph—whoever they decide to have manage the portfolio—shouldn't be pressed to make any quick decisions. I had always been a long-term investor, and I see no reason to change anything now. The checking account will need more money, so I call the broker and make a transfer, bringing the balance up to twelve thousand, which is higher than usual but won't be high enough to draw suspicion. It should be enough money to carry her through the first few months until she adjusts. But after reading my insurance policy, I'm shocked to see that suicide voids the payout. Crap, what now? I have never committed a fraudulent act in my life. The policy is for half a million dollars and with our savings, it would be more than enough for Betty if she lived to be a hundred. Then I rationalize the problem away. I would be dead in a few months anyway, and they would have to pay out the full amount then. So I'm not really cheating them.

I then wonder if she will ever remarry. I don't like the idea of some other man in my house with my wife, using my money. But there's a downside to everything, and I don't have much choice anyway. I decide to write my obituary, just for the hell of it, to see how it might sound. *Better do it longhand. Don't want it on the computer.*

"John Janne died on August whatever. He was born in St. Paul, Minnesota, on December 23, 1955. He received his bachelor's degree from the University of Minnesota and his law degree from the William Mitchell College of Law. Employed by Corker & Smith for thirty years, he specialized in construction law. As a senior partner at the firm, he was well known by local contractors and architects. He is survived by his wife, Betty (Wilson) Janne, and their two children, Alicia Cooper and

Ralph Janne, and four grandchildren, Kate Cooper, Joey Cooper, Marie Janne, and Morgan Janne. He is also survived by his mother, Alicia Janne, all from Minneapolis. His passions were tennis, golf, and his northern Minnesota lake cabin. Mr. Janne drowned while canoeing in the Boundary Waters. Services will be held at St. Francis by the Lake Catholic Church."

I read it again the following day and note that I have forgotten my brother and sister. I tear it up anyway. Noting my survivors gives me comfort, and I know my family can and will move on without me.

I'm trying now to spend as much time as possible with Betty without arousing her suspicion. I talk her into taking a walk after dinner, and we run into one of our neighbors whose husband recently died from ALS. I ask her how she held up for the three years she cared for him as he slowly wasted away without hope.

"God cared for me. He made me strong and helped me through each day, one by one."

So God cared for her but apparently didn't give a damn about him? Her comments piss me off. God must have lost interest in us after he created us. Maybe there are too many of us to keep track of. Maybe he just looks at the totality of us, like a herd, rather than as individuals.

It reminds me of one of Garrison Keillor's stories. I have this image of a little boy looking down at an anthill, musing about what they're up to. *Oops*—the boy steps on one. "Sorry, I didn't know you were there." Why are they all so busy scurrying around? Then he pulls out a magnifying glass and fries one or two. Next, he pushes a mound of dirt in front of a line of ants who are dragging white stuff back to the hill with a hole in it, but they just crawl over the mound, so he buries them with dirt. In the final episode of this saga, a bucket of water washes them away. Their "Revelation Day" had arrived.

Later that night, I see a poem written by Mary Elizabeth Frye in a magazine I am reading. It brings me to tears. I rip it out of the magazine, fold it up, and place it in my wallet.

> Do not stand at my grave and weep
> I am not there, I do not sleep
> I am the thousand winds that blow
> I am the diamond's glints upon the snow
> I am the sunlight on ripened grain
> I am the gentle autumn rain
> When you awaken in the morning's hush
> I am the swift uplifting rush
> Of birds in circling flight
> I am the soft star that shines at night
> So do not stand at my grave and cry

I know that when people are in a tough place, they often revert to religion, but I'm not there yet. Religious practice may be a necessary part of most people's lives, but I am beginning to think that the Bible is mostly mythology. In many cases, the early writings contain nonsense that clerics have desperately tried to revise.

Benjamin Franklin said, "It is convenient when you are a reasonable person to find a reason to enable yourself to believe whatever it is you want to believe. To do whatever it is you want to do and still be a reasonable person." I wonder if that is what I am doing. I wonder if I am becoming an agnostic or an atheist. I need to check out what they have to say, so the next moring I am off to the library again.

I see right away that most people don't even know the difference between atheists and agnostics, me included. Atheists simply say there is no god or afterlife. Atheists point out how dangerous religion has been over the years, the evidence being conflicts such as the Spanish Inquisition and even the attacks of 9/11. They make a good point; religion is at fault for many wars, but that doesn't prove that there's no God. Then I read that atheism is known as a "non-prophet" organization, and I chuckle to myself.

Agnostics believe that the existence of a God, one's soul, and life after death cannot be proven and are therefore unknowable. They simply say they are unsure whether there is a God. I think I may fall into this camp. Others refer to agnostics as "nones," because they have no religion. Crap, I do not want to be referred to as a "none."

Then I run across a troubling piece of text. *This is not good.* This atheist argues that if 20 percent of pregnancies are miscarried, is God not the greatest abortionist of all? Geez, if there is a God, he's going all the way down to that seventh layer of hell.

In England, there are 47,000 Christian churches, yet only 6.5 percent of the entire population goes to church regularly. In

France, most churches are in rural areas, and in some places, one priest covers as many as twenty-five churches. In Germany, one diocese shut down one hundred of its three hundred churches. So where did all those parishioners go? Why did they go? In our country, it's not only the faithful who are declining; the clergy itself is in decline. And I miss the nuns—they were the best part of the Catholic Church.

The Bible's authority in American culture was greatly diminished in the fight over slavery during the Civil War. Many preachers, like Thornton Stringfellow, preached that God had sanctioned slavery as lawful.

Richard Holloway was the bishop of Edinburgh who created quite a stir when he said that faith was of little help in determining the morality or immorality of mankind. Here is a man who came to this conclusion based on a lifetime of religious study. He rose to the highest position in his church, but he was roundly castigated by his congregation, and he ultimately left. As an agnostic, he maintains that there is morality beyond the Christian tradition. "I don't expect to meet my maker when I die, but if I do, it will not surprise me," he said. I wish I could talk to Holloway. I have many questions, and I would like to hear his answers. I need to decide soon just what it is I believe.

Democritus and Lucretius, two Greek philosophers, questioned the existence of a creator God. Jean Rousseau, the great thinker of his time and father of romanticism, also questioned the place of religion and the existence of a God. So atheistic thinking is not new. Many of the great minds of the time felt that religion was only interested in self-denial, suffering, and controlling the population by telling it that anything pleasurable is probably a sin. The French philosopher Andre Comte-Sponville is an atheist who believes that religion doesn't have sole authority over spirituality. One could have a moral life without a God. I agree. I love those Frenchies.

Darwin's theory of natural selection, or "survival of the fittest," drives Christians up the wall. Atheists think that someday there will be evidence that Darwin's theory of evolution will be beyond challenge. But many Christians believe in Creationism, holding that what the Bible says rules, and that God created man and woman, Adam and Eve. Apparently, half of us still believe this is true. I don't buy it, and many other Christians don't either. Another theory, called intelligent design, has it that, yes, we have evolved over millions of years, but we're so complex that only an intelligent designer—read: God—could have guided our development. Theologians say that the number of chemical and physical accidents—or "fine-tuning," as they call it—necessary for the creation of complex life can only be explained by the hand of the Creator. About a third of us buy into this possibility. And I think that includes me. Then there's simple evolution, which holds that we are indeed the result of a number of chemical and physical accidents that have occurred over many billions of years. I suppose this random chance for life would be one in many millions, but then, how old is the earth? Many billions; it could happen. Only about one-eighth of us believe this to be true. I believe it *could* be true. So then, what am I? A Christian, an atheist, or an agnostic?

Alfred Wallace, Darwin's cosponsor in developing the theory of natural selection, later came to agree that man's superiority proved that the theory could not apply to man. Man is special. Man's ability to think, memorize, and communicate sets him above the theory's conclusions on all of the other species. Man is the only species to develop far beyond the need to just survive; all other species stopped developing when they mastered their environment, while man continues to advance. This is a strong argument, but I'm not so sure I agree. Prehistoric man had a small brain, which grew over millions of years as he mastered his environment, step by step. Are we not still stepping? I would argue that we still haven't mastered our environment. So to me, this logic may be flawed. I'm not sure what to believe.

There's little doubt in my mind that we could have evolved from the first cells of life. For many people, this miraculous progression from a single cell to the many complex systems that make up our bodies is impossible to fathom. It's easy to understand how most of mankind has embraced a God as the Creator. The alternative leaves these people empty and hopeless. While science has proven evolution, it will never disprove the existence of a God. There is no possible way to prove the start of the universe without something behind the start. If it started with a big bang, who or what set off the bang? It seems only religion, and not science, can comfort the pain of the world and bring it peace.

Considering how poorly all the religions have acted over the ages, and even now, it would be easy to bag them all and be an atheist. These organized religions are all run by men who I don't accept as being any wiser than I am, and I cannot accept their blind adherence to ancient dogma. After reviewing all these religions, I'm confused more than ever. Is there a God or not? I need to make up my mind, because if there *is* a God, I don't want to have to explain myself to him when I get there.

St. Augustine maintained that science is insignificant in understanding Scripture. If science was in conflict with Scripture, science simply needed reinterpretation. Many Christians claim that if science completely disproves any of their religious tenets, their faith will simply reject the findings. How's that for an open mind? Evangelicals cannot believe that monkeys could be our ancestors. Why is it impossible to believe that God created monkeys for just that purpose?

Many have turned to atheism, and among the young, it's popularity is surging. Many are turning to simple spirituality in their lives, others to meditation and yoga. But most still yearn for the same answers. How is it that the universe and our world exist? What happens to us after death?

What's amazing is that almost all scientists do not believe in heaven or hell, while almost all average people do. This must be why evangelical Christians consider intelligent people to be elitist academic devils, out to destroy the country. Scientists who require evidence of God's existence are ridiculed as faithless. Well, of course they're faithless. Two-thirds of scientists are either atheists or agnostics. I guess they require proof that virgin births, resurrections, and miracles do, in fact, happen. No wonder the religious right looks down on the scientific community. If they don't believe in God, they can't possibly be right about anything, from global warming to evolution. Looks to me like our universe will be extinct before anything changes. Whoever is right will soon be known to me—or maybe not. Crap, my global warming might be down in that seventh level of hell.

The basis of Christianity seems to be spelled out in the Nicene Creed. Even I recognize the phrase, "We look for the resurrection of the dead and the life of the world to come." Christians, Jews, and even Muslims do agree on many concepts, so there must be some validity somewhere in religion. There's one God who lives in heaven; he is merciful; at the end of life he will judge all; and the good will live in heaven for eternity. But agreement seems to end there. The Puritans regarded even the Quakers as impure, and they imprisoned and executed many of them. While many people have created their own images of God, Southern Baptists make no bones about it. God is a Jewish man, and he looks like Jesus. Okay, but what did Jesus look like?

In Christian art, Judas is shown with strong Jewish features, and Jesus is not.

Karl Marx, a Jew, wrote that all men should unite to free themselves from exploitation, from the belief in God and the illusions of religion. Religion was oppressive in the struggle between the capitalists and its workers. No wonder he is so hated in our society.

The Christian Science Church was founded in the late 1800s by Mary Baker Eddy. She was dissatisfied with what she called the "cruel creeds" in the Bible, so she wrote her own book, *Science and Health with Key to the Scriptures*. She felt that church councils were guilty of teaching as if doctrine was only about men.

Mexicans celebrate Dia de los Muertos, the Day of the Dead. Family visits gravesites with music, drinks, and food, and they make fun of death, not the dead. This tradition dates back to the Aztecs, and I like it. It views death as a cycle of renewal, a new beginning. Since Mexico is Catholic, I wonder how this goes over with the old boys in the Vatican.

The Reverend James Forbes of the American Baptist United Church of Christ believes that "God is a force field of positive energy." *I like this thought. I think he could be right.*

I'm reminded of a funny joke. Seems that Muslims don't recognize Jews as God's chosen people, and Jews don't recognize Jesus as the Messiah, and Protestants don't recognize the pope as the leader of the Christian world, and Baptists don't recognize each other in the liquor store. I can't quit laughing. I might as well laugh, because I'll be dead soon enough.

Why is it that in all religion, the good is accompanied by the bad? The Dalai Lama said that we don't really have a soul. I think he's a Buddhist. They believe that this life is it, so live as such. To some Buddhists and Hindus, our present lives are an afterlife, as we're continually recycled through reincarnation. If you were good, you move up the chain, and if you were bad, you move down. If they're right, I'll most likely come back as an Arab woman or a goat in Afghanistan. For God's sake, what good is it to come back as someone who doesn't know he's lived before? I think I agree with the Dalai Lama when he says, "Whether a person is a religious believer does not matter much. It is far more important that he be a good human being." I think, all in all, I've been a good person. I see now why the Dalai Lama has such a large following.

The goat appears much too often in my research. What do you suppose they had against goats way back then?

And then we have Hinduism with their caste system. How could a loving God ever condone that kind of a life for anyone? And what's with all those cows running around loose? What do they have over goats?

All this investigation isn't helping me reach any conclusions. I skim a few more books but resolve that I'm done with all of it. I won't return to the library after today. My time has run out.

I've checked out God enough; better check out Satan before I go. Who knows? I might meet him, and he might be willing to negotiate. In the Bible's Book of Wisdom, the story of God and Satan's wager over Job captivates me. Satan challenges God, saying he's given too much to Job and that Job worships him only because he's awarded him with riches.

"If Job lost his wealth, he would curse you to your face."

God says, "Go and work your evil on Job, and we shall see his response." A messenger comes to Job and proclaims, "The Sabeans have made off with your five hundred oxen and five hundred donkeys. They have killed the servants, and I alone have escaped to tell you."

Then another arrives and says, "The fire of God fell down and burned up your seven thousand sheep and servants. Only I have survived to tell you."

Then another arrives and says, "The Chaldeans have raided and carried off your three thousand camels. They have killed all the servants, and I alone escaped to tell you."

Then another comes and proclaims, "A great wind has felled the house of your son and killed all of your sons and daughters. I alone am left to tell you."

Job falls to the ground and proclaims, "Naked I came from my mother's womb, and naked shall I return there. The Lord giveth, and the Lord taketh away."

God says to Satan, "See? He will not renounce me even though you incited me against him to destroy him for no reason."

Satan will not quit and again challenges God. "He will renounce you to save his life."

The Lord again tells Satan to go forth and do his work but not to kill him. Satan inflicts Job with sores from head to foot, but still Job does not renounce God.

This story raises a lot of questions in my mind. Is this a loving God or a vengeful God? Why would he let Satan incite him for no reason? Why would he condone the killing of so many innocent people just to prove a point? If he is all powerful, why does he tolerate Satan at all? Is God the reason I'm prosperous? I'm more confused than ever. This is a hard story to believe. "He giveth and he taketh away" seems to be more like he's just playing with us. If he allowed so many to be killed, does he care about all of us or just a few?

In modern Christianity, Satan is also known as the devil, Lucifer, or Beelzebub. Some Christians believe Satan is an angel who rebelled against God, along with many other angels. The other angels are considered demons. They have been condemned to the lake of fire. I assume that must be hell, but I don't like the reference to a lake, as I will soon be seeing a lot of lakes. The book of Revelation identifies Satan as a snake in one place and a dragon in another. Snake seems to have won out, however, as we aren't too scared of dragons, as no one's ever seen one.

In Islam, he is known as Iblis. He only has the power to place suggestions of evil into our heads. He was created by God but lost God's grace when he refused to bow down to Adam. He considered himself superior, because Adam was created out of dirt, while he was created out of fire. He deceived Adam and Eve, but they repented and were forgiven by God. God warned Adam and Eve that if they or their children fell under the spell of Iblis, they would be cast into the fires of hell. The Quran also says that Iblis, along with those who have sinned, will go to hell on Resurrection Day, while the good will be rewarded with paradise.

Then I come across information about people who worship Satan. Some groups don't recognize Satan outright but pay homage to a weird kind of horned God and his companion, the goddess of Wicca. There is a terrifying picture of a devil here called Baphomet. I don't dare spend any more time on these people, and I don't want to meet Baphomet in the next world. This guy would scare anyone on to the straight and narrow. It was not that long ago that Christians labeled these people as witches and hanged them. This must have helped convert people to Christianity.

Then there is Hinduism. Their ideas of good and bad are so confusing that I'm left with no idea whether they believe in heaven or hell, so I move on to Buddhism. Here, there is Mara, who is devil-like. He is seen as confusing people by convincing them that evil is, in fact, good. Well, he's succeeded in confusing me too.

This one in ancient Egyptian mythology is funny. Ausar is chopped into thirteen pieces by Set. Auset, who is Ausar's wife, collects the pieces to save his phallus. Their son, Horus, slays Set to avenge the death of his father. Ausar then rises from the dead and becomes the lord of the underworld. I have trouble understanding why the victim, Ausar, has to go to the underworld, but I can certainly understand putting one's phallus back together again.

As I get up to leave, the librarian calls me over.

"I have seen you studying in the religious section," she says. "I have something that might interest you." She drags me through the stacks and says, "You should look at this book." She pulls a book on Thomas Jefferson off the shelf.

"Why Thomas Jefferson?" I ask.

"Just look through it," she says and opens it to a section about how Jefferson made his own Bible by meticulously cutting out only the actual teachings of Jesus. Why, I wonder, would he do that? He believed that only the words of Jesus were to be followed. The words of Jesus's followers were embellished misconceptions and not to be trusted. He said the difference between them was like the difference between "diamonds in a hill of dung." I think he's right—and this was the main man who authored the Declaration of Independence! The Gospels were just copies refined from copies written many years after the death of Jesus. Jefferson spoke against the clerics and insisted that he was a true follower of Christ. He espoused that Christ's true and only teachings were to love one another, love your enemy, forgive those who harm you, and give up the need for power over others. He rejected religion as a driving force in politics, saying religion had led to wars and unjust persecution.

He makes some good points. When Jesus was nailed to the cross, he didn't proclaim his innocence; instead, he forgave the men nailing him down. Jefferson proclaimed that he was a disciple of the true doctrines of Jesus and didn't need or want anything more.

I think I agree with him. Those who impose their religion on others are out of line. How is it they can obsess about the sex lives of others and still condone divorce? How can they rail against abortion but not care for impoverished offspring? Why are they always so afraid of everything? Jesus said, "Be not afraid."

When we studied history in Catholic grade school, they never mentioned much about Jefferson, and now I see why. I'll bet if you surveyed people attending Mass, absolutely none of them would know this about Jefferson's beliefs. In fact, none of my friends know much about the history of religion at all. It must be that when you are young, you have too much to deal with at school, and when you are older, you are too busy raising a family and dealing with your job. I should have taken more time to explore these religious beliefs, but I guess better late than never. Or maybe not.

Jefferson reminds me of William Blake. I find Blake interesting because he also scorned organized religions but believed fervently in the Bible. He's also been dead for almost two hundred years. I remember a few lines from one of his poems that we studied in college.

> To see the world in a grain of sand,
> And a heaven in a wild flower;
> Hold infinity in the palm of your hand,
> And eternity in an hour.

As I leave the library for the last time, I realize the librarian has gotten to know my face more than I would have liked and may recognize me in the paper when my obituary comes out. But there's nothing to be done about it. I can only hope that she won't read the paper or recognize me. Or if she does, she won't say anything about my interest in the afterlife to anyone who knows me. I've learned much, but I still know very little, and I'm not even sure I've interpreted all that I have found correctly. I'm sure religious scholars would disagree with many of my interpretations, but it's all I have to go on.

Later that night, I come across an article in the newspaper by Oliver Thomas, who wrote the book *10 Things Your Minister Wants to Tell You (But Can't Because He Needs the Job).* I am now consumed by all things religious and read it with interest. He says the religious landscape is changing, that up to 15 percent of Americans are nonbelievers, and that they're the majority in Europe. I see myself being swayed also. The more I study, the more I become a skeptic. He says that "in the first hundred years after the crucifixion of Jesus, Christians still preferred spoken remembrances to the cache of writings that would become our New Testament." So they weren't so enamored at first with what has since been rewritten many times over and is now what I'm to live my life by? As Thomas puts it, "young adults are not interested in jousting over doctrine. They see Scripture for what it is: the witness of fallible humans to God's acts in history." I think many church leaders who take the Bible literally are clinging to childish metaphors that were intended to instruct an uneducated audience of the time.

As I read the newspaper, my wife says, "You don't seem that interested in the paper anymore."

"What?" I reply.

"You haven't turned the page for ten minutes."

"I was just thinking about a case I have at work that's turning into a problem."

"It must be bothering you a lot, because you've been like that for a week now."

"Yes," I say and quickly turn the page. Her comment bothers me—I've come too far and worked much too hard to establish my plan to let anything create doubt now. It is, however, difficult to show interest in a world I'm about to leave.

I start reading another story about a woman from Minnesota who's running for president. She says she believes women should be submissive to their husbands, as it says in the Bible. She also says, however, that this really just means you should respect your husband, even though she's been submissive in the past. The story goes on to quote a female pastor from Kansas who says "biblical teachings constantly are being reinterpreted." Ya think? I wish I had time to interpret my own version.

CHAPTER EIGHT

The Last Week

I promise myself to spend as much time with my family as possible this week. I go golfing with Betty and actually do pretty well. We usually walk the course, but I convince her that she's the one who looks tired and that we should use a cart. If I have to walk, I'm sure I won't have made it. I'm beginning to wonder just how far I'll make it paddling a canoe. It is a chore for me at times, when she's on the tee box, I stand back and spit blood behind the cart so she won't see it. She's happy to be playing with me, because I usually play with clients, but she does get upset when I smoke in the cart. Yes, I light up a cigarette, just like I always do when I golf. We have a good time and when we finish our round, we stop at the clubhouse for drinks. In the bathroom, I spit up more blood and take a fistful of painkillers.

Betty and I were sweethearts in high school and though we went to different colleges, we were inseparable during our vacations. We waited to get married until we were done with school, but after that, we didn't wait long to have a family. Raising our children was easy—they were active and never got into trouble. Betty and I enjoyed each other's company, and our family was considered a model, at least by me.

The next night, we go out for dinner at our favorite restaurant and talk about our kids—that everything seems to be going so well with them. I want her to remember that I'm extremely happy with my family and the way they all turned out. Then we head out to the theater to see a movie. She picks a chick flick, and I happily go along with her choice. Watching the movie hurt almost as much as my chest hurt, but she enjoyed it. The central theme is a wedding, which may or may not take place. I am against it, and Betty is worried he will back out. I frankly don't give a damn. Why is it that they can't make a good movie anymore? It's been years since I've seen a movie I thought was any good. That's one more thing I won't miss when I am gone.

The next evening, Betty says she'd like to go to the mall to do some shopping. She almost falls over when I volunteer to go along.

"I need some new clothes," I say, "and I could use your help picking some things out."

"Well, okay," she says with a quizzical look.

Unfortunately, I don't do well walking around the mall. I have to dart into the bathroom for more "killers," as I now call them, even though the real killers are my cigarettes.

"Do you want to look at clothes while I shop?" she asks.

"No, I'll go along with you."

This gets another quizzical look, and I realize I'm overdoing it, but I go along with her anyway. While she looks at one thing after another in the women's department, I sit on a chair and try to appear interested. I'm happy because she seems happy. When we pay, the cashier seems amused that I've waited patiently for my wife. I guess it must not happen too often. Over the years, I have been perplexed by the eternal male/female dynamic. Why are we so different from each other, and why does it take so long to figure each other out? It has taken me fifty years to figure out women, and yes, I do feel that I know what makes each of us tick. This valuable knowledge is soon to be wasted.

Then we go to the men's department, and she gets impatient while I browse. There is an obvious role reversal here.

"What are you looking for?" she asks.

"I am just looking right now," I say. Then I realize that's not what I said when we started, and I recover. "I need some new shirts and some neckties." After looking at the selection, I pick out a few. Since my son is the same size as I am, the purchases won't go to waste. They're all his colors, not mine.

That night I call my children and persuade them to come up to the lake for the weekend. It will be my last chance to get them all together. All kinds of excuses come up. Katy has soccer practice, Joey has a baseball game, and Morgan would have to be back early on Sunday for a birthday party. Then I use my trump card. "Your mother really wants you all to come up for the weekend." Mother rules. I was ecstatic when they finally agreed. It will be my last chance to create a memory—my last hurrah.

When they arrive at the cabin, everyone gets a hug and a kiss as the dogs run around as if the ride up in the car was disabling. It's early afternoon, so Betty makes tuna fish sandwiches for lunch. The kids get sandwiches and chips with soda pop, the wives get margaritas, and the guys drink beer. It's a nice day, maybe God's gift to me.

We have many toys to choose from at the cabin. Over the years, we've accumulated a speedboat, paddleboat, canoe, and a Jet Ski. The kids tell me they want to start the day by tubing behind the boat. The girls scream as they bounce around over the waves, and they're dumped, as usual, when I weave back and forth. While circling around to pick them up, I look down into the water and see my reflection. I see myself drowned and looking up from the depths. My heart stops at the sight of my future.

My son, watching from the back of the boat, calls out, "What's wrong?" When I don't respond, he calls out again with alarm in his voice.

Coming to my senses, I reply, "I thought I saw a big fish." We continue the ride, but later, when we return to the cabin, I'm shaken and need to take several pills and smoke a cigarette.

While the kids swim off the dock, I start drinking the hard stuff while the guys drink another beer. I think I'll have to be half shot to get through the weekend.

You would think that it would be the girls who would be the biggest screamers, but they are not, and it is Joey who can't seem to say anything without yelling it. Swimming off the dock, he is having a ball with the girls. I think he's still young enough to not realize he's actually playing with girls. But when he climbs up onto the dock and his trunks slip down to his ankles, the girls snicker because they do know the difference. He pays no attention to them as he pulls up his trunks and just keeps on going as

I also snicker. Maybe he does not have that much to learn about that male/female dynamic. Joey continues to jump in and lose his suit, over and over again, until Mother calls him over and tightens his trunks.

I visit my neighbors, whom I've known for at least thirty years and who have turned into our very best friends. They live at their cabin year-round and help police the lake and the cabins during the winter when most everyone else has shut down. He is the fisherman on the lake and never fails to tell me that God doesn't count the hours spent fishing. I guess I should have fished more.

"What have you been up to?" he asks.

I give him my usual reply, "Just trying to keep my sperm count up."

He always laughs like crazy at this joke. He lights up a cigarette and, as usual, offers me one. I really do not feel like a cigarette, as my lungs are burning, but he and I always have a cigarette and a beer together. I also want to appear normal, so I light one up with him. When he goes into the cabin for another beer, I turn toward the woods and spit out some blood. He's in his seventies, and I know he'll miss me when he hears of my drowning. "Damn, he was much too young to go," he'll say. I hope he'll have a cigarette and beer and think of me once in a while.

That evening, we all sit around and talk politics and the state of the economy while my son barbeques. My buzz is still with me, as the hard stuff goes down easy. We don't agree much on politics, but I don't care. I am on my way to eternity with a good feeling. For an instant, I think I'm getting better, but then I return to my senses, and I know that I'm not.

The next night, after another day on the water, we gather around the fire pit and sing. I'm usually the loudest, at least that's what my neighbors tell me. But tonight I don't have the lung power, so I mostly just mouth the words. With all the commotion around the fire, no one notices. The kids roast marshmallows and run around, trying to dodge the smoke. I am pleased and thankful that this get-together has come off so very well.

As they're leaving on Sunday afternoon, I give everyone another hug and kiss. After they drive out, I realize I'll never see them again. I almost pass out but can't because Betty is standing right behind me. I tell her I have some work to do in the garage, and she goes into the cabin to do the dishes. In the garage, I fall to my knees and am more overcome with grief than ever before. The pain in my heart is harder to bear than the pain in my chest. I wish I could die now and get it over with. "Oh God, take me now." My tears soak my shirt. When I finally compose myself and enter the cabin, I run up the stairs to change into a dry shirt. After she is done with the dishes and general cleanup, we load up the car and head for home. It's a three-hour drive, and I have nothing to say.

"Why are you so quiet?" she asks.

"I was just thinking about what a great weekend that was," I say.

"Yes, it was. It's more and more difficult to get them all together, with the kids involved in so many activities these days."

Monday is my last day in the office. I take a few antidepressants, paste on a smile, and prepare to say good-bye. I realize, when making the rounds, that there are more people in the firm whom I value than I thought. The first stop is the accountant's office, where I tell Dick that Anne is to have a promotion and a raise.

"Okay," he says, "if you say so."

Damn right, I think. But I wonder if he'll really process it when he learns of my death. I stop and see Terry, the junior partner, who will be handling most of my active cases. I wonder if they'll make him a full partner when I'm gone. I ask him if he's on top of everything.

"Yes," he replies. "I can certainly handle it while you are on vacation."

I want to say, *Oh, my boy, you're going to have to handle much more than that.*

"Tell me again when you'll be back," he says.

"We're planning on twelve days, but if we get caught in bad weather, we'll have to hunker down. So don't plan on my getting back for two weeks. I'll call you from Ely when we're done, so you'll know when I will be in. Remember, you can't call me up there. They don't have cell phone coverage, so you are on your own. I think you're doing a good job, Terry."

He has a big smile on his face as I leave his office. Terry was raised by a single mother, who struggled to help him through college and law school. He was in his late twenties when he graduated and was loaded down with student loans. I'm sure he can make it after I'm gone. He'll finally have a chance to make some big money.

I meander the floors, chatting with several people, and then return to my office. I look around to see if I should tidy it up but decide it would be a mistake to change anything. As I'm about to leave, Anne comes in and says, "John, will you please take this call before you go? This guy won't stop calling. It's over a remodeling project in his house, and he wants to sue the contractor. I told him you don't take small cases like that, but he won't take no for an answer and insists on talking to you."

"Okay, put him through." I wait a moment until I hear the call transfer to me. "Yes, this in John Janne. How can I help you?"

He tells me he had an agreement with a contractor to remodel his kitchen for $45,000 and that the work is unsatisfactory. The kitchen sink is crooked, there's a chunk out of the granite countertop, the wall cabinets aren't scribed to the wall, and so on. He wants to sue, no matter what the cost.

"Well," I say, "it could cost you up to forty thousand."

There is a long pause before he responds. "That much?"

"Yes," I say, "but there's another way I can try. Give me the name and number of the contractor, and I'll call him. He knows that if you sue him, it'll cost him a lot of money, too, and he might end up paying for the remedial work anyway."

When I call the contractor and identify myself and the firm, there is a long pause, and then he immediately agrees to send his best man out to fix the problems.

"Anne, call that guy back and tell him the contractor is coming out and has agreed to fix everything to his satisfaction."

"Shall we charge him?" she asks.

"No," I say. It would be my last good deed.

After gathering my things, I walk out to speak to Anne. "I'm going to cut out early," I say.

"So you're really going to do it?" she asks. "I hope you enjoy the time off in the North Woods."

I want to hug her, but I can't show that much emotion. "I put you in for a promotion with accounting," I say as I walk out the door. The smile on her face as I leave makes me feel good. Anne was a significant part of my success, and we both know it.

If Terry was my right hand, Anne Brisbane was my left. She started out at the firm in the secretarial pool, and fifteen years ago, when I made partner, she joined me full time. She was not a formally trained legal secretary but picked it up along the way. She was never married, to my knowledge but did have a live-in boyfriend until a few years ago, when she threw him out for some reason. I did not want to know why. Her passion now was dogs—show dogs. She traveled around the five-state area to dog shows at least once a month. Her weekends were spent on her dogs, four of them. She once brought her favorite into the office to show it to everyone. "Isn't she a darling?" she said. "She is a champion shih tzu."

The dog was barely ten inches high and twenty inches long. It had long hair sweeping down to the floor but looked to weigh less than ten pounds. The dog was gold, white, and brown and had a face like a teddy bear. It had a little red ribbon in its hair. "That's a girl?" I asked.

"Yes, she is descendant from prehistoric Chinese wolves. The name translates as 'lion dog.'"

I thought, *This dog is no wolf or lion and has been misnamed.* Then I said, "You have more just like . . . what's her name?"

"Her name is Queen of China, and I have three younger ones at home. They are a lot of work. Their hair needs to be brushed every day, or it becomes hopelessly tangled."

As the dog walked across my floor, I commented that Anne must not have to ever mop the floor. Anne did not find my comment funny, but the dog did look like a moving mop. My yellow lab Molly was a dog; Queen of China was a mop.

As I walk down the street to the parking ramp, I realize I'll never pass this way again. My career is over; my life is over. I sit in the car with tears rolling down my face for at least half an hour before I can get it together. On my way home, I stop to fill up the car with gas and take some painkillers and a handful of antidepressants before facing Betty.

Our evening together is as normal as I can possibly pull off. After dinner, she watches television while I just stare at it.

When I get up to pack my bag, she asks, "Do you want me to pack you?"

"No," I reply. "I can do it." Then I realize this is a mistake, because she always packs my bags. Then I explain, "It's no problem. I can do it. I really don't have much. The outfitter has almost everything we'll need."

Things to pack: rain gear, sweatshirt, socks and underwear, my favorite lake hat, and long underwear. You could call it packing, but I just throw it in the bag. I don't want to go to bed early, but it's expected if I'm going to leave early.

In the morning, I take a handful of antidepressants and eat

breakfast with Betty as best I can.

"You be careful now," she says. "You look tired."

"I am," I say. "I'm so excited to finally be going that I didn't sleep well, but I'll recover."

"Did you call that Peterson guy in Chicago and get everything set up right?"

"Yes. He's as excited to finally be going as I am." As I walk out the door, I give my wife a hug and a kiss. It's my final goodbye.

I'm only able to drive a few blocks, however, before I break down in tears and park the car by the curb. "Oh, Betty, I wanted to die in your arms." Memories of her sweep over me. Tears flow like rain. I wish I could have asked her to forgive my many faults before I left. "How thoughtless I've often been. I hope you'll forgive me and only remember the good times. I hope to watch you from above and always be near you. Please have a good life." I don't know how long I've been sitting here, but I light a cigarette and finally pull away forever.

The drive up Lake Superior's north shore is a new low. It's over now; I only have the end in front of me. All my planning is done and so far, as far as I can tell, my plan has worked well.

When I get to Duluth, I go to the airport. I'm not sure why, because no one's going to be there, but I thought it might be wise to call Betty from there so she can hear the background noise of the airport. "He wasn't on the plane from Chicago," I say.

"Really? What's going on?" she asks.

"I called his office and got his secretary. She told me he left for the airport to catch a plane to Duluth to start his vacation. But the plane's here, and he's not on it," I told her. She said she'd try to find out what happened and call me back, but before she could I got a call from him. He was in a car accident on the way to the airport. He says his arm and shoulder are banged up, and he doesn't think he can handle the strain of paddling a canoe that long. He was very sorry and apologetic, but he can't come. He was calling from the emergency room."

"So, you're coming home then?"

"No, I'm too into it," I say.

"No, you shouldn't be going alone."

"Well, I've already paid for it, and it took so long to set it up that I want to go ahead. Besides, I'm pretty sure I can hook up with some others or at least tag along behind. If it proves too much, I'll just turn around and come back."

She sighs deeply and says, "All right then, but how much fun is it going to be going alone?"

"It'll give me time to reflect and enjoy it in a different way," I say. "When I get to the outfitters, I'll ask them if there's a problem with my going alone, and I'll call you back, okay?" I start to lose it, so I tell her I love her and hang up as soon as possible.

When I arrive in Ely, I drive all the way through town and back again before spotting Alan's outfitting shop. There are over twenty outfitters here. How on earth can there be a need for so many? Ely reminds me of an Old West frontier town. It is truly an unusual town. There's the North American Bear Center and the International Wolf Center. It's interesting how often I see the Canadian flag flying with the US flag. There's the Dirty Dog Manufacturing Plant, Bloomers Floral, the Ely Steak House, the Chocolate Moose, the Boathouse Brewpub, and Kat's Drive-In Liquor. Then I see that Ely was once named Quam Chep, which means "Land of the Berries" in Chippewa.

I decide that Kat's Drive-In is a discreet way to get my scotch. I don't want anyone remembering my storing up on liquor and then drowning because I was a drunken fool.

"What would you like?" the woman at the window asks.

"Scotch."

"What kind?"

"Your best."

"The twenty-five-year-old stuff?"

"Yes, that'll do. Give me two bottles."

When she wraps it up, she says I'm getting a good deal because they've had it for many years, and I'm probably getting forty-year-old scotch at the old price.

Great, I think. Just what I need now, to save a few bucks. "Oh, yeah. Give me a pack of cigarettes, too."

"What kind?"

"Pall Malls." I knew I couldn't smoke a whole pack now, but I think some should be found in my stuff. I make sure no one's looking when I slip the two bottles of scotch into my bag in the trunk of the car. *This is the really good stuff. I intend to go out in style.* I wonder how it tastes with lake water. What the heck? I'll just drink it straight.

The first thing I do when I arrive at the outfitters is call

Betty. "Hi, honey, I'm in Ely. The guy from Chicago called again and said the doctors told him he'll be in a sling and can't use his arm."

"What are you going to do?" she asks. "Have you changed your mind? Are you coming back?"

"No, I'm here now, and I'm going to try and hook up with three other guys from the cities that I met in the store a few minutes ago." Lies, all lies. "They've already left, but I'll catch up with them shortly. I won't have a chance to call you again, as the cell phone coverage up here is spotty." I can barely get the words out. This is the last time I'll hear her voice. It doesn't fit my plan well, but I say "I love you" for the last time. I go into the bathroom to compose myself before meeting Alan the outfitter.

Alan appears to be in his early thirties. He wears his hair tied back in a ponytail and tops it off with a baseball cap turned backward. You can tell he's living his dream up here in the woods. I peg him as a hippie environmentalist. He walks with a slight limp, and his heavy boots clop noisily on the store's wood floor. His dog follows closely behind him, but then discovers me and starts sniffing my shoes.

"He likes the smell of feet. Stop it, Smoky," Alan says, and Smoky trots over to the counter and lies down. I feel sorry for Smoky and give him a few pats on the head.

Alan must have heard me talking to Betty about the cell phone coverage, because he says, "Every year there's this big argument over cell phone towers in the wilderness area. How can it be a wilderness with towers four hundred feet tall, flashing across the sky and waters? But many feel that with all the accidents that occur, if just one life could be saved, it would be worth it. There are usually eighteen to twenty-five emergencies each year. But then, who wants to see the flashing lights day and night?"

I can't tell which side of the argument he's on, but I do need to know if there's coverage in Quetico Park.

"No," he answers. "When you'd *want* to make a call, you can be sure you won't get a signal."

That's what I want to hear.

"You must be Mr. Janne," he says.

"Yes."

"You're here first. Mr. Peterson isn't here yet."

I tell Alan that Mr. Peterson was in an accident and isn't going to make it because he's busted up his arm. "Is this going to be a problem?" I ask.

"Well, you can go out alone, but we prefer there to be more than one in a party. Are you an experienced canoeist?"

"Yes, I know how," I lie. "Last year I went down the Brule River in Wisconsin; we ran the Lenroot Ledges and the Highway 13 rapids."

"Oh," he says, "they're rated class 2 and 3. I guess you'll be okay then."

Good show, John, I think. All that planning is paying off. "Would it be possible to catch up with another group?" I ask.

"Yes, if you can find another party that wants additional company."

"I've come this far, so I am going to go ahead."

"Might as well," he said. "You've already paid and would not get much of your money back."

CHAPTER NINE

The Outfitter

Alan is so kind and concerned for me that I know he won't respond well to my death. When he sees what I'm wearing, he says, "You shouldn't wear blue jeans."

"I'm going to leave them in the car. I just didn't want to wear the nylon ones on the way up." We go over the clothes I've brought along, and I assure him that I have the synthetic shirts, pants, and underwear he recommended.

Alan lectures me on how important it is to be prepared for all kinds of weather. "You need to have the right clothing. It could rain all day long, and you'll have to get off the lake if there's a thunderstorm."

I muse silently that it might be okay to get hit by lightning. It would be fast, and it wouldn't be suicide. I've made the right decision to come here—there are so many ways to die. Alan goes on for ten minutes about snow and hail and says that one year at this time, it snowed for three days in a row. I smile and again think that yes, I have made the right decision.

"You want to travel light, because you'll be carrying everything on your back." He then proceeds to load me up with more stuff than I would have expected. The list of stuff he says I need seems endless, and I'm not going to buy and carry around all that stuff, just so he, no matter how nice a guy he is, can make a bigger sale.

"Propane stove and two bottles of propane."

"No," I say. "I prefer an open fire."

"You may regret it if you can't find any dry wood. Cooking pots and pans."

"Okay, one deep pot that I can make soup in and one frying pan, so I'll have two to bang together."

He laughs and says that should be enough. "Can opener. You'll want to take some foodstuffs in cans."

"Okay, put one in. How heavy can it be?"

"Eating utensils and dish."

"Yes, but the knife has to be sharp for cleaning fish," I say, even though I have no intention of cleaning fish.

"A couple of food barrels."

"What's a food barrel?" I ask.

He shows me a barrel, and it does look like something I'll need.

"It's for everything that isn't dried or canned."

"Okay, but one is enough."

"Towels for washing up the pans."

"I have towels." I only brought one.

"A shovel."

What the hell was I suppose to do with that? Bury myself? "Why?" I ask.

"Poop. If they catch you not burying your stuff, they'll throw you out and fine you."

The shovel has a short handle but still looks heavy. It seems the shovel is nonnegotiable.

"An extra paddle," he goes on. "You'll be charged if you lose the one you're getting in the package. You'd be surprised by the number of paddles we buy each year. I think we should start tying them around their necks. They'll give you one when you get your canoe at the resort." He looks back at his list, "First-aid kit."

I don't need it, but I can't say no. It would appear strange to decline it.

"Tarp and rope."

"The rope yes," I agree, "but I don't want a tarp."

"Hatchet for wood."

I rebel and say it's too heavy.

"You'll be sorry," he says but recants somewhat by thinking out loud. "Well, it *is* easier to find kindling in Quetico than in the Boundary Waters. They pick it clean in the Boundary Waters." We settle on a small folding saw.

"Water filter."

"I'm not worried about drinking from the lake."

"Yes," he says. "Me either. There's nothing wrong with the water in these lakes. The Forest Service recommends you filter and boil water before drinking, because you risk consuming a parasite that causes severe diarrhea that requires medical treatment. Many experienced people here just take their water from the lakes, but you want to get as far away from the shore as you can when you take it. I drink it straight from the lake, and it hasn't killed me yet."

"It will probably kill me."

He laughs, but I know as soon as I say it that I shouldn't have. It wouldn't be prudent to get sloppy now. We settle on a water bottle.

"Small tent."

I don't want to sleep in the rain, so this is a must.

"It's a Eureka Timberline tent. The best one we can find for the Boundary Waters," he says. "Sleeping bag and pad."

"I'll just take the bag. I'm used to camping out and sleeping on the ground," I lie.

"*Ground*," he laughs. "You'll most likely be sleeping on rock, but at this time of year you can find leaves or use pine boughs. Crazy creek chair."

"Can't I find a stump or something to sit on?"

"I'll take that as a no. Bug repellent. This isn't optional with Alan The bugs are way down," he says, "but you cannot take any chances, as they will eat you alive."

"Give me two."

"Sunscreen."

"No, I'm not worried about sunburn."

"Maps and compass."

"I have maps but will need a compass."

"But do you have a waterproof pouch for the maps?" he asks.

"Oh, okay. Is there no end to the stuff I need?"

He doesn't respond. "Waterproof matches."

I didn't know there were such things as waterproof matches.

"Headlamp."

"I'll need this for sure, as the days are getting shorter."

"Yes, you do need a headlamp. If you miss a campsite, and it gets dark, you'll be glad you have it. Mosquito head net."

"Okay." It doesn't weigh anything.

"Rain gear."

"I already have it in my pack."

"Toilet paper."

"Wow. I would have forgotten that."

"How many rolls will you need?" he asks.

Good Lord, does anyone know how many rolls they go through in a week? "For two weeks, how many do you think?" I ask.

"It's up to you," he says. "If you run short, I don't want to be blamed."

We laugh, and I say two is enough.

"Don't forget to bury it with the poop."

Next it was time to pick out my menu. I tell Alan that I don't want to spend much time cooking, so we go from there. Breakfast would be oatmeal, Tang, dried milk, coffee, and bagels. Lunch would be sandwiches with salami or peanut butter with grape jelly in those small packs that restaurants have. I also buy a bag of trail mix and a small pack of single-slice cheese. Dinner's the tough one. Dried soup, apples, oranges, and canned kippers, which I love, and a can of beans.

"Do you want some spam?"

"No. I don't like spam."

"You'll have to bring the cans back with you," he says.

I guess I knew that but had forgotten. "Well, I will just have to catch fish for dinner," I reply. "I don't want to haul around too many stinky cans."

"Just cut the ends off and crush them. Keep them in this plastic bag, and they shouldn't be a problem. You should take some flour, onions, and potatoes. Together with fresh fish, it makes a great stew; it's one of my favorites."

"All right, but just one onion and two potatoes."

"Quetico has more lake trout than anywhere in the world, so you should be eating well."

Why not? I think. *Why not eat well for my last meals?* I decide to do some fishing—or at least try it.

For chow, he recommends protein bars and some freeze-dried stuff that looks god-awful to me. "These are the most popular food items," he says. "For ten or twelve days, you'll need six packs of some kind of freeze-dried chow." We agree on a few packs of pasta and rice, and a few foil tuna packs. "They are good on pita bread."

"No pita," I reply. "I don't like pita bread. Give me a loaf of real bread; it can't weigh that much."

"The protein bars are great to eat when you can't or don't want to stop paddling. What kind of rice do you want?" he asks. "White or brown?"

As if I'm worried about eating healthy rice now. "Oh, give me the brown—my wife always buys the brown kind."

He offers me a GPS device and a satellite phone for rental. I laugh and say I'm not interested. *Really not interested,* I think.

"Are you sure? You'll be out there alone. I'd feel more comfortable if I could call you."

"No, I've always hated cell phones. Always hated being constantly on call just for someone else's convenience. Not only that, I'd most likely lose it the first day."

"Okay. Finally, we have the Duluth pack. This is the traditional Boundary Waters pack," he says. "It's been used here for over a century. It was designed by a French Canadian in the 1880s. You can rent it or buy it."

"I'll probably use it again, so I'll buy it."

"For $140, you get the olive drab one; the colors are more."

The $140 is enough money to reinforce the impression that I'm in fact planning to come back and use it again.

"Do you want padded shoulder straps?"

"No," I say. The Duluth pack is made to last forever. I wonder who will use it after me.

"You have your fishing gear with you?"

"Yes."

"Where's your rod and your gear?"

"I don't like to pack a clumsy rod, so I have my stubby Popeil rod."

He starts laughing so hard that I think he's going to have a fit. "You're not a serious fisherman, are you?" he asks.

"No, but I have fished, so I should be able to catch one or two for dinner. What about the canoe?" I ask.

"You'll get that at the resort. Everything in our package has been personally tested by our staff and guides. We have the lightest Kevlar canoes with bent-shaft paddles, and you'll get a lightweight paddling life vest."

I won't need the vest, but I say nothing.

The pilot walks into the store, and Alan introduces the two of us. At first, he scares me, as he looks like he'd be a better crawler than a flyer—scruffy as hell and definitely an alcoholic. But then I think, *What the hell. If the plane goes down, that works too.* Alan talks him up, and he does seem to be a nice guy, and he is thankful for the work this late in the year.

I spend considerable time talking to the outfitter and Joel, the pilot, about how I'm going to get back. "How will I contact you? Will you just come at a certain time? What if I'm late?" I want to seal the impression that I'm planning to return, so there's no question about my motives. They answer all my questions, but I don't really listen.

"Be careful out there," Alan says as he bids me off. "It's slippery on the wet rocks, and you can get hurt falling with a canoe and pack on your back. That's how I hurt my leg. I slipped sideways, and the canoe came down on the side of my knee."

"Wow. Did you go to the doctor?"

"No, I don't have medical insurance. You have insurance, don't you?" he asks.

"Yes, I have insurance." *And it's the right kind for this trip.*

"And wear that life jacket. If you fall, it can cushion the impact and save your trip. The water is cooler now and can be deadly, so wear the damn life jacket."

"Okay, okay," I say.

He seems to think I'm a loose cannon. "Remember, there will be no one to bail you out."

Good, I think. Then I get the bear lecture.

"Leave your campsite clean, and hang your food pack from a tree at least ten feet up from the ground. Never keep food in your tent."

As we leave, I turn to Alan and ask, "How can you make a living up here with so many other outfitters?"

"None of us is getting rich, but we love this lifestyle. We love the lakes and the woods. I'm friends with many of my competitors, and we frequently go fishing and hunting together. In the winter, I shut down and move in with my parents in Las Vegas for a few months."

"You're not married, then?"

"No, there aren't many women who think I'm much of a catch."

When we step outside, I quickly spot Joel's truck across the street. I know it's his, because it looks like him, the same ambiance. He throws my gear in the back of the truck with a pile of junk that I don't recognize. We get in and drive to the plane, which is moored on a small lake about three miles from town. I am sure that at one time it was a very nice plane—again, the same ambiance as Joel and his truck.

The plane engine grinds, and Joel swears at it for not starting right away. I can tell he hasn't flown it for a few days. It starts and sputters for a while as it warms up. Joel takes off and heads for the opposite shore. He doesn't seem to be picking up enough speed, and the trees are getting closer. As they get closer still, I wonder if Joel has cancer too. But then, up and away, we lift off the lake and clear the trees with at least two inches to spare. I ask him if he can tell how much older his plane is getting every year by how much closer his plane comes to the trees. Sitting behind him, I can't see his face. He laughs but doesn't answer.

The plane trip reminds me of my youth. My uncle in North Dakota had a light plane, with no top and sheet metal doors, that he used for hunting coyotes. It wasn't very fair; he would shoot them from the air and claim a ten-dollar bounty. That's how he paid for his plane. He had pictures of himself and his hunting buddy in front of the plane with at least forty coyotes hanging from the wings. He wouldn't let me hunt with him, however, because he was afraid I'd get overly excited and shoot off the propeller. He said teenagers were not to be trusted.

He'd also use the plane to catch rattlesnakes in the Badlands. He milked them of their venom and sent it somewhere in Florida, where they turned it into a vaccine. He'd fly into the Badlands and land around the buttes. He knew where all the rattlesnake dens were, as he had been doing this for years. He'd throw rocks in, and the whole place would rattle as they came pouring out. Then, using a three-foot-long pronged grabber with a handle on one end, he'd pick them up behind the head and drop them into a gunnysack.

He kept them in a box that looked like a small coffin in the garage at the back of his Ford dealership. Watching him milk a rattlesnake was something else. He'd hold them behind the head and force their mouths open. Then using one of those Ball canning jars, he'd hold the edge of the jar behind the curve of their fangs, and the venom would drip into the jar. The rattlers would be pissed. He took me along to the Badlands once, but riding back in his plane with the gunnysack full of snakes at my feet was not good. It was a once-in-a-lifetime experience, and I decided to keep it that way. My uncle had a twisted sense of humor. There was a shelf directly in front of his front door with a stuffed bobcat that looked like it was lunging at you. Every time I entered his house, that bobcat made me jump.

After we climb through the air and level off, Joel says to look to the left. "Can you see that small island?"

"Yes!" I shout back.

"That's the remains of a fire started by a lightning strike in the summer of 1995. That was the hottest and driest summer I ever saw up here, and I've been here for over thirty years. Look ahead, and you can see some remains of the great Boundary Waters Derecho."

"The what?"

"The Derecho is what we call the straight-line winds that took out over twenty-five million trees. It was a ninety-mile-per-hour wind that cut a swath thirty miles long and ten miles wide. See how they're all laid out in the same direction, like dead bodies in the cemetery?" His analogy doesn't do much for me. "It happened on the Fourth of July 1999, when there were a lot of people around. It's amazing that only one person was killed. You can see the prescribed burns the US Forest Service did and some logging. It's a shame they couldn't log more of 'em."

"Are those portages down there, Joel?"

"Yeah, they're usually just cleaned-out old animal trails that were well worn through the woods from one lake to another. When you're on the portages, be aware that the bear and the moose still use them too. Down there is Twin Falls. That's where you'll start." He starts laughing.

"What's so funny?"

"Well," he says, "you'll be starting off right from the beginning of your trip with a tough portage. Not many trippers want to start off with a portage. Then you'll be going upstream." He starts laughing again.

Good, I think. *There shouldn't be many other people about.*

After a few minutes, Joel yells out that the resort is just below us. "I'll circle around a few times so they know I'm here, and they'll come out to pick you up."

As I look down, I see that the resort is nestled on the shores of a bay off Lac La Croix. The cabins are tucked in with the pines along the shoreline. There are more cabins than I anticipated, and I wonder out loud how busy they are.

"Not too busy this time of year," Joel says as he finishes his last circle and heads in for the landing. The lake is smooth, and Joel shows me his expertise. It's a nice glide in, and he maneuvers slowly around several boats to dock the plane next to a huge rock.

CHAPTER TEN

The Resort

"Hi, I'm Al Goodman. You must be Mr. Janne. But you're alone. Where's your partner?"

"He was in a car accident on the way to the airport. He called me from the emergency room; his arm is in a sling. He's very sorry, but the doctor said there's no way he could paddle a canoe. I've decided I'll go alone—it's paid for."

"Are you sure you should go alone?" Al asks. "Are you experienced?"

"Yes, I can handle it. I own a lake place and have some white-water experience."

"Okay, but are you sure you still want to go up the Maligne River? It's one of the more challenging trips. You could just stick around here and go fishing."

"I wasn't intending to just fish. I'm more interested in the scenery and the exercise."

"Well, let's go into the lodge and get you settled." Al is thin as a rail and wears blue jeans with one of those flannel shirts all the North Woods men wear. They all wear blue jeans with the shirttails hanging out. It is amazing how much you can tell about a person from his dress. It was not surprising that Al was thin, because I know the running of a resort is endless work.

"John, I see you're a lawyer," Al says. "You know, we get a lot of professional firms and companies coming here for bonding experiences. Maybe your firm would be interested in something like that?"

A few years ago, when my firm had an especially good year, our human resources department proposed we go on a bonding adventure to bring the partners closer together. Since the firm would pay for it all, it went over big with everyone—except me. I said nothing, however, as there would be no stopping a free vacation. After proposing several experiences, a week at a dude ranch in Tucson was chosen. There we were, all fourteen of us. We each climbed up on the back of a nervous horse. My daughter had horses growing up, so I knew how to ride. Only one other partner also knew how. For the rest, it was a new adventure. We rode out into the Arizona desert and spent the night on the ground in sleeping bags. Lawyers aren't used to sleeping on the ground.

In the morning, half our shoes were home to scorpions. Two guys had fallen off their horses the day before and were bruised, so they had to be driven back to the ranch, along with another partner who decided he didn't like horseback riding after all. Only nine of us made it back to the ranch two days later. Back in the office on Monday, everyone, including me, walked in like we still had the saddle between our legs. It was a bonding fiasco; several partners found they really didn't like each other. Any form of the word "bond" was never mentioned again.

"I'll mention it to my partners when I get back."

"Great," Al says. On the way into the lodge, he tells me all the cabins have been modernized with fully equipped kitchens and comfortable furnishings. I think he's trying to sell me on staying. After signing in, Al says he'll introduce me to Ozaawizi at dinner.

"What?"

"Ozaawizi," he replies and laughs. "Brownie is his name. He is Chippewa. He'll boat you over to the falls to start your trip. All of our guides are native Chippewa. They all belong to the Lac La Croix Guide Association. They know the waters like the backs of their hands."

Then I, with all my gear, am deposited in cabin number two. "You can go to the lodge anytime now for dinner, but don't wait too long. It's getting late."

"I'll be over in a few minutes," I reply. The cabin looks nice enough, but I can't wait to get outside and have a cigarette. Sitting by the shore, I smoke and enjoy the twilight, puffing away until my lungs burn and I start spitting up that crap again. I go into the cabin and take a painkiller and then head for the lodge.

The dining room is much bigger than I expected, but people are sitting at only two of the tables. There are four men at one and a young couple at the other. I sit by myself, next to the kitchen, in an uncomfortable chair. The four who appear to be retired sportsmen are talking about golf. They'd been playing in the North Woods and extended their stay to include fishing—a lifestyle I wouldn't live to enjoy. The young couple is busy eating and can hardly shovel it down fast enough. Al had mentioned a couple who were boating and hiking, and this must be them. Their appetite doesn't leave any room for words.

Al guaranteed that all the home-cooked meals were delicious. An older woman comes out of the kitchen and introduces herself as Kim. "We have fresh-caught walleye tonight, and I also have baby back ribs. Or you can have some pork tenderloin from yesterday. I decide on the walleye.

"What would you like with that? I have beans, mashed potatoes, creamed corn, and Brussels sprouts."

"Bring me the last two," I say, and she leaves me with a cup of coffee.

The four men discuss their catch of the day, and they don't seem to be all that happy. I hear ten walleye, three northern pike, and two bass. They had portaged into a nearby lake, Gun Lake, and didn't think the portage work had been worth it. They will fish Lac La Croix tomorrow. The young couple get up from the table and leave quietly.

Kim returns with my dinner. Three large fillets is more than I can usually eat, but I skipped lunch, so I eat it all. Just as I'm finishing, Al comes out of the kitchen with a burley young man.

"Meet Brownie," he says as my hand disappears into Brownie's. "When do you want to leave, Mr. Janne?" Al asks me.

"I'd like a good breakfast, and I'd also like to get a reasonable start on my day. How long does it take to boat over to the falls?"

"It will take about a half hour. The portage up the falls isn't too long, but it's not an easy one and will likely take you another half hour. What do you think?"

"Okay, how about eight o'clock?"

"That's fine. Brownie will pick up your gear at eight in front of your cabin and load it into the boat. You can pick out the canoe you want then, before you leave."

Brownie is not very talkative.

Kim brings me a big piece of apple pie and a nice hot cup of coffee. She then closes the kitchen door and disappears.

I visit the store, or "the trading post," as they call it, to look around and kill time. They have much more than I would have thought. There are groceries, tackle, and souvenirs. Kim comes in to ask if she can help me find anything. Kim is a short, somewhat overweight . . . well, just plain overweight woman who I think was Al's wife. Al's thin from all the work of running a resort. She's apparently heavy from doing all the cooking. I ask her if they live here year-round.

"Oh, no," she replies. "We go to Tahiti during the winter."

That's about the last place I expect to hear. "Tahiti!" I exclaim.

"Yes, we have a place on the beach. We've been going there for seven years now. We spend two weeks closing up and winterizing everything in October, and then Joel comes in and flies us out. We come back in April and spend two weeks getting everything ready. It's a lot of work, and we couldn't do it if we didn't get a good break. People who come here have no idea how much work it takes to run a resort. We get up at five in the morning and go straight through until ten at night, seven days a week. This place started out as a trading post, trading with the Indians in the '20s, so it needs a lot of work to get ready in the spring."

"So, you're about ready to close it up?" I ask.

"Yes, it slows down quickly this time of year. Will you need any bait?" she asks.

"No, I have lures, and I'm here more for the experience and the exercise."

She shows me the local treasures: jams, maple syrup, hand-carved decoy ducks, moccasins, Hudson Bay blankets, and—get this—"Sounds of Nature" tapes. I don't have the heart to tell her no one buys tapes anymore. I fill out the fishing license form, pay for it, and leave. "Good luck," she says as I go out the door.

Later on that evening, I go out for another cigarette. My mind is racing as I sit alone, looking out on the lake, the sun casting shadows on the water. Why did I rush through life? Why were all those meetings so important? What good is all that money now? I think of all those hockey games my son played that I missed. My daughter's dance recitals—missed. Anniversaries and birthdays—missed. Vacations cut short. Who cares about all that stuff in my closet, in my garage? It's clear to me now that making a living is not the same as making a life. My lungs start to hurt now, and I become depressed. Most dying people want a loved one to hold their hands and pray with them. They don't want to be left alone in their nightmare. No one will be there to hold my hand. I start to cry. I wonder if God will forgive me my sins. I will soon find out. I wonder if there is a God. The sun disappears, and the darkness is complete now. I begin to see death as the friend who will end the pain in my chest. Back in the cabin, I eye the scotch but know I can't be hungover in the morning, or they may not let me leave.

For breakfast the next morning there's French toast made from cranberry wild rice bread, with pure maple syrup, extra thick bacon, scrambled eggs, and fresh orange juice and coffee.

"Eat up," Kim says. "You'll need all of that and more to paddle up the Maligne River."

I eat up and enjoy it, as this will be my last good meal on this earth. As I finish, Brownie joins me with a cup of coffee in his hand.

"Good morning," I say.

He just smiles and nods his head.

We gather the gear I deposited in front of the cabin and carry it down to the dock. There are several canoes from which to choose. "No," I say to the yellow one. "I don't like yellow." I request the white one, as it will be the least visible. It's lightweight and shaped like a dart. The new paddles are lightweight composites with bent shafts. This is high-tech stuff compared to the flat wooden oars we use at the lake cabin. They fit me for two paddles. The extra one is lashed to the canoe. The sermon on losing a paddle is repeated. I will have to pay for it if I lose it, and they are not cheap. They laugh and then explain that they have a large supply of paddles because so many do lose them, and that's why I need to take two. I wonder if they'll charge for the extra paddle when they get the word. Brownie ties the canoe to the top of a rack built over the motorboat and stows the gear in the boat.

Al walks down to the dock to see me off. "Be careful," he says. "There are high winds projected for the middle of the week, gusts up to 35 to 40 miles per hour. You don't want to get caught in open water. Stay away from the middle of the lake and hug the shore. You'll have to carefully look for the campsites because they're not marked like in the US. In Canada, you can camp anywhere, so look for flat areas that have been used before. All the campsites have good landing spots for the canoes and a good spot to pitch a tent. But they can be hard to spot, so you have to know your map and keep a sharp eye out for them. There aren't any campsite signs or portage signs out there, so be vigilant. You'll find that all the sites have beautiful settings and views. Give me your route so I'll know where you are."

"It's route number 47. I figure ten days and maybe a couple of extra days for fishing and bad weather."

"But you have no fishing gear."

"I have a compact fishing rod and lures in my pack."

"Have a good trip, and we'll see you back in a couple weeks."

"Okay," I reply, and we take off across Lac La Croix to Twin Falls.

Brownie might be the last human being I see in my life, so I'm not going to let him get by without talking to me. But we do more yelling than talking, as the motor is so loud. After badgering him, I find out he's a member of the Lac La Croix First Nation and lives on the lake year-round in a small village. "Do you have a wife?" I ask.

"Yes."

"Do you have children?"

"Yes."

"What are their names?" I ask.

"Flower and Hunter," he says.

"Do they have Ojibwe names?"

"Yes, Waabigwan and Gilwosewinini." I soon realize just how introverted he is and am sorry I asked. He doesn't seem comfortable talking to a stranger about his wife and children.

I pull out my map to see if I can figure out where we are. As we leave the main body of Lac La Croix, we enter a narrow inlet around what the map indicates is Bell Island and then go around Lou Island to the foot of the falls. The pristine waters sparkle in the sunlight next to the rocky, pine-covered shore. There is no wind today, so the water is flat. It's a good day to start out.

After a half hour, we arrive at the foot of the falls and Brownie pulls the boat up to the shore at the foot of the portage. I would never have guessed this is the entry to the portage. The boat is wedged up into a huge V-shaped boulder at a 45-degree incline. I can hardly get out of the boat. Brownie throws the gear out on the rock, disconnects the canoe from the boat rack, and pulls it up to the top of the boulder where the portage begins. I cringe when I see the grade of the portage and I turn to Brownie as he gets back into the boat to leave. "Would you like to make a few bucks and help me haul the stuff to the end of the portage?" I ask. "How about twenty bucks?"

He smiles, and I imagine him thinking that I'll never make it two weeks. He grabs the canoe, and I take the backpack and off we go.

The path is every bit as bad as I thought it would be. It's heavily worn, and there are stones and roots sticking up all over. I feel like I'm playing hopscotch, trying to keep up with Brownie. But the path is short and on arrival I think, *That wasn't so bad after all.* Then it occurs to me that I'm just carrying the backpack and not the canoe. Still, my lungs burn and I spit crap all the way up. We arrive in about twenty minutes and Brownie drops the canoe on the shore, looking to me for his twenty bucks.

"Thanks," I say and give him the money.

"Bye," he says, "and good luck." And away he goes. When he is out of sight, the reality of what I am about to do sinks in.

CHAPTER ELEVEN

Day One

After popping a few painkillers, I decide to get going. I strap my backpack to a cross brace in the canoe, along with the life jacket. I push the canoe into the water and start paddling. The Maligne is moving fast. They told me that the flow is down in the fall. *Okay, what the hell is it like in the spring with the melting snow?* As I paddle farther away from the falls, the current seemed to slow, but I'm hardly able to breathe and soon have to pull over into a quiet pool on the side of the river.

The map shows a campsite at the top of the falls but it's only ten o'clock in the morning, too early to stop. The next site looks to be about three miles farther, and I'm not sure what kind of progress I can make. I decide not to worry about it.

The shoreline is endless solid granite. It reminds me of the coastline in Maine. This rock was carved in the Ice Age. Random boulders lie scattered about like an old game of marbles. The landscape was carved out by a million-year-old glacier, and there are scrapes and gouges where the glacier pushed in and out. Blue-gray cliffs rise from the water's edge up forty feet, topped by deep green pines. The face of the cliff is covered with moss and lichens. Many boulders have thin veins of different colors running through them. On closer inspection, the veins are mostly rose-colored and a few are white. They're glassy and have a crystal-like structure. I think they're quartz, but I'm not sure. On many of the boulders, there are scratches of varying depths and widths. They all run parallel to each other in a northeastern to southwestern direction. This must have been the direction that glaciers took as they moved back and forth, with each advance pushing these huge rocks over the last bunch. Hard to imagine the size and power of the glaciers, but as I see the remains, the piles of rocks, and the carved topography of the landscape, I can't help but be awed by the power of nature. All these lakes and rivers were scraped out in a random pattern by the glacier.

It's the end of August, and the color of the forest is just beginning to show. Under the trees, the ground is carpeted with ferns and flowering plants that contrast in color through the deep green; many stands of birch and aspen provide a white backdrop. It's amazing that the forest can be this mature with a growing season of only four months. How did they get this big and healthy while standing in the cold for eight months, with their roots fighting their way into rock? The colors are surreal—the verdant forest framed by a purple sky and the grayish-white of the granite bluff. Their reflection echoes on the lake. The leaves are turning colors and just beginning to fall. Soon it will be winter, and this fabulous landscape will grow dormant. It will return in the spring, even though I will not.

The birch trees glisten white in the sun. Many of the trees are dead at the top. If lightning were to strike this stand, the fire would race a long way. They're dying from the top down.

Reminds me of my mother's Alzheimer's. If she were aware, she would be saddened to see her son die first.

The trees remind me of my beautiful green sports car, which I'll never see again. I begin to cry, but the thought of my passengers screaming when I hit the accelerator, with the front end rising up like I'm doing a wheelie, actually makes me laugh. Then I hit a rock, jarring me back to reality.

It's beautiful here; I'm sad to think I'll never see this again. The Indians believe that in death, their spirits will walk the land again. I hope they're right and all those Christians are dead wrong. I start to laugh again. Dead wrong seems to apply pretty much to me. I'm hoping for a peaceful death, but how does anyone know what that is?

The vista is so wonderful I think there *must* be a God. I can only sit in awe at the splendor of creation and wonder how this could all come about without a God. I've come to the right place to die, and somehow I feel more alive here than I ever have. My plan is a good one; I'm at peace. There is harmony here, a harmony with nature that man has lost.

We fill in swamps and bulldoze hills, and for what? More parking lots? We pollute the air and the water, and for what? Bigger cars and more air-conditioning? I think the Bible holds us responsible for the earth. Why do we ignore this directive and follow so many other directives that seem to make little sense? Why do we wage war when the Bible says to love one another? We live on this earth; why do we take such poor care of it? The time will come when all we have left to mine are our own garbage dumps. My lungs are burning—it's time for pills.

Then suddenly, a small island appears in the middle of the river, with small rapids on both sides. I must quickly decide on which side to take it. I go to the right, paddling harder than I had been, and as I clear it, I'm exhausted but must keep going, or the current will take me back through it. I remember from the map that the rapids are only one mile from the falls, and it's already almost one o'clock. I have two more miles to the campsite. I start to panic but then remember: *What do I have to worry about?* I paddle a while until I find another quiet pool off to the side, and I rest.

I'm soon joined by a large bull moose coming out of the woods. He stops when he sees me, only about forty feet away at the other side of the pool. We look at each other for a long time, at least five minutes. He is fat; my guess is he's storing up for the winter. His rack is huge, and I wonder whether I could get away if he charges me. But then again, what do I have to worry about? So we continue looking at each other. He is over seven feet tall. He must weigh over a thousand pounds but is supported by legs that look like thin stilts. His rack has sharp points. He has a long bulbous nose and a waddle. He's homely yet magnificent at the same time. The moose sloshes around and starts nibbling on a pine bough, totally ignoring me as I slowly pass by.

I remember reading about the moose on Isle Royale in Lake Superior. The moose on the island became so numerous without any predators that they ate themselves out of house and home.

They ate all the trees down to the ground and were starving to death. Then, apparently wolves came in one winter over the ice and thinned the number down to a population that could survive. This moose must use the area as his dining room because the branches I see are pretty well denuded.

He also brought along a swarm of black flies and mosquitoes that soon find me too. What the hell? They told me the flies were gone at this time of year. They told me the mosquitoes were down this late in the summer. Crap, if this is down, what must they be like in the middle of summer? They're all around me, and they bite. I quickly dig out the insect spray from the backpack and then take off with inspired energy. It takes my mind off my other problems.

When that energy wears off, I look in the backpack for painkillers and soon feel much better. A cigarette would taste good but my breath is short and I decide to wait. It was a nice day, and I did enjoy the scene as I paddled along. The trees and rocks, with the clean blue sky, are drop-dead beautiful. *Drop dead.* Yes, I think I will.

A flock of geese fly overhead in a V formation. They're heading south for the winter. They fly so that one cuts the wind for those behind, and when the lead tires, he falls back and another takes over. If one becomes sick or wounded and drops out, two will fall out of formation. They will stay with the goose until it is able to fly or it dies. I start to cry. I will die alone. There will be no one to stay with me. I also will never fly again. All of a sudden, I feel very alone but then remember the old saying, "If you're lonely, you're in bad company," and I tell myself to get over it.

About another mile up the river, there is a large bog off to my left. I'm not sure what it is at first, but when I see there are ducks in the bog, I realize it must be wild rice. At one time, the Indians must have harvested this patch, beating the rice off the stalks, down into their canoes.

The pain in my shoulders and back begins to overwhelm the pain in my lungs. I'm not used to the paddling, but I know I must keep going, because there's no place to pull over with all the huge rocks on the shoreline. I see few opportunities to beach the canoe. Just when it seems I can't paddle anymore, the campsite comes up around the bend on my left and the water widens at the entrance of Tanner Lake. The site is on the south side of May Island.

I couldn't have paddled any more. My legs are numb and my shoulders and arms ache so badly that I forget about the pain in my lungs and chest. Here, there is fresh air and room to breathe, if only I could. I took two painkillers an hour before, and they have already worn off. My body seems to be adjusting to the meds, and I think I'll need to take even more at a time.

The campsite is surrounded by pines and spruce, forming a canopy over the ground cover of lichen and moss. There's a gravel shoreline, and as I ground the canoe, it lets me know it's not happy by groaning loudly. Getting out of the canoe is difficult, and I fall sideways on the gravel into the shallow water. But the cold water feels good. After dragging the canoe up, I unhook my backpack and sit down with the scotch and a cigarette. It's five o'clock, and I estimate that with actual time spent paddling, it took me close to six hours to go three miles.

It starts to get dark, and I have to get a fire going. It just about kills me to forage for firewood, but I find enough and start a fire. Foraging would have been easier if I'd remembered I had a saw in my backpack. Not taking that propane stove may have been a mistake. There's a flat spot where others had placed their tents, and I use it too. At least the tent is easy to set up. I use my frying pan to heat up some of the freeze-dried stuff. It ends up charred on the outside and cold on the inside. I'm not even sure what it is. Washing the frying pan in the gravel is a new experience, and I'm sure that if I were to do this long enough, I would die of food poisoning.

Next, I try to hang my backpack from the tree. Anyone watching would have died laughing, and even I laughed after it was done. It looked ridiculous. I wonder how this could work, because a bear can climb up the tree and chew through the rope, and the bag would just drop to the ground. Maybe I'm not doing this right. *Whatever.*

It's finally dark, and I'm not feeling very well. I take my cocktail of painkillers, antidepressants, and sleeping pills, along with a shot of scotch, and I sit on a rock, watching the moonlight on Tanner Lake. I hurt all over—arms and shoulders, my lungs, everything hurts. As the fire dies out, I crawl into the sleeping bag and soon, the rhythm of the waves lapping against the granite shoreline lulls me to sleep. Well, I don't fall asleep as much as pass out. I had decided to survive as long as possible before implementing my plan. If I die the first day out, I'll be remembered as a dumb greenhorn. My plan is to go as far into my last adventure as possible.

CHAPTER TWELVE

Day Two

When I wake up, the sun is shining, and it's late, but I can hardly move. Lawyers are not cut out for this sort of activity. Oh well, I would not be a lawyer very much longer. I should have taken the pad with the sleeping bag. I untie my backpack and go for the painkillers first, washing them down with cool lake water. It's almost ten o'clock when I start the fire again. For coffee, I boil water in the pot and just dump in some grounds. I have no idea how much to dump in—this was not covered in law school, and why the hell didn't Alan mention a coffee pot when we went through all that rigmarole? I drink my coffee filled with grounds and smoke a cigarette, waiting for the pills to work. Then I heat up the dried milk with lake water and make oatmeal for breakfast while eating an apple. Sitting down with coffee, I look over the map.

The trip to the next campsite looks to be about two and a half miles across the wide-open waters of Tanner Lake and then up the Maligne River again. It should be easer paddling, because the lake is calm, the river is much wider, and there are no portages. I estimate it to be no more than four hours. I wonder if I can go farther but decide I can't, because the campsite after that is another four or five hours, with three rapids.

After packing up the gear, I strap my bag to the canoe cross-brace and head out. Then I realize I should take a crap now, rather than later. I remove the small shovel from the pack and head into the woods. It would be nice if I could find a stone to sit on, and I spot one not far from the campsite. Squatting on the stone, I realize it won't work like a toilet seat. So I move into the woods with my shovel and wonder, *Do I dig the hole first and try to hit it, or do I just go and then bury it?* I decide to just go.

There it is on the ground, and then it hits me—the toilet paper is in the backpack. I'm not going to walk back in this condition. Looking around, I see a pile of dried leaves that will have to work. "Yuck." Then looking down, I think, *That's a nice tight stool, not the sign of a dying man. My digestive system is not my problem.*

I thrust the shovel into the ground and hit rock, jarring my eyeballs. The dirt was only about half an inch deep, so picking up the stool in the shovel, I move farther into the woods and try again—with the same result. Moving farther into the woods, the stool rolls off the shovel and under some leaves. *Fine, I'm not going to do this again.* I don't care if the rangers find out. What the hell—the moose aren't picking up. On the way back, I decide I don't even want to take the shovel with me again, and I leave it at the campsite. Others will just figure someone forgot it.

I climb into the canoe and take off into the open waters of Tanner Lake. My muscles scream at first, but I recently took the pain pills, and I know more won't help much, so I just soldier on. My arms and shoulders soon settle down to the point where it's only my lungs that bother me. I cough up a lot of crap and spit it into the lake. I can see red blotches in the clear water and wonder when I'm going to decide to let go. If I let go too soon, all those people back at the resort and the outfitters will think I'm just a stupid greenhorn. That doesn't sit well with me; I don't want to give lawyers a bad name.

The sun gradually gives way as dark clouds move in. Then rain starts to fall, and the sky darkens—and then the gusher hits. It's too late to get out the rain gear, and the downpour drenches me immediately. The misery of being totally wet makes me forget my aches and pains but does nothing for my mood. Just as soon as it came on, the rain lets up, the sky brightens, and the patted-down lake is smooth. It's amazing how a bright, sunny, clear sky can cheer up even a dead man.

There are three beautiful small islands in the middle of Tanner Lake. The shore is lined with white and red pines, jack pines, and aspens. A flock of ravens fly right through the forest as if the trees aren't even there. Overhead, there is a large group of turkey vultures. Most people confuse them with eagles, but I've made the mistake before and know better. While they're difficult to distinguish from eagles, eagles don't fly in packs like that. I also see a bird with a white belly and a mean-looking beak, but I don't know what it is.

As I leave the islands behind, Tanner Lake widens out to what looks like a mile across, and I'm in the middle of open water. My mind begins to wander as the paddling becomes monotonous. I think of my time at the library and remember a poem that got to me.

So grieve a while for me, if grieve you must
Then let your grief be comforted by trust
It's only for a while that we must part
So bless the memories within your heart

But when we're gone, our footprints in this world fade. And soon even those who remembered us are also gone. It all seems so useless and temporary. Suddenly, a sense of loneliness and despair befalls me. I will die alone. Krishnamurti, an Indian spiritual leader, was once asked how to say good-bye to a dying man. "Tell him that in his death, a part of you will die with him, and he will not be alone." Oh Lord, I'm going to die alone, but I know that Krishnamurti is right—a part of my loved ones will die with me. I did not want it to be this way. I've let them down. Those damn cigarettes.

My mood is broken by three loons who seem to pop up from nowhere in front of the canoe and then dive when they see me. I'm almost clear of Tanner Lake and about to reenter the Maligne River. Pulling over for a break and rummaging through the pack, I come up with some meat sticks that Alan the outfitter must have just thrown in. While eating, I spot an eagle sitting in a tree above me. *Damn, they're mean-looking.* He seems to be deciding whether I would be good to eat. I think it was Ben Franklin who didn't like the eagle and thought the turkey would be a better symbol for the country. Eagles really are aggressive birds, and I think I might agree with Ben. They have piercing eyes and curved beaks, but when they soar in the sky they *are* majestic. The new resident eagle near our lake cabin tried to carry off the neighbor's small dog and ruined his welcome. I move on before this one decides to carry me off.

Shading my eyes from the sun, I think I can see voyageurs coming around the bend in giant canoes loaded high with furs or whisky, lustily singing their *chansons*. Chansons are epic poems that were mostly sung in that era in France. Sounds romantic, but it must have been a tough way to make a living. Every fall, from 1750 and on for about a hundred years, the voyageur carried trade goods through the Boundary Waters as far as Canada's Northwest Territories. Much of it was carried on the Maligne River. The voyageurs were mostly Frenchmen who came down from Canada. They spent the winter in the interior, trading with the Native Americans and even married many of them. They traded with the Indians for furs, giving them cheap goods and liquor in return. One has to watch those Frenchies . . .

When the ice went out of the lakes and rivers, they returned with beaver and other pelts. The Canadian border with the United States is somewhat defined by their routes, often going right down the middle of some lakes.

The exploits of the voyageurs are most likely exaggerated. Stories tell that it was common for them to carry two-hundred-pound bundles of furs over portages. They could paddle and portage as many as fifty miles a day, with as little as four hours of sleep. How could anyone do that while being attacked endlessly by mosquitoes and black flies? Those fur pelts must have been worth a lot of money. Legend has it that if you couldn't sing the chansons of France, you weren't worth your salt as a voyageur. Their names are everywhere, along with the Indian names. There's Lac La Croix, Grand Marais, and Dieu River, as well as many others. As one might expect, they plied the Indians with drink when trading. Rum and blueberry mash made a potent drink that they consumed prior to trading. Over time, the beaver population was decimated, all for the sake of hats for fancy European ladies.

I close my eyes, and I can see them ahead. Their canoes are large and their paddles move in rhythm with their song. Furs are piled high in the canoe. There are eight men singing as loudly as they can for the enjoyment of only themselves.

Up ahead, a small stream joins the Maligne River on the right. The map shows it as Poohpah Creek, and the campsite is just a little bit past the creek on the right. The shore at the campsite is gravel again, and the canoe screams again as I land it. I wonder if that Kevlar can take all the abuse the canoes must get. There are rocks everywhere. The first thing to do is grab the bottle of scotch and have a cigarette. It's only a little after four o'clock, and I have plenty of time to get everything done before dark.

I decide my time will come when my bottles of scotch are gone. I'm going to enjoy them to the last drop. This time, a little lake water goes into the scotch. I suppose I'm stretching out the liquor if it's going to be my drop-dead signal.

The map shows the next campsite is a bit more than two miles up the Maligne. The river narrows, and there are three rapids but no portages. The campsite after that is only a little more than a mile farther, but there are three portages. That doesn't appeal to me, so I decide not to try it. My butt has joined the pain in my shoulders and back. The seat in the canoe doesn't match my rear end very well. With more scotch and painkillers, I lie down and stretch my body. Even the rocks feel good. This time, before setting up the tent, I go into the woods with my saw and cut some bushy pine boughs to lay on the ground under the floor of the tent. Then I gather wood for the fire. The fire is difficult to start because the wood is wet from the afternoon rain, but it finally gets going, and I put on the pot for coffee.

At five o'clock, I lie down to rest again. Then, out of the woods comes a scream that jolts me. *What was that?* Then I hear voices. I'm not alone. Where are they? No one was in sight when I was on the river. Looking up and down the river, I see no one. Then I hear the voices again. They seem to be coming from the direction of Poohpah Creek, which I passed earlier. Are they screaming because they're in trouble? I run toward the creek. Well, I don't exactly run. I'm much too sore, and navigating through the brush is slow going. The creek forms a point as it flows into the river, and there they are—a young couple on the other side of the point from my campsite. They are less than a block away, and they are naked, goofing around in the water. I drop down so they don't see me spying on them.

What to do? What to do? Should I let them know I'm here, or should I just ignore them? While trying to figure it out, they rush out of the water and dive into their tent.

Maybe they're horny, but I don't think so. The water is cold, so when he dashes for the tent, he looks like her, only with muscles. Returning to the campsite, I decide to go over and talk to them. The smoke from my fire is drifting their way and might panic them into thinking there's a fire coming their way. Why not talk to them? My last conversation with Brownie was not very satisfying. It will be dark soon, so if I'm going to go over, it should be now. Going through the brush in the dark would be difficult.

As I step out of the woods, I see they're outside, getting ready to cook. "Hi!" I yell out.

They stare at me as I approach. "Hi," he says. "Are you a ranger?"

"No, I'm just tripping, like you. My campsite is just on the other side of the point. I heard a scream and was concerned."

"Oh," he says, "that was Brook. We went into the water to wash off, and she thought it was too cold."

"How did you come to be here?" I ask. "I didn't see you on the river."

"We were coming off the Poohbah Lake and wanted to shortcut over to the Maligne River, and we saw this creek that looked like it would connect. We did okay until it was too low, and after a couple portages, we gave up. We tied the canoe with a rope and pulled it as we waded through the stream. We're exhausted. It was a big mistake, and we should have known better, but we thought we were experienced enough to make it."

"Are you alone?" she asks.

"Yes," I say and tell them my lie about my partner's last-minute accident.

"If you're alone, have you eaten yet?"

I can't pass up the invitation. While we chat, she cooks up a dinner of bacon and beans with hard rolls. The bacon is to die for, but I remember being told that it would attract bears. Still, it would have been worth it. I learn they're from Iowa, and this is their third trip to the Boundary Waters. They're both tall and thin and appear to be in their late twenties. It's obvious they're both fitness freaks—the kind who go jogging every day, the kind who belong out here, versus me, the kind who isn't active enough to eat bacon every day. Her hair is a mess, but she seems unconcerned about her appearance—not your typical female. Her hair keeps falling in her face, but she just keeps pushing it back. He's wearing one of those stupid baseball caps so many young men wear backward. They were very nice, and I'm happy I joined them. Both work for the same insurance company.

I'm not sure if they're married, because she isn't wearing a ring. But then, you shouldn't wear rings out here anyway. I'm wearing mine but for different reasons. When he finds out I'm a lawyer, he expresses his desire to go to law school someday soon. As we sit around the fire, he and I talk about law school. She sits quietly and listens.

"How long have you been out?" I ask.

"Seven days," he says, "and we need to get back to the resort within three days, so we're going to have to move it in the morning. The trip down that damn creek set our timetable back. Then we fly into Ely, rent a car to Duluth, and fly out of Duluth.

When it starts to get dark, I tell them I need to return to my campsite. "Be careful," I say as I walk away. "Just before you get to the falls, the river quickens, and it is not that far to the falls. Watch for the portage—it'll be on your right."

Their youthful enthusiasm is good for me to see, but as I lie in my tent, it depresses me. I'm so exhausted that I no longer feel the soreness in my body, and I soon fall asleep.

CHAPTER THIRTEEN

Day 3

It is daylight already when I wake up; I've never slept this hard in my life. Exhaustion works well for a deep sleep. My muscles are still very sore but seem to be getting somewhat accustomed to the paddling. There are still some embers in the fire pit, so adding more twigs starts it up enough to boil water for coffee. I'm not hungry, but I know I have to eat something so I just spill some of my coffee water into the oatmeal and eat it with the coffee grounds. Then I make Tang with cold water from the river and wash it down with a few painkillers as I review the map.

The river narrows considerably, and there are two rapids right off the bat and then a third just before the next campsite. I know that as the river narrows, the current is going to be much stronger than anything I've encountered over the first two days. Crap, this is going to be much tougher. At least there were no portages on the first two days. The next campsite beyond is only about a mile and a half farther, but there are three portages, and I see no way I can pull that off. I load the gear into the canoe and take off.

The river quickly narrows, and it seems as if the woods are closing in on me when I come upon the first rapids. The water pouring over the rocks and the trees growing up to the edge are gorgeous, but I fixate on exactly where to hit the rapids with the canoe. I can't tell where it's the deepest, so I go for the middle and paddle like crazy. I make it through without hitting anything, but I am exhausted and my shoulders hurt. The current doesn't let up, so I continue to paddle. I only go a few hundred feet and then stop to rest, but the current carries me backward, and I panic. Adrenaline kicks in as I keep going, only to encounter the second rapids. I now know why two in the canoe is better. This one looks even worse than the first rapids. The river is much narrower and the water is coming faster, but I know more about what to expect. I hit it hard, paddling like crazy. I come through it with less stress and am proud of myself. When spring comes and the snow melts, this river must roar and be nearly impassable for all but the most experienced canoeists.

An otter appears ahead of me about twenty feet from the canoe. He barks and disappears, only to appear again and bark some more, as if to tell me to get out of his world. He's about three feet long with short legs, and he looks to be bodysurfing in the fast-moving water ahead of me. I think he's playing with me. He continues to move ahead until he sees a frog on the shore. He goes for it and then disappears for good. No doubt his world is in the water.

Around the next bend, I find an amazing scene—a moose standing in the water, facing off with two timber wolves. The wolves see me and turn back into the pines. They should thank me. I don't think they would have won that fight. It is a very big bull moose who doesn't seem to be too worried.

The river slows, and I relax a bit. It is again a nice day, and I enjoy the scenery. There's a slight breeze from the west, and it brings the smell of pine with it. I watch a large school of crappies below me, and as they move in unison, they almost hypnotize me. I'm mesmerized by their movements, until a northern pike appears, and they scatter in all directions. I see the pike with a crappy in his mouth and wonder which one God was watching out for: the crappy or the pike.

With thoughts of God, my mind turns to the library and my confusion over what I've learned about the afterlife and religion. I have to make up my mind soon. Is there a God, or isn't there? Is he a loving God or a vengeful God? My library time didn't answer my questions.

The artist Van Gogh was widely considered to be mad. He believed he lived in a world created by a God who didn't know what he was doing. After seeing the world spin, I'm not so sure Van Gogh was all that crazy.

Would a good and forgiving God cast me into hell forever? Is there no moral good without religion's threat of hell? How could something like the earthquake in Haiti, the Japanese tsunami, and the floods in Thailand happen if there's an all-powerful and loving God? I've noticed that most TV preachers don't talk much about hell—it scares off the donations, I think. But if there is a divine justice, how can there not be a hell to balance the scales? Old-time religion preached fire and brimstone and an angry God, but now it seems we'll be blissfully reunited with loved ones. Many Christian preachers now say that heaven is whatever you want it to be, but how do they know?

We seem to have inherited religion from the many generations that have embellished it over the ages. My review of religion was brief, and I know it was most likely riddled with inaccurate observations. *I'm sure priests and rabbis would disagree with many of my conclusions, but I have nothing more to go on.* Religion, as far as I can see, has many contradictions, having been revised so many times throughout history that it's now just a mishmash to me. It's no wonder many educated people have rejected it. Man seems to have spent thousands of years rewriting ancient literature and refining the same beginning in different ways for different religions. The only common concept is that of a supreme being who will receive us in heaven or banish us to hell, but then, many of those Asian religions don't even believe in heaven or hell.

Who really believes that Jonah was in the belly of the whale, that Noah built an ark and gathered all the animals, and that the creation story is true? I'm not sure, however, that I'm ready to reject God just because I have such a low opinion of the Bible and organized religion.

I remember reading about a seventeenth-century philosopher, Blaise Pascal, who first proposed that it's rational to believe in God, because you have nothing to lose if you do. If there is a God, you're ahead of the game, and if there isn't a God, so what? Without belief, you may lose nothing or—heaven forbid—lose heaven. I think this is a very dangerous approach. An all-knowing God is going to know you're just playing the odds, and the lack of sincerity might condemn you to that seventh layer of hell. And how can anyone believe that hell has seven layers? In Paul's letter to the Romans, he says that on the Day of Judgment, God will judge the secret thoughts of all. Well, there you have it. Those people who say they believe in God because they have nothing to lose by doing so are going to be in trouble, because God is going to read their minds.

I've worked myself into a snit; all those religions are full of it. I need to pray for guidance. But then I hear the rush of water, which must be the third rapids ahead, and I need to focus. The river is very narrow here, and the water is fast. This is the worst of the three rapids, and I'm tired, so this may be the end. I hadn't wanted the end to come too soon in the trip. I don't want the people back at the outfitters and the resort saying, "We shouldn't have let him go alone. This is our fault too. He didn't even make it past the first few rapids." I know my wife and children will feel that way, no matter where or when I drown on the trip.

Paddling as hard as I can into the middle of the rapids, I seem to stall and go backward for a moment, but then the adrenaline kicks in, and I manage to pull through. Exhaustion sets in, but I remember that the campsite is only a quarter of a mile past the rapids. I'm determined to make it. My lungs are bursting and I can hardly breathe, and then the campsite comes up on the left. Beaching the canoe on the shore, I can only sit. I don't have the strength to get out of it. But then . . . I'm amazed to hear my cell phone ring. Turning around to get it from my backpack is painful, and it takes me so long that it quits ringing before I can get to it. I sit in the canoe for at least ten minutes before leaning over, falling sideways on the rocks, and then twisting to stand up. Walking slowly, I reach a boulder and sit down to rest. After another ten minutes, I pull the canoe up out of the water and remove my backpack and the cell phone. The call was from my wife. I'm surprised she called me when I happened to be in a spot with coverage. I go back and forth, trying to decide whether I should return the call. After all, I've already said good-bye, and I'm not sure I can keep myself from breaking down. I decide to think about it and maybe call her back later.

It's after four o'clock but already starting to get dark, as the sky is overcast. I hurry to make a fire from branches that have been left behind by the last occupant. While building the fire, I hit the bottle of scotch with two painkillers. I decide to call Betty after eating. An antidepressant might be a good idea but not if I'm going to sound all right when I call her back. I'll take the antidepressants afterward; I think I'll need them.

This campsite is nestled in a larger stand of aspens, and the night breeze whispers to me through the trees. After setting up the tent, which I'm now getting good at, I make a salami and peanut butter sandwich and have an orange with cold river water. Unable to stop for lunch, my stomach isn't satisfied, and I need a second sandwich. Then I repack the backpack and hang it from a tree. It's time to call.

The phone rings twice and she's on. "Oh, my God, I've been trying to reach you every day since you left and was about to give up."

"You must have just caught me at a hot spot."

"Why didn't you answer right away?"

"I was in the canoe and couldn't get to it in time."

"How are you?"

"I'm sore as hell from all the paddling, and I'm tired. I just came through three rapids on the Maligne River, which is the toughest part of the whole trip. So you don't need to worry, because I'm about to leave it and enter Sturgeon Lake. The going from here is much easier. How is everything back there?"

"The kids have called, wondering if I'd heard from you. They don't think you should have gone alone either."

"Has anyone called from the firm?"

"No, no one has called," she says. Then she asks, "Are you alone? Did you hook up with those people in the store?"

"Well, yes and no, but I had dinner with a young couple from Iowa last night."

"So there are people around. That's good."

"You know, the odds of your getting through to me here are almost nil. I told you that there wouldn't be coverage here, so don't be so concerned about it." After more small talk, I tell her I love her. I'm not as emotional as I thought I would be, but I'm depressed and take two more pills with some coffee.

It's dark now, so I take out the headlamp for the first time. The map indicates that there are three portages ahead. I haven't even done one portage yet, and now there are three in one day? The next campsite is about two miles ahead, but for some reason, there are four campsites together, about half a mile apart. So if

I can do it, I'll have a choice of different sites. The first portage starts right at the campsite. According to the map, it's 42 rods. I cannot remember how long a rod is but I do remember figuring that 16 rods would equal about a city block. So the first portage will be two and a half blocks long. I'll be fresh, so I should be able to make that. About a quarter mile up the river is another set of rapids. Then another quarter mile more, a sharp turn in the river is apparently impassable because the second portage is right there. This one is 64 rods. This would be—crap, almost four blocks long. After another quarter mile, the third portage comes up. This one is 52 rods long. *Not to worry,* I think. *I'll be dead by then.* If I do make it that far, up the river from the first campsite is a cluster of three more campsites about half a mile apart.

I have a cigarette with coffee, and my lungs burn, but I smoke it anyway. They've already killed me, so what difference does it make? I crawl into bed but have trouble falling asleep, as an owl close by keeps saying, "whosnooks, whosnooks." I get up and feast on a variety of pills and finally go to sleep.

CHAPTER FOURTEEN

Day 4

When I put on my pants the next morning, I'm shocked to see that I'm in a smaller notch on my belt. I've lost an inch on my waistline. Geez, why didn't I do this when I was healthy and could have enjoyed it? Untying the backpack from the tree, the rope slips through my hands, and the pack hits the ground hard. My pot now has a big dent in it and doesn't sit straight. *Oh well, I'm not sitting straight anymore either.* I start the fire from dry leaves and twigs, and it's barely hot enough to get my coffee boiling. I eat an orange, some cheese, and some of the trail mix. A tear comes to my eye when I think that I'll never have pancakes, bacon, and eggs again.

Sitting with my coffee and a cigarette, I take out the map for another look. The first portage is inland and doesn't follow the water's edge. It doesn't look too bad, as I can see up the start of it from where I'm sitting. There's another set of rapids almost right away at the end of the portage, and it looks like the river narrows even more, from what I've seen so far. After that, the river narrows to almost nothing, as it turns 90 degrees to the left. This is where the second portage is, and it's the long one—64 rods. I think I'll have to rest at the end of this one before taking on the last portage, which is over three blocks long, and then another half mile to the next campsite.

I load up, and off I go. I spot the owl looking at me with big yellow eyes. He's sitting in his nest in a large oak tree, looking down into my bloodshot eyes. His nest is a tangled mass of sticks, and I remember that owls don't build their own nests but take over abandoned ones from the previous year. They hunt at night, and the sound of his hooting and wings flapping is what kept me awake last night. All of the campsites are fertile ground for mice, so he knows dinner's close by. I yell back at him, "Whosnooks yourself." *Don't follow me, or I'll sue you for disturbing the peace. Oh, wait. I'm disturbing your peace. Never mind.*

The first portage is awful; my pack and the canoe are heavy and unstable. Then at the end, the rocks are muddy and slippery. I slide all over the place and fall sideways with the canoe, giving a loud, hollow thud and taking skin off my ear. It's difficult to get up again, but I'm not really hurt. They warned me about the rocks, and they weren't kidding. I vow to be more careful in the future. They should have a medical clinic at the end of each of these portages.

It takes about a half hour to go the two and a half blocks. I try to time myself to figure out how far I can go in a day and make it to the next campsite. After resting a bit in the canoe, the rapids are straight ahead. The sound of the rushing water is intimidating, and as I approach, I see it's flowing even faster than the rapids I've already been over. The spray off the rocks soaks me as I fight my way. This is the most treacherous one yet, and the rocks below scrape the bottom of the canoe. When I reach the middle, total concentration takes over; there is no time to be afraid. And as I pass through, even though part of me just wants to let it go and let the journey be over, I have an overwhelming sense of exhilaration. When life gets like this, the brain seems to go on automatic pilot and block out the fear.

A small island appears ahead in the middle of the river, and as the map indicates, the next portage is just past it. The island is gorgeous, with pines growing out of the rocks. It would have been a beautiful spot for a cabin, with the water crashing into the rocks and swirling all around it. You would have risked your life getting to it, however.

At the portage landing, I decide I'd better rest before taking it on. Then I remember I didn't poop before leaving, so out in the woods I go. Before dropping my pants, I actually look around to see if anyone is looking. *What an idiot.* Then, for the second time, I forget the toilet paper. *What an idiot.*

A few blocks down the portage path there are wild blueberry bushes that are loaded with berries. *Why not?* I think. *Good spot to rest.* I love blueberries, so I stop, drop the canoe, and wander into the bushes to gather some. After eating a few handfuls, I hear a noise in the woods—and it gets louder. *Oh, my God, bears and blueberries, bears and blueberries and me—a bear's favorite foods. Get out of here.* Picking up the canoe, I take off as if the devil himself is after me. Just as I'm ready to drop, I reach the end of the portage at the water's edge and collapse on the rocky shore.

I am so exhausted that I think I might slip into a coma. My life flashes before me. I clearly remember, as a teenager, lying in bed and wondering about my future—what kind of job I'll have, who I'll marry, if I'll be successful, how long I'll live. Forty years later, it's all come to pass, but back then, forty years was incomprehensible. Where did all that time go? Oh God, and now it is over. Here I am, about to die, and I still don't know anything. I think life should be about happiness. Was I happy? I think so. I made a lot of money and I think that helps, but there were hard years getting there.

Then I hear a noise behind me and there he is—the biggest bear I've ever seen. We just pause, looking each other over. Coming to my senses, I dash to the canoe and hit the water like I'm a twenty-year-old. I look back, half expecting the bear to be chasing me, but he is only drinking from the river. The river widens now, and the paddling is easier.

I paddle past an old log cabin that looks abandoned in the woods. I think how beautiful and simple it would have been to live that way. There would be no expensive cars or houses to maintain, no professional persona to project. How did I get to the point where I needed all this stuff? Does it make for a better life? I think of Thoreau's book that I couldn't finish. He went into the woods to experience the simple life and extolled its virtues. His message beat into me, chapter after chapter, was more than I could take. I'm not sure I agree with him—if he could have seen my little sports car, he might have changed his mind. And even he couldn't stick it out for more than two years. But I do envy him. No computers, e-mail, or cell phones. Thoreau's finally proven his point to me, however.

Here, one realizes one doesn't need much to live or at least get by.

I look up ahead and see a series of rapids on my right and the portage on the left around the bend, just as I remember from the map. But as I approach, I'm uncertain where the portage begins exactly. I waste time going back and forth by the shore, but I finally spot what looks like a small pile of garbage and decide that must be the spot. It will be hard to get ashore, because there's only a rock ledge touching the water. I stand up in the canoe and then flop down on the rock ledge on my butt, with my feet still in the canoe. Then, as I grab the canoe and try to stand on the rock at the same time, I lose the paddle in the water. *Damn!* I get back in the canoe and grab the paddle before it floats away. This time, I throw it on the shore before pulling the canoe up behind me. If I were dead by now, none of this would be happening. But I sense the timing isn't right. I decide to sit down and have some scotch and a cigarette before continuing. Then, trying to get up, I realize I also need some painkillers. This last portage, if it doesn't kill me, will be over three blocks long.

I'm quickly learning how to portage. If I lift the canoe up just a little with my arms, it doesn't cut into my shoulder blades as much, and the backpack does provide a measure of ballast that stabilizes my footing when it gets slippery. But the portage is still miserable, and when I hear a woodpecker rattling away on a dead tree above me, I stop to rest and watch. It's a big bird, the size of a chicken. He has a flaming red head and a black-and-white body with a long neck and one big pecker; I suppose

I should say one big *beak*. He is not a very good-looking bird. I recognize him—he is a pileated woodpecker—from seeing one near my cabin at the lake. One lived in a dead pine tree there. Woodpeckers are supposed to go after the carpenter ants and grubs in dead trees, but that one angered me when he went after a healthy hundred-foot white pine in my yard. The pileated woodpecker is the noisiest native of the Boundary Waters. His endless hammering away on trees can be heard for a mile. While noisy, he's also shy and rarely seen. This one is hard at work and pays no attention to me. I move on.

When I finally reach the end of the portage, I rest and take another look at the map. There are three campsites within reach, two of which are on small islands. The next day's trip is a long one over what looks like two miles of open water on Sturgeon Lake, so I decide to go for the farthest campsite to cut the next day's trip as short as possible. On the map, it appears to be a very small island. Some scotch and a cigarette would taste good, but it's getting late and the sun's going down. I can't take a chance on finding that island in the dark. The river is much wider now, and the paddling is a bit easier. Then the first island comes up on my left, and I can see one other campsite to the right on the shore. The first island site is tempting, but I paddle by it and see the one I want another quarter mile ahead. I go for it.

When I arrive, there are three deer standing on the campsite, looking at me—a buck and two does—and they seem to think I'm not going to stop. I have to stop; it's too late to go on. This is one big buck—he looks to be over two hundred pounds with at least a twelve-point rack. He would never have survived to get this big if they allowed hunting up here. The buck seems to think he can run me off and does not move. The two does run away, but he doesn't move. I grab the paddle and wave it at him in a menacing way. He doesn't move. Then, remembering this might be mating season, I yell at him that his girls have run off and he better follow. I can't help but laugh when he does. Then I see that this is a very small island, and we're going to have to share it for the night.

It's getting too dark to look for firewood, but I luck out. I find a pile of dry driftwood and get a nice fire started. After a few day's practice, starting a fire has become easier. Birch bark and pine needles are excellent fire starters when dry, not so good when wet. Alan the outfitter told me back at the store (God, that seems like a lifetime ago) that it's customary to leave firewood for the next party at the campsite when you leave. But there's been little or no firewood waiting for me. And I'm no better, as I rationalize that it's late in the year and there's no point leaving firewood now.

Then comes the routine of setting up the tent and digging out something to eat. It seems there are no bears on this small island, so the backpack will stay in my tent tonight. After a skimpy dinner, I pull out the scotch and have another cigarette but cut back on the painkillers as I feel better tonight. I think my body's beginning to adapt; my shoulders and back are not that sore anymore. Then, just when I feel that maybe I'm not really that sick, the coughing starts in from the cigarette, and I spit up blood.

The air is so clean here that the moon is the brightest I've ever seen it. I look at it as if I've never seen it before; I study every crater and spot as if to memorize them. Why have I not taken the time to look until now? Why is it only *now* that I study each rock and tree? All those years and I've come to this—how sad that in dying I've come alive. I think death is overrated as a tragedy. There comes a time when the pain and loneliness are no longer bearable. Digging my mantra, my poem, out of my wallet, I read it, even though I now know it by heart.

> Do not stand at my grave and weep
> I am not there, I do not sleep
> I am the thousand winds that blow
> I am the diamond's glints upon the snow
> I am the sunlight on ripened grain
> I am the gentle autumn rain
> When you awaken in the morning's hush
> I am the swift uplifting rush
> Of birds in circling flight
> I am the soft star that shines at night
> So do not stand at my grave and cry

I listen for the howl of a wolf or the hooting of an owl, but I hear nothing but the trees swaying in the wind, lulling me to sleep. I dream about a poem I read in the library by Philip Larkin. Only a few lines come back to me:

Yet the dread of dying, and being dead, splashes afresh
to hold and horrify
Total emptiness forever
The sure extinction that we travel to . . . nothing more
terrible, nothing more true

Then the devil greets me. It is Baphomet. He charges me, screaming. I wake up in a cold sweat and realized that it was I screaming. When I finally go back to sleep, I'm greeted at the pearly gates by St. Peter. I've gone to hell and heaven in a single night. God help me, I know not what I do.

CHAPTER FIFTEEN

Day 5

During the night, the wind strengthens and shakes the tent. It wakes me, and when I leave the tent to pee, it is cold, and the trees wave violently over my head. Then it starts raining. I now know enough to grab some fire starter—pine needles and birch bark—and throw them under the canoe. Then I grab my backpack, which I'd forgotten outside, and bring it into the tent. The woods groan in the wind, and the sound of branches whipping and dropping to the ground keeps me awake. When the rain falls more steadily, the pitter-patter on the tent reminds me of the sound of rain on the tin roof of my beloved lake cabin, and it saddens me.

The sound of the wind through the pines is so sad, it sounds like all the dead in a cemetery quietly wailing at once. I quickly dive back into my sleeping bag. The sleeping bag feels like a body bag. Lying in the bag tonight, all squished and looking up, reminds me of lying in a coffin. Thank God that isn't going to happen to me. If they forget I'm supposed to be cremated and instead put me in a coffin, with all those people looking down at me, I swear to God I'll stick my tongue out at them. Depression overwhelms me until exhaustion forces me to fall asleep.

Then the weather gets even worse, and I wake up to thunder racing across the sky. Lightning frames spider webs on the side of my tent. Thunder bounces across the lake. The lake is alive; the waves slam the rocky shoreline furiously. There is a flash of lightning across the lake and then a thunderbolt roars, followed by the thud of a tree falling to the ground. It's somewhere across the lake, but it sounds very close. When the great blow-down came through, at least one person was killed by a falling tree. Maybe with some luck . . . no, the odds are too high.

Checking my watch, I see it will be light in a couple of hours, but there's no chance for any more sleep. I close my eyes, and I see the ghosts of the past—the voyageurs, the Indians, and the animals as they might have been hundreds of years ago. I'm the intruder. When I die, though, I'll join them. The dead of all time are in the dirt of the earth. All beings and all their history lie in the dirt, and I will be there too. Peace will come at last, and my adventure will be complete. Keats argued that life in this world is only schooling for the education of souls, preparing us for the next world.

I'm convinced now that I'm not prepared—my schooling's been inadequate. Sometimes I think all the organized religions would have you believe this life should be nothing more than getting ready for death and the next life. We tend to fear that which we don't understand, and we *should* fear what we don't understand. I don't understand death, and I fear it. I think most young people feel that death only happens to others. I now know that I am one of the others. We bury mortality in the back of our minds; it makes life—the long process of dying—more bearable. I had no idea that life could end so quickly.

When daylight comes, I poke my head out of the tent. Angry gray clouds are rolling in, and there are white caps on the lake. The wind is coming from the northwest, which is the direction I need to take across the lake. No way. It's at least two miles across Sturgeon Lake, and the wind is gusting up to forty miles an hour. It isn't raining, but I can't leave this campsite today. It's more than three miles of paddling and four portages to the next campsite. Even without this terrible weather, it will be my biggest challenge yet.

Stuck on the island, sitting on a rock by the water's edge, I watch the fog slide across the lake and the clouds race across the sky. The only sound is the wind—the birds are quiet, but the trees are not. I think, *I'm just sitting on a rock killing time, waiting to kill myself.* But then it starts to rain again, and the sky is dark, with claps of thunder in the distance. I could stand out in the rain and maybe get hit by lightning; it *could* happen. But I would more likely get pneumonia and die. That would take too long. Then the rain comes down hard.

Back in the tent I change my clothes and open my backpack to find something to eat. I don't call it breakfast anymore, because no one would choose to eat this stuff for breakfast. Then the wind blows the tent down. I set it up again, and the wind blows it down again. I try to imagine what an experienced camper would do. Crawl under the canoe? *That's stupid.* I turn the tent to better cut into the wind, and it finally stays up, so I crawl in.

What am I going to do here all day? I feel bad and think that I can't die in my tent this way. There would be an autopsy, and they'd find my cancer.

The gusts are howling, and I sit in my tent with the flap tied back, looking out at the bleakness of the day and watching the clouds roll angrily across the sky. I light a cigarette and let it hang from my mouth as the melancholy overtakes me. Falling into deep loneliness, I take a handful of antidepressants. It would be nice to have a companion to talk to now, and yes, to help me carry the canoe once in a while.

I think of my childhood and of grade school and the old nuns, one in particular, who came at me from behind and slapped me with a ruler on the back of the hand. To this day I don't know what I did. She must have hit me for practice. It was always the older nuns who were grouches and the younger ones who were cheerful. I wonder if the cheerful ones, in turn, became grouchy. My personal favorite—well, not really—was Sister Bernadette. Sister Bernie, as we all called her, was all business; any nonsense was intolerable and quickly punished. She frequently instructed us to bring money from our parents, for everything from crayons to paper to the next holy book. She watched every penny. I now think she was running a brokerage from the convent. If she were still alive today, she'd be trading derivatives for Goldman Sachs on the side. It doesn't matter anymore, though, because there are no more penguins around.

In the sixteenth and seventeenth centuries, many aristocratic families made a habit of dumping their unmarried daughters into convents. Unable to afford dowries for more than one or two daughters, the rest were cloistered. At times, they greatly outnumbered the seriously committed nuns, which caused endless problems, including one instance where they burned the convent down and escaped. They were not all brides of Christ.

I think of when I was in high school, sitting in Mabel Planner's history class and thinking, *In the year 2000, I'll be fifty-eight years old.* I thought it would never come. When I was eighteen, I never thought of mortality. Yet here I am, terminal at fifty-five. My lungs hurt. I know I'm taking more pills than the bottle says I should, but what the hell? Are they going to kill me? Then I realize that all the bottles have the doctor's name and full description of the medication on them. When this is over, I don't want this to be found. I don't want anyone tracing this back and finding out about my cancer. It would ruin my plan. I rip the labels off all the bottles immediately and put all the pills together in one big bottle—I know what they all are anyway. This was a sloppy hole in my meticulous plan, and it makes me wonder if I made other mistakes.

Studying the map, I notice that on the back of it, there's a long list of Dos and Don'ts for maintaining the pristine nature of the Boundary Waters. I'm interested to see how I've done so far. Besides the poop.

"Choose equipment and clothing in subdued colors." I did this because I didn't want anyone to notice me, but what would be wrong with seeing other canoeists in bright colors?

"Stay on the designated portage trails." Are you kidding me? The trails are hardly designated. And one would have a hell of a time trying to walk through these woods the wrong way for more than a block. The portage trails are hard enough as is.

"Choose a designated legal campsite that will not be damaged by your stay." No problem, I've found that damaging rock is beyond my abilities.

"Do not burn food packaging and other trash." They should explain this one, because I'm not sure what the problem is with a few ashes if it burns completely.

"Pack out all trash, yours and others that you find." I would, but someone else will end up packing out my trash. Sorry.

"Human waste is to be buried at least six inches deep and at least 150 feet from the water." Well, okay. I'll do my best, but I should have kept my shovel.

"Pack your toilet paper out." No comment. They wouldn't want to know what I'm thinking. I seem to be using more leaves than paper anyway.

"Campfires are hard on the environment. Use stoves and candles instead." No one told me that. What's the problem? Half the fun of camping is sitting around the fire.

"To wash yourself or your dishes, carry the soapy soiled water 150 feet away from the lake or stream and spread it around." I have no idea how this would work, but I don't think I will have to worry about it, as I have no soap. Alan didn't mention soap; maybe he doesn't use it.

"Take wood only from downed or dead trees." Come on, wood from a live tree won't burn anyway.

"Never leave the fire unattended." No problem. I'm as close as I can get to keep warm.

"Never feed the wild animals." That's what I keep telling the animals.

"View the animals from a distance. Do not approach them." They should honor the same rule.

"This is the animal's home. You are a visitor." I may be more than a visitor.

"One must admire the concern expressed in these requests and how few blemishes you see in these waters."

I peek out of the tent to see that the weather has cleared, but it's too late to start out on the next leg. It's still windy, and I'm bored and hungry. I dig out a piece of the nine-grain bread and spread it with peanut butter. It's hard to chew, and I throw the crust into the woods. While digging through my pack, the Popeil fishing rod falls out, so I decide to go fishing. Izaak Walton once said that God never made a more calming activity than fishing. I'm feeling very nervous this morning, so I figure I'll take him up on it. After cleaning up the campsite, I grab the Popeil, hook up a lure, and take off to look around the island with my backpack.

After the rain, all the black lichen on the rocks has turned to a bright, iridescent green, and branches knocked down in the storm are everywhere. The air smells freshly scrubbed. I break my "no exploring" rule and go to the other side of the island to fish. The island is no bigger than a city block. The wind and the water are calmer here on the other side. It's close to the mouth of the river and should be a good fishing spot. The deer are nowhere to be found and must have decided to swim across to the shore. I soon have a nice walleye on the line and as I try to land him, I almost slip off a rock into the river. *I don't find this calming, Izaak.* I go to my pack and pull out a half empty bottle of scotch and drink a good bit of it with painkillers. *This is what's calming, Izaak.* The fish's mood also improves as I release him. I sit there for quite a while, smoking a cigarette under an evergreen canopy. I realize this is the most beautiful campsite yet.

I feel like a normal canoeist, enjoying the scenery. Across the water, the shoreline is forested with tall evergreens. In the background, oaks, maples, and birch are in full fall color. I start to think about my family, wishing they could see it with me. I start crying like a baby. I just can't think about my family anymore. It disturbs me, and I lose focus.

Catching a fish on almost every single cast, I decide I have enough to eat and just sit there until I realize it's getting late. I've kept one of each: a bass, a walleye, and a trout. Heading back with the Popeil reel in hand, I have to laugh at those experts back at the outfitters who belittled me for bringing a Popeil. It worked perfectly and was so easy to pack with a few lures.

Since I have more time to spend on dinner, I decide to make it a feast. I get the fire going for coffee and then open a can of beans. I wonder if there's any difference in taste between the bass, walleye and trout. The bass and the walleye are a good size, about two pounds, but the trout is smaller, maybe just a pound. I'd never caught a trout; there weren't any in our lake. It has shiny red spots on a black-and-green background with, a cream-colored belly and orange stripes on the edges of its fins. It's a colorful addition to the Boundary Waters. Fresh fish for dinner sounds good after what I've been eating. The problem is my knife—it's not sharp enough to clean fish, and I'm not skilled at it. Lawyers don't clean fish. My wife always cleaned the fish at the lake. My policy at the lake was simple: I wouldn't go fishing with her if I had to clean them.

They're big enough so that even though I massacre them, I'll get plenty to eat. This will be the stew Alan said was to die for, and it's the first time I've ever made anything like it. But just in case Alan is wrong I will heat up some beans too. I cut up the onion and potato and throw them into the water with the flour and fish—this feels strange to me, as I am no cook. There will be plenty of bones to pick out. All the fish mix together so I can't tell which is which, but they're all good. The smell of the stew and coffee sparks my appetite, and the meal is delicious, rivaling the best restaurant in Minneapolis. I eat it all and then clean the pans with some sand in the water. I crush the bean can flat and put it into a plastic bag. When they find my body, they'll know this guy was an experienced camper, no city rube.

Studying the map in the little daylight that's left confirms my suspicion that I'll need to get an early start, at daybreak. It's a long way across Sturgeon Lake and then a two-block portage just to get on Jean Creek. Then I see there are *five* portages, not the four I counted before. Jean Creek is very small, according to the map, and has four portages. They're all short, however, each under a block long. The portages must be there because the creek is so narrow. The creek goes another mile before it lets off into Rouge Lake; the next campsite is on a point into Rouge Lake. It's becoming apparent that the campsites are set up for one day of travel. But then I wonder if that's true as I am paddling alone with bad lungs and am most likely not making very good time. Two people paddling and portaging together could easily go twice as far as one sick person.

I sit by the fire before going to bed. A fire in this darkness is a magical event. The warmth, the leaping flames, and the bright red coals with sparks rising into the darkness are simply wondrous. In my solitude, I wonder who else has sat in this very spot. It must have been used by the Indians, most likely the voyageurs, the loggers, and maybe even prospectors. They're long gone, and soon I'll join them. The saying "dust to dust," comes to mind, and it reminds me that soon I'll be dust also. Scooping up a handful of dirt, I wonder who I might be holding. There is no moon tonight. The animals and birds have fallen silent. It is so quiet and dark now, it seems as if I'm already dead and residing in the next world.

A small ember in the fire grows larger and hypnotizes me. Then it breaks out into flame and grows larger still, until it reaches out to the cold night air and then slowly reverses itself back into a dying ember. To me, it represents birth to adolescence, then adulthood to old age, and then death. I see myself in the top of the flame. I won't live to go backwards, like my mother regressed. My time is now, and I will go out on top, at the very peak of the flame. For the first time on my trip, I fall asleep with a full stomach.

CHAPTER SIXTEEN

Day 6

In the morning, the birds foretell the coming of dawn. This is a birdwatcher's paradise. Every morning there are seagulls swooping into the shoreline to feed and in the evening, the loons call across the lake to each other. All day long, I hear the song of birds in the woods. I cannot identify them from their song. Well, what the hell; I am a lawyer, not a birdwatcher.

I find I've been sleeping on a rock and now have another pain to deal with. The first thing to do is start a fire, but the woods have been picked clean on this small island, and I don't find much that looks like it will burn. I spot a high branch that looks dead, so I jump up, and it breaks off, hitting me in the head. There are so many bumps and bruises on my body now that it hardly matters. After I start the fire, I boil the coffee and take down the tent. There's a small tear in the fabric from the wind, so if it rains again, I'll be wet.

After oatmeal and an apple, I stuff the backpack and am ready to go. The Indians and the voyageurs ate only two meals a day, starting their day without eating and then stopping at midday and again at night. That is not for me; I need to eat something before I start my day. Besides, there isn't always a place to pull over at midday. No matter how sick I am, at the end of the day all this crazy food starts to look delicious, but it isn't.

Looking across Sturgeon Lake, it's difficult to tell how long it will take to cross to the other shore. It's seven o'clock, and I hope to make it in no more than three hours. The map shows submerged rocks close to the shoreline, so my route will be on open water. I'll need to pick a point on the horizon to paddle toward to keep from zigzagging and wasting time and energy.

Off I go as the morning sun burns through the cold fog. Having loosened my grip on life, my mood improves, as does my lung capacity. I'm overcome with bliss. I'm sedated. I am at peace with the Lord today. *Did I really say that!* The water is like glass this morning, and the wind has died down to a gentle breeze. These Kevlar canoes cut through the water like a knife. After about half a mile, though, I realize that while my back and shoulders are getting used to paddling, my lungs are not. My capacity has gone down throughout my journey. My time is short.

Up ahead, a pile of granite rocks support a dead white pine, its bleached bones home to an eagle's nest. The owner soars high on the currents of the wind; he doesn't flap his wings but spreads them wide. Circling down, he checks me out as my canoe glides by his home. I wonder where my bleached bones will find a home.

The landscape is exhilarating, each bend holds a new formation of rock, trees, meadows, and sky. Just ahead is a group of rocky islands with a majestic cluster of huge red Norway pines that look like they survived the logging days. They must be old growth, over a hundred years old. As I pass, I see that their roots are deep into the rock, which makes one wonder how they could ever have received enough sustenance to live that long. Off to the side, the colors of autumn blare out to me in the sunshine. It looks as if it was painted by a higher hand, with colors from a different world. Everything is beautiful. The combination of colors and texture in nature and the interplay of the sky with the water, rocks, and the trees are the very definition of beauty. I wonder whether prehistoric man could recognize this scene as beautiful. He might have been too busy running away from or chasing animals to be concerned with the beauty of his surroundings, but I could be wrong.

Paddling the open water becomes monotonous, and my mind takes off. I think that everything I have ever known in my entire life is still somewhere in my brain, and as I paddle, my brain begins to leak. I think the brain is like a symphony orchestra, each neuron like an instrument that can play separately or in concert. When the body and brain die, the sound lives on, maybe in heaven. The interaction of these sounds, learned over a lifetime, is your soul, your symphony, your very being, not that organ that pumped your blood.

The brain is run by electrical circuits, so maybe when you die, the circuitry leaves the dying brain as an electromagnetic force field and lives forever. But does your brain wiring create God, or does God create your brain wiring? I remember that scientists at UC Berkeley programmed computers to decode brain waves and were able to replay them as words. My body is only a vehicle for my brain, and my vehicle has a stripped transmission. My time is short, so I must decide soon. Do I believe in God? I want to believe that God is merciful, because that's what I *want.*

What is the point of this life? The solitude and mystery of the wilderness are affecting me in ways I didn't anticipate. Is this God, speaking to me? There is no past for me now, and there is no future; there is only the present. I need to put my family out of my mind. I have to make the most of my last days. I feel one with the spirit of the Boundary Waters now, one with the warm sun and the stars, one with the water and the land, and one with God. A serenity is intrinsic here.

I remember reading somewhere that if you love the earth, you'll come to see the mystery of the divine. The things of daily life, the difficulties that seem important, are insignificant here. As the Bible says, "Know thyself, God is in you." *I think now that he truly is.* A clear picture emerges, and my mind is in communion with God. As I leave this world, my wish for it is that man can come to an agreement with nature and live together. I've lived a good life and have no regrets, no reason to complain that it is over now. Now I know that only man's spirit is eternal.

In Minneapolis, my life was one day at a time, one week at a time. The sounds on the street were hectic; the pace in the office was hectic; my clients were always in a hurry. Out here in the wilderness, the only pace is that of the sun rising and then being replaced by the moon. There is no mealtime, only time to eat when you are hungry. There is no bedtime, only a time to put out the fire. Some people take life so seriously that happiness eludes them. When they are dead, what does it matter? Why did I not come here sooner? I'm at peace here; still waters have restored my soul. I think God might be sending me a message. He hasn't given up on me. *Please, God, show me the way!*

In the sky there is a long jet contrail. I can't see a plane and wonder whether it's a passenger plane or a fighter jet from North Dakota. At such a great height, it doesn't harm the silence of the place, but the sight of it does interrupt my solitude. There are no motorboats allowed in the Boundary Waters, at least by the visitors. I'm not sure about the rangers. The silence and beauty of the place would be destroyed by even the smallest motorboat. The only sounds here are the rush of the water against the rocks, the wind in the trees, the birds and insects, and oh yes, the wolves.

Christian and Jewish dogma holds that the world was created out of a void, out of nothing. But how can anything be created from nothing? Was our universe always here? Humankind sees a beginning and an end in everything. The animals, the plants, and humans always have a beginning and an end. Everything I have ever known has a beginning and an end, a birth and a death. Not only the animals and plants but the earth itself had a beginning, and the way we are going, it too will have an end. Everything is born, lives, and then dies. If the universe was created by a God, did God also have a beginning? If he did have a beginning, why is it a stretch to think that the universe also had a beginning without a God? The only explanation I can think of is that God must exist outside of time, as we know it. Therefore, he is eternal, and then maybe he doesn't care that much about any one of us. This is all so confusing, but my time is short, and I must decide what I truly believe. I am still going back and forth.

Our universe, according to the big bang theory, is 13.6 billion years old. Scientists have determined that since the big bang, the universe has been expanding steadily and will continue to expand forever. Wow, try getting your mind around that one. It took thousands of years for them to determine that there are other solar systems with planets; we've thought we're the center of the universe. Many scientists now think the universe didn't require a creator—God won't be happy with that observation. Some cosmologists believe there may be an infinite number of universes; this theory is called "multiverse theory." And if true, it would mean that there are multiple copies of each one of us. And that we may never identify them, as they may exist in different dimensions.

I think of infinity, and it drives me crazy. It frustrates me. Many mathematicians have gone mad trying to prove or solve infinity with numbers. Some believe it to be God's proof of his existence. That he is infinite. I think we are therefore unable to comprehend our existence. Maybe there is a God, but we can never verify his existence in this world.

A large group of Canadian geese fly overhead. Their honking and the flapping of their wings jolt me back to reality. There are too many to count as they spot the sky, heading south. I see a large inlet where Jean Creek and Sturgeon Lake meet. It's surprising that I've crossed Sturgeon so quickly without having noticed. The inlet narrows to the first portage and, pulling the canoe ashore, I'm ready to take it on.

The first portage is about two blocks long, but its beauty takes me by surprise and I hardly notice the pain on my shoulders. I should not have declined the padded shoulder straps that Alan the outfitter offered me. When I get to the end of the portage, I see that Jean Creek is really much smaller than I thought it would be. In many places, I could almost touch both sides of the shore with the paddle. It's now obvious why there are five portages on the creek before Rouge Lake.

After being on the wide-open water of Sturgeon Lake, the small creek is pleasant. The trees are right on top of me, providing a nice break of shade here and there. At least, it's pleasant until the second portage appears.

This portage is not like the other portages. It is muddy with scummy water, but it looks like I have to go through it. There's no other way. Holding the canoe on my shoulders, the water suddenly rises up to my waist. I sink to my ankles in muck, and I can't move. I panic and have trouble breathing. I don't want to die in the muck—it stinks to high heaven. I stand there, for what seems like a long time, with the canoe on my shoulders and the pack on my back. I start to sink in further. Next to me, there's a small patch of orchids that seem to hypnotize me. *Damn, I have to do something.* Finally, I lower the canoe down alongside my waist and try to belly up on top of it. The muck almost sucks my shoes off, but after several tries, I get up and slink back the way I came in. I figure my best bet is to back up. I move back to where

I can walk out. Lying on the ground, exhausted, it dawns on me: this is no portage.

As I pant for breath, I look up at the sky. Only one small cloud is visible and part of it begins to split off and slowly disintegrate into the air. My mind begins to identify with it, and then another piece separates and thins into nothing. This continues until there's only a small cloud remaining, which also disappears, and only the bluest sky remains. Tears flow down and wet the earth as I see my life disappearing with it. Then, a bald eagle circles high overhead and slowly sweeps downward in circles toward me, as if God himself has come to take me. I think I hear him sing.

"Be not afraid. I go before you always. Come follow me, and I will give you rest. Then sings my soul, my savior God to thee. How great thou art, how great thou art! When through the woods and forest glades I wander and hear the birds sing sweetly in the trees, when I look down from lofty mountain grandeur, and hear the brook and feel the gentle breeze. And he will raise you up on eagle's wings, bear you on the breath of dawn, make you to shine like the sun, and hold you in the palm of his hand."

A chipmunk runs across my legs and jolts me back to reality. Being filthy and wet, I have no choice but to shove off in the canoe and find the right portage. But do I go backward or forward? Logic says forward. Then farther up, I see a spot on the shore that looks like it might be the right one. It's not marked, however. This portage is short, and as I move through it, I laugh about the instruction that I should follow the designated portages. So far, only a few have been designated. The next three portages are short and aren't a problem, but if I were to take this trip again, I would not choose this route.

Then after the last portage, Rouge Lake and the next campsite is in view a short distance across the lake.

It's late when I arrive, but after the experience in the muck I know I'm lucky to get here while it's still daylight. My clothes are dry, but the pants and shoes are dirty, and I need to clean them before leaving in the morning. The campsite is on a peninsula that juts out into Rouge Lake with spectacular views in all three directions. There's a huge rock next to it that gives it a sense of enclosure. If I were with my family, this would be a great spot to spend a few days, fishing and relaxing. I must get these thoughts out of my mind. My time is growing shorter.

After going through my daily routine of building a fire, setting up the tent, and making a meal, exhaustion sets in, and I'm ready for sleep. Then I remember I have to hang my backpack first. I've grown to hate stringing that damn bag up in the trees. When the sun sets, the first call of a loon is so soulful that it only amplifies the silence. With their bright red eyes, these magnificent birds are the soul of Minnesota lakes. They reach up to thirty pounds and live up to thirty years. It seems all the lakes in Minnesota have at least one mating pair. They lay one or two eggs a year, and the male and female take turns guarding the nest. They're not the best guardians, however, as many of their offspring do not survive. This is evidenced by the fact that there never seems to be an increase in the number of loons on a lake.

The loons on this lake are in full conversation. I have no idea what they're talking about, but the sound of them calling back and forth turns my mood dark. My mind goes out of control, and sparks in different corners bring forth different memories from the past. I'll never be with my family again. I'll never call to my grandchildren, never again. I listen to the echo of the loons calling each other across the lake and to the water as it washes against the shore. Exhausted, I fall asleep.

CHAPTER SEVENTEEN

Day 7

I wake up to strong daylight, and my watch shows it's nine o'clock. I've slept too long, and I panic. I'll have trouble making the next campsite. I dress quickly and let down my backpack, and then I check the map. The next site is only about a mile and a quarter and—*hurray*—there are no portages. So I calm down and start a fire.

Skipping lunch most days is catching up with me. My weight is down dramatically, to the point where my body will look anything but normal when my wife identifies it. I need to start eating lunch and eating more of it. My food supply has dwindled by more than half, but my time is short so I don't care. I eat a big breakfast. Anyway, what's to worry about when you have plenty of scotch left?

After cleaning up the site and stuffing the tent into my backpack, I study the map again. Heading north up Rouge Lake, there's a fishhook in the long connection to Burntside Lake. The connection is narrow but looks much wider than Jean Creek was. The trip looks short, and if I make good time, I can reach the next site, which is about half a mile farther across open water. That decision can be made later, so I don't worry about the late start.

As soon as I shove off in the canoe, the weather begins to change. The wind picks up as I go. The lake narrows, twisting through forests of cedar, spruce, and balsam. In the narrows, where the trees are closer, the wind doesn't seem so bad, but the treetops are moving. There are downed trees everywhere, and maneuvering around them takes time and is nerve-wracking. The fallen trees face the same direction, and I realize they must be victims of a blow-down. With their roots splaying up into the air, it's as if nature itself abused them. It's ugly to see so many lying there.

There is a small creek flowing into the narrows. Two beavers are waddling around carrying something toward a dam on the creek. They are funny-looking, with short front legs and webbed hind feet, and it looks like their flat tails are not really attached but simply just dragging behind them. Their dam looks to have been damaged, and they're rebuilding it. One is dragging an aspen branch, and another looks to be carrying mud. They're so busy that they don't notice me watching from the canoe. They have chewed down a stand of small aspen, and there are wood chips all over the forest floor. The dam's construction is amazing. It's curved to withstand the flow of the creek, and in the center is a small mound that appears to be their lodge. I'm not sure how they make it through the winter, as the whole thing must freeze solid. They are protected now in the Boundry Waters, and their dams are everywhere, although this is the first active one I've seen. I can't imagine these beavers would make a good hat.

I hug the shoreline as much as possible as the wind is becoming stronger and stronger. I do all right until I reach the tip of a fishhook in the riverbed. The water swirling off the bottom of the hook and around the tip, along with a blast of wind, hit me and the canoe at the same time, snapping the front of the canoe 90 degrees. Over I go into the water, with the canoe flipping over and hitting me on the head. Dazed by the hit, I let myself go, slowly drifting to the bottom of the lake and twirling around with the cold, swirling water. *This is it,* I think. *This is it.* I see the surface slowly disappearing. I'm looking at the interface between the last life and the one to come. My life is slowly disappearing above me.

A great calm comes over me, and nothing matters anymore. I had no idea death could come so quickly.

My lungs are bursting. Then all of a sudden, my arms and legs thrash in the water. They won't listen. *Let it go,* I think. *Let it happen. Stop flailing around.* Then my feet hit bottom and push up violently; my body is taking over from my brain. Arms and legs kick like they're not ready for this. They're not the part of my body that caused this problem, and they won't give up without a fight. My subconscious is fighting me. As I near the surface, my lungs give out, and I take in water. I break through, coughing and spitting out water and a lot of blood.

I float in the water with no canoe in sight and no easy shore to climb. After floating a while, a rock ledge comes up, and I crawl halfway up, with my legs still in the water. *Crap, now here I am, without any food, tent, or canoe. I'm all wet, and I should be dead.* Laughing, I think that at least my shoes and pants are clean.

Now what? I'll simply freeze to death tonight. It would have been better to drown, but no, part of me doesn't want to die that way. Damn, this part of my plan isn't going to work. All that planning, and it's not going to work. But then, an inner peace envelopes me, I feel I'm not alone, but I am.

My body simply refused to let me drown. There must be another way; there has to be another way, because I can't go back. I guess I can always just walk off into the woods until I drop. I could simply walk out into the woods and keep going. But then what? How would anyone find me? Would they *ever* find me? If I eventually collapse on the ground, deep in the woods, no one would find me for years, if ever. My body would be eaten by wolves, for sure, *Oh, my God, wolves.* They'll rip my throat out, and I might not even be dead yet. What a horrible way to die. But I have no choice now; I'll just have to chance it. At least there won't be enough of me left for an autopsy. They would wonder how I got so far into the woods, but it would be so long ago that not many but my family would care. There would be a good chance my remains would never be found, and that's okay with me. That can be my new plan. My family will suffer longer, not knowing what happened, but when the snow falls in two months, there won't be any doubt that I'm dead. If and when they find me, years from now, there will only be a skeleton with a watch on it.

Oh, crap. I look at my watch. I have a very expensive watch that seems to still be working, even with the soaking I gave it.

I've always taken good care of it, and I've always wanted my son to have it someday, but I forgot to mention it in my will. I want him to have something to remember me. He'll have to wait for it now.

After lying on the rock a while, the sun comes out. Re, the Egyptian sun god, finally comes out, and the wind dies down. There's nothing to do now but start walking into the woods. Might as well. There's no food, no tent, and no canoe. Nothing. Might as well start walking. This is going to be a tough way to die, but there's little choice now. I know that over the years, many bodies have been found in the woods here. Finding me, one or two years from now, won't be unusual.

When I stand up, I'm amazed to see the canoe. It's caught on the roots of a downed tree a few hundred feet away. Should I just forget it and start walking into the woods, or should I go get it? My body tells my brain to shut up and get it. Since I'm already soaked, I go back into the water and float down to the canoe. It's floating upright in a tangle of roots. After years of canoeing at the lake cabin, I know how to get into a canoe from the water. Turning the canoe sideways, I easily flip up into it. There's no water inside; it's bone dry. How is that possible when it tipped me into the water? The backpack and the life jacket are still latched to the cross bars and are also dry, but my paddle's gone. Now I know why they made me take a spare. Why there is no water in the canoe is a mystery until I feel the bump on my head and realize that when the canoe hit me, it must have bounced back upright without taking in any water.

Resting a while in the canoe, I take out the bottle of pills and swallow a handful. There's no going back—I have to try the fishhook again. Maybe this time, I'll come from the other shore, where the water isn't so swift and I'm more aware of the current.

When the hook comes up, the wind is down, and the canoe goes through. But then I see another hook up ahead that's flowing in the reverse direction, so I have to take it from the other shore. It's wider, and the current isn't as strong, so the canoe handles it easily. Finally, the narrows is left behind, and Burntside Lake looms ahead. By now I've forgotten where the next campsite is and have to check the map again. It is not that far ahead on the left. The next one, which I thought I might be able to make, is out of the question. I'm tired and wet and need to change clothes, so I beach the canoe at the first campsite, change my clothes, and sit down to rest with a cigarette and the last bottle of scotch. My plan is in shambles. I can see no other option than walking into the woods. But when? Now or later? Because I feel better with dry clothes and because the underbrush here is so thick that I can only see ten steps ahead, "later" is the clear winner. Mark Twain once said he would like to die in Manchester, England, because his dying there would be unnoticeable. The woods are my Manchester.

Next to the campsite is a downed tree with small branches and dead leaves. It'll make a good fire without all the work of foragingthrough the woods. The branches snap off easily and make me think of Alan the outfitter, who wanted me to take that damn ax along. That's one point for me, but he's still ahead on the count.

I make the biggest fire yet. Anyone across the lake will see it burning in the distance. At first, my concern was that I'd run into too many people on the trip, but now I don't care anymore, and there's no one around anyway. I place the banged-up pot on the fire for coffee, and soon the water is boiling away. I toss in the grounds. I've decided that coffee with grounds in it isn't so bad, but that just shows how far down the scale I've fallen. Exhaustion quickly sets in.

My experience at the fishhook wore me down. I'm lucky this campsite was so close. If my partners at the firm could see my meal of dehydrated chuck-wagon stuff, they would laugh their asses off. I add too much water to it, so I lay it out on a dish by the fire to dry out. This stuff isn't even good when you fix it right. Then a whisky jack flies down from the tree above, and before I can say Jack Robinson, he swoops down on the dish and starts eating. There's never a dull moment in the Boundary Waters. "Get the hell off my dish. Quit eating my dinner," I laugh. He doesn't seem to like it either and flies away.

Then a red squirrel in a tree about twelve feet away starts chattering. The cheeky little devil sits on his branch and sasses me until I launch a rock at him. At our lake cabin, these red ones chase the larger gray squirrels and try to bite their tails off. Without their tails, they lose their ability to maintain balance in the trees. It's a death sentence.

I am struck by the beauty of the place and become melancholy. Dusk falls into darkness, and my mood follows. I hear the loons calling to each other across the lake, and my depression returns. The moon shoots rays of light across the lake that dance hypnotically on the water. The stars are out. The sky here is so clear, free of city lights and city smoke. There are stars everywhere. There are so many, I have trouble finding the dippers. All those other constellations are there, but I don't know them. Why didn't I ever take the time to know them? I am going down the road to perdition if I don't believe in God, and he does exist. I must decide what I do believe. Was all that time at the library a waste?

When the flames die away, sparks fly into the darkness, and I climb into my body bag. Tonight, it's the timber wolves' turn to speak to me. They're howling somewhere behind me. Then another pack of wolves across the lake answers. Hard to tell if they're friends or foes. Hard to tell if both packs are just baying at the same moon. Then they howl together and a shiver goes down my spine. *Crap, maybe a few more branches in the fire would have been a good idea.* It sounds like there are a hundred out there, calling for me, as if they can't wait.

I think about my sweet yellow lab, Molly. She hates loud eerie noises, like thunder. When an airplane would fly overhead, she'd push her head in between my legs and pretend she was protecting me, but we all knew better. If she were here now, she'd be in the sleeping bag with me.

Later in the night, I hear a hollow banging sound, and then I realize it's the canoe. I didn't pull it up far enough and now, thinking it might float loose, I dash out into the cold and pull it up. This shakes me. Without the canoe, I'd be walking out into the forest tomorrow. I have trouble going back to sleep.

CHAPTER EIGHTEEN

Day 8

When I wake up, the first thing on my mind is the plan. I am apprehensive about my new plan. It won't be an easy way to die; it will be an excruciating and miserable way to die. Walking into the woods until I fall from exhaustion and then waiting to die would not have been acceptable in my original planning.

How do I it? It can't be from a campsite, because they'll know where to start looking. There must be no indication of where I might have been. The canoe should be fully loaded and set adrift. They'll think I drowned and won't be able to find me. If they *do* find my body in the woods some day, they'll think the canoe got away from me, and I started walking for help. *The poor stiff just didn't make it.*

To set the canoe adrift and have it actually go anywhere, it will have to be from an upwind location on a large lake. I look through the pack to find something to wear. Being warm won't work, as I'll just suffer longer, so light clothing it is. I'll take the rest of my pills all at once and throw the bottle away. That should work . . . but maybe not. It could make it all the more excruciating. Is this what I've come to? It dawns on me that the fishhook was a pure accident. It wouldn't have been suicide. It could have happened to anyone. What a missed opportunity. I didn't know my survival instinct would be so strong. My brain said let it go, but it was overruled by my subconscious. Get over it, and start looking for the right opportunity. Either that, or go back and die in bed. I've come too far to go back.

I poke my head out of the tent, and there's a blue heron sitting on top of the overturned canoe. He takes off when he sees me and leaves a big white blotch. But the little things don't matter anymore, now that I'm looking at death. It's a nice day, and the birds are singing. Their songs are like a symphony. It's hard to be depressed when the day is bright and the birds are so happy. I imagine for a time that I'm not sick. I can't seem to go on unless I do.

After starting the fire and putting on the coffee, I pull out the map. There's one campsite ahead on Burntside Lake, but it's too close for one day's journey. But if I don't stop there, the next one is a long portage into Jean Lake. It's seven blocks long, and then the campsite is off to the side, a short distance down the side of the lake. I don't think I can make it any farther than that, but then, I don't care anymore.

Breakfast isn't appealing and I'm not worried about losing weight anymore, because they'll probably only find my skeleton anyway. I don't eat much besides a handful of pills. I didn't hang the pack in the tree the night before, so I stuff the tent in the pack, load the canoe, and off I go.

I think I'm losing my focus. The thought of walking into the woods and dying that way has disturbed me. I'm nervous and forgetful. I would have thought of a better way to die if I'd known it would come to this. Oh God, what am I to do?

Before getting too far, I realize my pills are sitting on a rock back at the campsite. There is no choice but to go back. This rattles me; my mind is all over the place, trying to work out everything at the same time. When I finally return to the site, I grab the pills and take off again. As I paddle through the wide-open space of Burntside Lake, I think back to my research at the library, and it helps settle me down.

I must decide what I truly believe, as my time is gone. I have been gone for nine days. I have not warmed up to religion. All those pedophiles, rogue popes, and TV preachers have left me cold. I think that the authority of the church's hierarchy was supported by the ignorance of the masses through their inability to read the Latin Bible. How else can you explain roasting the man who translated the Bible from Latin into plain English? Keep them dependent on the hierarchy rather than allowing them to figure anything out for themselves. Where did all this hierarchy come from anyway? There was no Vatican in the beginning. Jesus made no mention of a Vatican. Jesus said to *go and spread the word.* He didn't say, *Go and you will all be bishops.* We've inherited this religion, and clearly it's been embellished over the ages to entrench those who would make it their career.

Religion has always been used by the powerful to keep the people in line. Even Robespierre, the bloody leader of the French Revolution, used religion as a tool to keep the people under his control. Too many people believe their God is the only God, and that all others are evil. It's not hard to see why we're always at war.

Everyone creates a heaven to fit religious beliefs. I think our vision of the afterlife says a lot about who we are and what we hope for. If heaven is only for the good, for all of eternity, where's the excitement in that? I wonder again whether all the interesting people are in hell, but I'd rather not find out. All my life I've tried to make myself into the person I want to be, yet I'm not sure I accomplished all I wanted for myself. Guess it will be for others and God to determine whether my life was a success. I hope somehow I can know the verdict when I'm gone.

How could my existence on this earth even be possible without a higher power? The concept of "universalism," where everyone goes to heaven, regardless of sin, is what I'm hoping for. Given the number of times I've called out to God on this trip, there must be a part of me that does believe. I still find mystery. As John Henry Newman, a Victorian cleric, wrote: "Take away this light and we are utterly wretched, we know not where we are, how we are sustained, what will become of us, and of all that is dear to us, what we are to believe, and why we are in being."

I can't buy organized religion, and I can't accept everything in the Bible. But I do have to give religion credit for establishing moral values—if only the leaders would follow their own teachings. Traveling through this unspoiled country and seeing the universe at night has convinced me that there is a God. While I do not have much respect for organized religion, I do believe in God—God the creator. Having settled my position (as a lawyer I must have a position), I paddle on and a calm comes over me.

I become more aware of my surroundings. *Yes, I do believe in God—God Almighty who created me and this wondrous landscape.*

It's a beautiful sunny day, and it's getting hot. The yellows and reds of the hardwoods are stunning against the deep greens of the pines. Framed by the clear blue sky and shimmering blue water, the picture causes me to stop and think that it is okay to die here.

On one side of the lake, there's an odd construction of some sort with rusted cable and some kind of machinery. When I look closer, I see a sluiceway; it's part of an old logging camp. And there's a rusting hulk of an old sleigh used to haul the logs out of the woods to the water. Farther back in the woods, there's a collapsed bunkhouse. The surroundings are pristine, but I think about what this camp must have looked like in its prime, during the winter, still beautiful but cold and forbearing. No one but the hardiest could have managed it.

This area was heavily logged many years ago, but the new growth is substantial and looks mature to me. Every so often, an old-growth tree shows its majesty above the canopy to remind me of what was here before the loggers. Soft white pines were the loggers' favorite tree. Red pines, which are hard and straight as an arrow, seem as if they would be much better for building. The mills didn't like the reds, however, because they quickly dulled their saw blades. The reds are my favorites; they seem to like the buddy system, as they grow in groups of two or three. The whites spread their branches all over the place looking floppy and disorganized but still majestic in their own way.

Pulling over for a rest, I think of what life must have been like at this camp. In death, I will join those who toiled here. I wonder whether a lawyer could fit in with that group. It must have been a hard way to make a living. I often forget how good I've had it.

A seaplane flies over, disturbing the silence as it waves its wings at me. I lustily wave back, not wanting to appear dispirited or in need of help. They said there were no planes allowed here—must have been a park ranger. Then a group of small islands appears, and the next campsite comes up. It's a beautiful site, but it's much too soon to stop, so I paddle on.

Then I think I hear someone yelling. This startles me—I haven't heard a human voice for a while. Where did it come from? I look around and see a canoe in the distance. At the far end of the lake and barely visible, there appears to be a man and a woman. I panic and start paddling as hard as I can. They're fishing and don't even notice me, so I slow down. They must have caught a big one, judging by all that yelling. It's amazing how sound carries across the open water, because I can hardly see them.

The portage is ahead and this one finally has a sign. I load up the backpack and the canoe, and off I go. This is the long one, over five blocks long, and a rest or two will be needed. After walking just a short distance, a tall group of aspen and young balsam start drumming. I'm not sure what it is at first, but then I remember hunting in North Dakota and the sound of grouse gathering. I look closer and see a large group of grouse doing some kind of ritual. It isn't mating season, so what's the occasion? Since I'm not a fox or wolf, they don't seem to pay attention to me. I watch for a while and then move on. My feet object to this portage, and I become concerned that a blister might be on the way. Lawyers do not spend much time walking. *Crap, just put one foot in front of the other and get on with it.*

Birch trees choke off parts of the portage trail, and the smell of damp soil and wet leaves rises with the hot sun. The moss on the rocks makes for treacherous walking with the canoe on my back. To the side of the trail, there are odd mounds of moss and lichens that don't look natural. Kicking one in, it exposes itself as an old stump. Red rotted wood falls under my foot. The moss and lichens had been feeding on the stump. My back hurts from carrying the canoe, and I feel I have something in common with the old rotting stump. After walking a way, I hear a hissing sound coming from up above, and I stop to look. Up above is a large nest with what appear to be chicks peering down at me. Then a small hawk lands in the nest, and the hissing stops. The chicks disappear, but the mother watches me.

When I finally reach the end of the portage, there are three snakes on a rock at the edge of the bank. *Papa, Mama, and baby*, I think. There are not supposed to be poisonous snakes in the park, but these are definitely rattlesnakes. They apparently never got the word. They're rattling like crazy as they sun themselves on a rock. They are warning me away. They have dark brown crossbands on a yellowish-brown background. Papa has at least twenty rattles on his tail, Mama looks to have about twelve, and baby has three or four. Papa is about four feet long, Mama about two and a half, and baby is less than two feet.

Why not death by snakebite? I think. I impulsively approach them, kicking gravel. The big one coils and feigns a strike but pulls back. Damn, he's ugly and vicious-looking. His fangs are over two inches long. Then Mama coils and also feigns a strike. Baby seems to just be watching and learning. As I kick more gravel at them, the rattling gets louder, and they become more agitated. I approach them more aggressively and kick at them. The big one turns and slithers off into the brush. Then I remember my uncle telling me that the old ones aren't the most lethal. The younger ones are more lethal. Baby also leaves, leaving Mama alone to face me. Whether or not she bites me, I'm going after her. Kicking out again, she strikes and bites me on the foot. Her fangs are deep into the toe of my shoe. Stupid snake. You just got the end of my shoe, and now you can't get your fangs out of the rubber tip. So there I stand with the snake flailing violently on the end of my shoe. There's nothing to do but step on her with my other shoe and crush her head. It takes a while, but soon she's dead. Pulling back, her fangs finally come out, but they tear the tip off my shoe.

Later, as I paddle along the shoreline to the next camp, it occurs to me that would not have been a good way to die, because there would be an autopsy. I also remember my uncle telling me that very few people actually die from snakebites; most only get very sick. Getting sick out here would not have been good when what I really want is to die.

After a short stretch, I see a campsite sign. There seems to be more signs in this area of the park. It must be a more heavily traveled route than the one I've been on so far. There's even a metal grating on the fire pit. There is damage at this campsite. A large group of ferns has been trampled down for seemingly no reason. They're off to the side and not in the way. Why were they not respected as part of the wilderness experience? Who thought they had the right to destroy them this way? Even I, who will never go this way again, would not violate the spirit of the park this way. There's a pile of debris in the middle of the ferns, and there are fish heads and bones by the rocks.

I'm covered in sweat. Today has to be wash day. Anytime my clothes smell like this has to be a wash day. I strip down and then walk out into the cold water and wash for the last time in my life. It's been over a week since I had a bath, and the smell from all that paddling is too much to handle, even for a dead man. I wash my clothes and actually beat them on a rock, but they still smell from sweat and wood smoke. My partners would have paid big bucks to see me whipping my clothes on the rocks while naked. Screw them.

I eat a slice of bread with peanut butter slathered on. Then I eat another. I make a sandwich with salami and eat that too. A couple chipmunks approach and go after the crumbs, so I spend some time feeding them. Time to pull out the scotch. I wonder what Alan would say if he knew my dinners consist largely of scotch and pain pills.

The sun starts to go down, and the shadows get longer as I sit by the fire. A small pine tree growing out of a rock catches my attention. Its roots are firmly set in a crevice in the rock. It seems to be fighting for survival. Its branches are almost bare from facing the northwest wind. Still, it hangs on. For a moment, I think that I should try to be more like the little tree and not give up. But it's too late for me—my roots are shot.

The night sky is full of stars. The Milky Way is the milkiest when the sky is this clear. Even the northern lights make an appearance at the edge of the horizon. I feel as if God is entertaining me with the wonder of his universe. Maybe he's welcoming me aboard. I can see the insignificance of my life in the stars. Life is challenging and complex, but under the northern lights, it seems so simple.

Later in the tent, I hear an owl somewhere, hooting. He knows there are chipmunks and mice around. A light rain starts to fall, and the sound of the drops on the tent lulls me to sleep. But I wake an hour later, having to pee, and I don't sleep well after that. My mind races.

CHAPTER NINETEEN

Day 9

In the morning I feel as if I didn't sleep at all during the night. Going over the previous day's thoughts on religion and coming to the same conclusion, however, is reassuring. *I'm now committed to God.* I dress quickly and when I leave the tent, I see that the campsite is still wet from the night's rain. I find what I think is dry wood and pine needles for a fire, but when the wood starts to burn, it creates a lot of smoke that blows everywhere. My lungs take in a lot before I can get out of the way. I run into the woods, coughing and spitting blood all the way. I stand in the woods, waiting for the fire to burn through the moisture.

I need to take more pills. The pain is bad today, and the smoke didn't help. I remember reading the label on the bottle and start laughing, because I'm taking more than twice as many pills as the prescription allows. But what the heck? I'm six foot two and weigh two hundred pounds—I should be able to take more than the average man. I wish the pills would kill me. Dr. Davis prescribed enough pills for two months, but now I am almost out.

After the fire settles, I make some coffee and eat my last orange and some oatmeal. Oatmeal made with lake water is like grazing in a field like a goat. This food is so unappetizing to me today that it makes dying easier. Between this food and all the exercise, there won't be much left of me for the wolves.

After eating, I decide to show my new faith in God and kneel down on the rocks to pray. The rocks hurt like hell, but that can be my penance. *Crap, he is not going to make it easy for me.* After saying a few Hail Marys, I say, "Dear God, please forgive my skepticism. I still cannot buy into the people who represent you on this earth today. Somehow, I think you're not all that happy with them either. They say that suicide is a sin, even though at one time, it was not. But I think that maybe it is a sin. Please forgive me for what I must do. It may be suicide, but remember, there are only a few months left for me anyway." Then I realize I'm arguing with God like a lawyer. God can't be impressed. As my grandmother would say, "You made your bed, now go lie in it." Why are grandmothers always so religious?

"Oh, God. Hear my prayer:

> Our Father, who art in heaven, hallowed be thy name.
> Thy kingdom come, thy will be done, on earth as it is in heaven.
> Give us this day our daily bread.
> And forgive us our trespasses, as we forgive those who trespass against us.
> And lead us not into temptation, but deliver us from evil.
> For thine is the kingdom, and the power, and the glory,
> For ever and ever.

"Oh, God. I do believe.

> I believe in God, the Father Almighty, Creator of heaven and earth.
> I believe in Jesus Christ, his only Son, our Lord.
> He was conceived by the power of the Holy Spirit and born of the Virgin Mary.
> He suffered under Pontius Pilate, was crucified, died, and was buried.
> He descended into hell.
> On the third day he rose again.
> He ascended into heaven, and is seated at the right hand of God the Father.
> He will come again to judge the living and the dead.
> I believe in the Holy Spirit, the holy Catholic Church, the communion of saints, the forgiveness of sins, the resurrection of the body, and the life everlasting.

"Oh, God. I do believe. Well, except for that last part."

In Paul's letter to the Romans, he says that for everyone who does good, there will be glory and honor and peace. For everyone who does evil, there will be wrath and fury. I think my life has been one of good. Maybe I'll be all right when I am judged.

Sitting on a rock by the lake, smoking a cigarette, I watch water bugs dance around each other. I throw stones into the water, and the ripples as they spread remind me of the impact my life might have on this earth. Will I be remembered? Will my footsteps count? The first ring is big and close to the splash.

It stands for the remembrance of my wife and children. As the ripple spreads, it becomes smaller and more distant—it is the remembrance of my grandchildren. It spreads further and becomes smaller still. This is how my great-grandchildren, who will never know me, will remember me. Then finally, the ripple disappears. Eventually, I'll only be remembered in someone's genealogy chart. My name will be in a box and maybe there will be a picture. But it doesn't really matter; all of us fade away. Even the great men and women in history are nothing more than a picture and a short story in a book. In time, they'll fade away too. We remember them, and then we forget. I recall a phrase from the book of Ecclesiastes: "The living know that they will die, but the dead know nothing; they have no more reward, and even memory of them is lost."

I look at the map. Looks to be about an hour or so across Jean Lake to a bay and the first portage. It's a short one—about one and a half blocks long—and then into a small, unnamed lake, across another short portage, and finally into the Quetico Lake chain. There are four campsites clustered around the last portage, so it must be a heavily traveled route. I should be able to make this by noon. Then it looks like the current will finally be with me. Going downstream should double my distance for a day.

The water is unbelievably flat and pristine after the night's rain. The shore is lined with tall pines and edged with rocks; it is a picture anyone would enjoy. I'm in a good mood now, as the pain pills are kicking in, and I've made my piece with the Lord. The sun is so bright this morning, and it reflects off the water into my eyes. As I try to avoid it by canoeing close to shore, I hang the canoe up on a rock with a loud, scary screech. I need to pay better attention to where I'm going.

The memory of my meeting with the snakes yesterday disturbs me. It wasn't right of me to kill that snake. They meant me no harm. They made no attempt to attack me. This was their home, not mine. I was the aggressor; I attacked them. God created all the animals of the earth, and I've just killed one. But wait, the devil was a snake; did I just kill the devil? I don't think so. There are people who are absolutely certain that all animals go to heaven. Their reason is that animals do not sin. If they're right, I hope the snake can forgive me. Catholics believe that in heaven, all we do is sit in adoration of God. If all the cows and turkeys I've eaten are there, it's going to be difficult to see him behind the herds and flocks.

Ahead, I see a quiet pool, where a bass jumps after a swarm of black flies. The swarm is so dense, it reminds me of the black smoke monster on the TV show *Lost*—the black smoke that dragged people off, yelling and screaming, into the dense jungle. Damn, now I know what that was and why they were so afraid of it. Grabbing the insect spray, I prepare to be attacked, but they go back into the woods. Apparently, I'm not juicy enough.

Then a strange bronze-colored bog with a pungent smell appears, and at the edge is a small furry animal. As I approach, I see that it's a cranberry bog. The little guy nibbling at the edge is a porcupine, and the "fur" is actually his quills. My neighbor at the lake cabin says you don't want to get close to porcupines because they can throw their quills, but I don't see how that's possible. The Indians must have picked these berries; I think they ate pretty well in those days.

At the end of the bay, there's a structure that I at first think is a beaver dam, but no beaver cuts down whole logs. It must be a relic from the logging days. It creates a small rapids, so I skirt off to the side, but the canoe gets hung up on a log. I panic at first, but then I remember why I'm here in the first place. Adrenaline kicks in, and I pass through. Off to the side is an old wooden rowboat. It's rotting and the joints are wide open. I wonder how old it is and who might have used it last.

My portage is easy, and paddling through the unnamed lake and tackling the next portage is a breeze. My muscle tone has improved over the week, but my lung capacity is worsening quicker than I had hoped. The four campsites are picturesque. During the busy season, when four parties are here, they must all get together for a good time. It's noon, and the next campsite is an hour up one of Quetico Lake's fingers. This next leg will be about an hour, and then I'll turn left down Quetico. Finally, my paddling will be with the current, and I can relax more. I stop at the portage before launching to eat some of the gorp and rest before taking off into Quetico. I try to smoke a cigarette but can't inhale it. My lungs will no longer accept the smoke. I'd throw the cigarettes away, but I think I should be found with them. Details like that are important to me.

The next portage is marked with a sign hanging upside down on the side of a tree. The trail is narrower than the others and meanders around rocks and fallen trees. The surface is hardened from centuries of traffic, except where a tree recently shed its leaves. There's one soft spot, with deer tracks everywhere. Then ahead, there's a small stream with moss-covered rocks. I decide to rest before crossing. It looks slippery.

When I cross, I tiptoe my way along, feeling my way as best I can with my feet. One fall on the rocks was enough. The canoe feels heavier, and the hill ahead looks formidable. After paddling, it feels good to use different muscles, but crap, this is enough portaging. At the top of the hill, I hear the welcoming sound of water. The trip is over.

Taking off in the canoe, I soon come upon another abandoned logging camp and the strange, rusted remains of an old car. I wonder how they ever got it in there, because they sure did not get it out. It was probably driven in over the ice, which would have been exciting. I wonder how beautiful the woods would have been in the winter, covered with snow. But I can't imagine anyone enduring the cold. The lake narrows, and as cliffs close in on both sides, it takes on the appearance of a river gorge. But then it widens out again, and there's another campsite on the point where my route turns to the left. I'm disappointed when there really is no current. The lake is just calm, but at least the current isn't fighting me and carrying me backward when I stop paddling.

A hawk comes toward me, cruising down the river, gliding on a cushion of air. When he is over me, he begins to circle and dives at me. He comes so close that I hear the flapping of his wings, and I think I can even smell him. Then he continues on down the lake. I imagine that it's God, assuring me that he's with me, and I break out in song.

> "Amazing grace, how sweet the sound,
> That saved a wretch like me.
> I once was lost but now am found,
> Was blind, but now I see."

The sound bounces off the high rock walls across the lake and repeats my words. It's as if the Lord himself is singing with me, so I continue.

> "'Twas grace that taught my heart to fear,
> And grace, my fears relieved.
> How precious did that grace appear
> The hour I first believed."

I love this song. It was written by John Newton in the eighteenth century, and I always belt it out in church.

> "Through many dangers, toils and snares
> I have already come.
> 'Tis grace that brought me safe thus far
> And grace will lead me home."

Crap, I wonder if anyone can hear me singing. Sound travels a long distance over the water and echoes off the rocks, back and forth. But so what? I continue and paddle along in rhythm with the song.

> "The Lord has promised good to me.
> His word my hope secures.
> He will my shield and protection be,
> As long as life endures."

Truly listening to the words as I sing breaks my heart, and I pause to cry.

> "Yea, when this flesh and heart shall fail,
> And mortal life shall cease,
> I shall possess within the veil,
> A life of joy and peace

I cry so hard the words barely come out, but I'm determined to finish, no matter what.

> "When we've been here ten thousand years
> Bright shining as the sun.
> We've no less days to sing God's praise
> Than when we've first begun."

After resting for a while, I sing it all again.

The sky is clear, and in the distance is a small rocky island covered with tall spruce, outlined by the sunset. The sun is slowly setting across the water, and the loons begin to call to each other. Then it dawns on me that it's late, and the campsite I was aiming for hasn't come up. Paddling on, it still doesn't come into view. The lake is about a half mile wide here; I must have missed it while canoeing down the middle. I was so absorbed in my song that I went right by it. I decide it's God's will. The question is, *where am I?* Looking at the map, I see that the next campsite is a good two miles past the one I was looking for. But how far in between the two am I? There's no way to tell from the map. There's no turning back, so I start paddling harder and harder as it gets darker and darker.

It's getting too dark to read the map, but I remember that there are two campsites off a point, just past a small bay on the right. And just when I think I'll end up spending the night somewhere in the canoe, I see the campsite right where I thought it would be. Patting myself on the back for adroitly reading the map, I remember that I did "adroitly" miss the campsite I was looking for.

Pulling over, the first thing I do is get out the headlamp. It's too late to look for firewood and start a fire, so I eat the last can of beans cold with a salami sandwich. I take the backpack into the tent with me. The beans would be with me all night, along with a big black fly that refused to leave the tent. In the light of the headlamp, I remove my poem from my wallet and read it. It gives me strength.

Do not stand at my grave and weep
I am not there, I do not sleep
I am the thousand winds that blow
I am the diamond's glints upon the snow
I am the sunlight on ripened grain
I am the gentle autumn rain
When you awaken in the morning's hush
I am the swift uplifting rush
Of birds in circling flight
I am the soft star that shines at night
So do not stand at my grave and cry

The music of the water lapping on the rocky shoreline puts me to sleep in spite of my aching body.

CHAPTER TWENTY

Day 10

Staring out from my body bag in the morning, the fog is thick, and there's a damp chill in the air. It looks like a good day to die. It suits my mood. The air over the lake is steamy and gray. Fog covers the entire campsite, and I struggle to decide what to wear, because I know it will soon warm up. Getting dressed quickly, the next thing I do is get rid of those damn beans. Heading off into the woods, tooting all the way, it occurs to me that if I have diarrhea in the canoe, it won't be pretty. I use half of the roll of toilet paper. There isn't much left, so it comes down to this: the timing of my demise will be determined by a roll of toilet paper.

Skipping the fire this morning, my breakfast is Tang made with cold lake water and a pack of tuna that actually tastes good. My apples, oranges, and gorp are all gone now, and there's not much left to eat but oatmeal. Then, at the bottom of the pack I see the dried milk, which has gone unnoticed. It would have been better in oatmeal than lake water, but I forgot I had it.

The map shows Quetico Lake is huge; it's at least six miles long. There's about four miles left for me with one portage into Beaverhouse Lake, where there's a campsite. Quetico wanders all over the place, with many large islands to go around. It will be a confusing route, but it doesn't really matter anymore. Loading the tent into the backpack and the backpack into the canoe, I start my day's journey.

It's still early, and the channel ahead is covered with mist. I can't see very well and hit a rock head-on. The impact jars me, and my body reminds me that it's wearing out. Then, as the fog begins to lift, I see a marsh to my right and a female grouse with three chicks, wandering around and pecking at the ground. They don't see the eagle perched above, watching them. I don't know what happens next, as I glide by too fast, but I think I know. I think the eagle is just waiting for them to fill out.

Far into the woods, I see a huge boulder. The pine trees around it are at least a hundred feet tall, and still the boulder towers above them. The glacier that placed it must have been massive. Paddling on, mindlessly passing two or three islands, my mind wanders. I have to keep paddling now, because when I quit my arms shake.

I know I haven't been thinking clearly. I'm running out of time, and my mind is out of control. I begin to think maybe I shouldn't go ahead with my plan. I begin to go through those stages of grief again. Maybe I should have gotten another opinion; maybe I am not that sick. Then comes, *Why me, Lord? I am too young to die!* Then anger comes—*Damn it, why me?* Then acceptance comes, and I know I must go through with it. I'll take all my pills at once and drink the rest of my scotch. I'll walk off into the woods. I'll know when the right moment comes.

I think about my family and cry like a baby. I paddle along, not paying any attention to where the canoe is taking me.

Faulkner said, "The past is never dead; in fact, it's not even past." I relive the past in my head as if it's not the past. I think of happy times with my family as if they're happening in the moment. I remember when my father died; his last words were ramblings as he relived good times from his past. Are these my last words? I realize now I also am rambling.

My brain sparks in different corners like fireworks, bringing up all sorts of thoughts in no coherent sequence. I can't seem to stop it. Then a big fart brings me back. I never should have eaten that whole can of beans.

Ahead, I see a steep rocky shoreline with what looks like scratches on its face. Coming closer, I see that the scratches are stick men. Paddling right up next to the rocky cliff, I recognize the pictographs I'd read about. They are right next to the waterline and must have been done while in a canoe—that would not have been easy. They are red like the rust of the iron oxide commonly found in northern Minnesota soil. There are handprints, drawings of moose, a man running with a bow, and figures in a canoe. They're crudely done. These drawings must have been created hundreds of years ago by the Indians who lived here. Some of the figures can be identified but many look like ancient symbols. The shoreline there is vertical, and the rock is smooth and receptive. A few of the figures are suns and moons, but most are animals. The handprints are most likely the signature of the artist. I wasn't supposed to go this way; my route wasn't supposed to be by these pictographs. After a brief moment of panic, I calm down because it doesn't make much difference where I am now. But just where *am* I now?

After examining the map, it's obvious I've gone the wrong way around Eden Island, a huge island in the middle of Quetico Lake. Paddling without paying attention, I'd taken the wrong fork in the lake and am now a very long way from the portage into Beaverhouse Lake. If I'd paid attention to the sun, I would have known which way to go. Maybe it was fate. Maybe God wanted me to go this way.

I've gone about four miles over open water, and I'm not sure how hard I was paddling. It's already getting late. The days are getting shorter at this time of year. The map shows a campsite fairly close to where I think I am. It's on a bay that connects to Cirrus Lake. Paddling on, I see the campsite where the bay narrows down to a small stream flowing in from Cirrus Lake. At least I know where I am now. I land with enough daylight left to set up the tent, find wood, and start a fire.

Crap, then my pot with the big dent tips over and puts the fire out. After getting it going again, I use the hot water for dried soup mix and coffee. I also fix my last pack of tuna fish. After washing the dish and pot with sand and gravel, I return them to my backpack. There's a good tree to hang the pack. I loop the rope over the tree, and I tie it to the trunk, just like the book says. When I walk into the woods to shed the last of the beans, I see my roll of toilet paper is dangerously small.

It's late, but I'm not ready to go to sleep. My mind won't stop; it races, going over my relationship with God. I add wood to the fire and the flames leap into the air. I pull out the scotch and sit down. There are only a few cigarettes left in the pack, and I try to smoke one but it doesn't taste good, and my lungs burn. Damn cigarettes, they've killed me long before my time. I take a good swig of scotch and a handful of painkillers, and in about a half hour, I feel a bit of relief from the pain. There's less than half a bottle of scotch and a few pills left. I need to save them for my last journey.

Sitting down by the fire and looking out into the lake is a good setting for prayer. After saying a few prayers, I call upon God to forgive me. "Please accept what I'm about to do. Please make my last journey as painless as possible. I'll pray all the way, asking for your forgiveness until I drop to the ground. Please let me die as quickly as possible. Please ease the pain of my family."

The loons are calling, and the moon flickers on the lake as the clouds fly by it. Back in the tent, I cry myself to sleep.

CHAPTER TWENTY-ONE

Day 11

As I wake up, I hear something going on outside the tent, probably a fox or squirrel. But then I peek out of the tent and see two bears sitting on the ground, looking up at my backpack. They have their backs to me, I duck back inside. *Crap, what to do? Should I just stay quiet in the tent, or should I go out?* While I dress, I realize the pots and pans I'm meant to bang together are packed away in the backpack. I decide to go out and yell at them. What the hell? If they come after me, that's okay too. When I climb out of the tent, the scene fascinates me, and I just stand there watching. It's a mother bear and a youngster. She is about five feet tall and two hundred pounds, but with all that fur it's hard to tell. Her paws are huge, but strangely, the back paws are much larger that the front ones. Her belly and rump are also much bigger than her chest, which looks out of proportion to her big head. The youngster is about two and a half feet tall and maybe eighty pounds, but it's thin and looks like a big dog. They're just sitting on the ground, looking up at the pack.

She must be getting ready for winter and is so hungry that she is more interested in her stomach than anything else. She doesn't even notice me. *Damn it,* I think. *You're supposed to be eating nuts and berries, not my food.* Then with some grunting from

Mama, the cub climbs up the tree. The screech of its claws as it shimmies up sounds like nails on a chalkboard. She watches her cub climb out on the limb, trying to dislodge my backpack. The cub has trouble on the limb. The tree is a white pine, and the limbs are soft and spongy. The cub is having a hard time just holding on. After trying for a few moments to swat the backpack over the limb the cub just hangs on for dear life and stares at it.

When Mama sees that the cub is not getting it done, she loses patience and climbs up to where the rope is tied around the trunk of the tree. She bites on the rope and with a few good chomps and then a few swipes with her giant claws, the rope tears loose. This bear is a pro. She must have read the manual. When the limb is set free of the rope, it springs up sharply, pitching the cub off the limb and onto the ground. The pack falls to the ground, and my pans clang together loudly. So much for that noise scaring them off. The cub whimpers and limps around. I expect the mother to console it, but she goes to the pack instead, leaving the cub to fend for itself. She opens the pack with her claws, which must be at least three inches long. She obviously has done this before; her skill set is impressive. .

The cub wanders over toward me, but is still in pain and doesn't show that it sees me. Then it occurs to me that being killed by a bear would not be a bad way to go out. It would be quick and less painful than walking out into the woods. I remember when we were on vacation in Yellowstone with the kids many years ago, the rangers repeatedly told everyone that they were never to get between a mother bear and her cubs (or for that matter, between her and food). So what could be a more fitting end than to be done in by a bear? That couldn't be construed as a suicide. It would be painful, but quick, so without thinking much about it, I go for it. Walking slowly, I move to a spot halfway between the cub and its mother. I stand there waiting and say a small prayer. Then the attack comes—only it comes from behind.

The son of a bitch wraps itself around my leg like a dog and bites me in the ass. I kick like a mule but can't get it off of my leg. Its sharp claws dig into my flesh; the pain is excruciating. Mother bear sees us but doesn't move. She just stands there with both paws on the loaf of bread, holding it like a concertina. I lose it. I have the high ground and am about eight steps away. With the cub still on my leg, I charge her. *You stupid bear. You're supposed to protect your cub, not feed your belly.*

She stands frozen in disbelief. *The campers always run away. You stupid camper. You're running the wrong way.*

After a few steps, I'm moving full tilt downhill, and the cub falls off my leg. The mother doesn't move, and as I lower my head to hit her, her jaw comes down on my forehead just above my nose, scraping a chunk of skin from my forehead and pushing my head back. I ram my chin into her chest and knock her over. Her breastbone is as hard as a rock and dazes me. Together, we lie on the ground. I'm on top of her, with her legs wrapped around me in a hug. She stinks, and her fur feels greasy, coarse, and heavy. She rolls me over and rakes my ear and cheek with her claw. Then she takes off, hardly giving her cub a glance, but it follows her into the thicket, and they're gone. I lie there for some time. The skin is gone off my forehead, blood runs down my cheek, and my lungs are burning from my valiant charge. This is not going according to plan; I'm dying by bits and pieces. Why does nothing seem to work?

Everything in my backpack is scattered all over the ground under the tree. I find the first-aid kit. The big Band-Aids look like they'll work on my rear end. Dropping my pants, I only see scratches where I was sure there would be big holes. I check out my legs, and there are only punctures where the cub grabbed me. It feels like there's only a bite mark where I was sure a chunk would be missing from my ass. At least I can't feel that there's a missing chunk, but I can't really see the back of my ass. I've lost so much weight that there isn't enough ass left to bite. It's my ear and cheek where she raked me that hurt the most. I use my towel to blot my wounds, and a good amount of blood comes off my face and neck. I have no mirror, so I try to see what I look like in the lake. I can't tell much, because I now have a heavy beard, and the water on the shore ripples. It's hard to see exactly how bad it is, but I can tell that there are too many cuts and they're too long for the Band-Aids in my kit to be of any use. After dabbing a while with the towel, the bleeding stops. I try to wash the towel, but it comes up pink no matter how many times I try. I leave it on a rock to dry. I sit next to it and mentally lick my wounds. There can't be too many people who've hugged a bear like that and lived to tell about it. That was a *real* bear hug. I have to laugh, though, because I won't live to tell about it either.

Looking at my watch, I see that it's still early. The whole scene with the bears lasted less than half an hour. What do I do now? There are still only two options: walk into the woods, or go home and die in bed. The bed sounds pretty good now, but I have gone too far to go back. *Please, God, show me the way.*

I gather up the mess the bears left—there are two cans of fish, the oatmeal and dried milk, the salami, peanut butter, and just three slices of bread that aren't mashed or dirty. They didn't get a chance to eat anything. I start a small fire, and use the newly discovered dried milk in the oatmeal; it tastes good. My coffee's gone, spread all over the dirt, but the Tang is still intact. It is now later in the morning, and I am unsure what to do. Should I go on or stay here?

The map shows that I'm on the north side of Eden Island, and the next campsite is on a small island a little more than a mile ahead. It's a long way to the campsite that I should have reached yesterday on Beaverhouse Lake. I'll just start out and see where it takes me.

Paddling while sitting on my ass hurts like hell. Maybe I should have put that big bandage from the first-aid kit on it. Pulling out the first-aid kit, I try to drop my pants and find the spot on my backside, but there's no way to see exactly where to put the bandage, as I cannot see my backside. There's no way I can stand up in the canoe, drop my pants, and find my ass without tipping over. *So live with it.* It must be God's will.

The shoreline here is all rock cliffs, and I see more scratches ahead. Coming closer, I see the scratches are more of the same stick men. Paddling right up next to the rocky cliff, I recognize the pictographs and wonder if they're the work of the same artist. They're right next to the waterline and again must have been done while in a canoe. There's an Indian with a bow and arrow and several lying down. They must be dead. If there were something to scratch with, I'd add myself to the dead. It could be my tombstone.

Paddling along, it dawns on me that today is my birthday; I'm fifty-six years old today. Birthdays never meant much to me, so the thought passes quickly, except that it brings my family to mind. I have lived the good life, and I pray thanks to God for all that he has given me. *Thank you, Lord, for my wonderful wife, two great kids, and four grandchildren. Thank you, Lord, for a successful career, and as an afterthought, thank you for my beloved little green sports car. Thank you for my parents who loved me and raised me and saw to it that I got a first-class education.* Then I realize for the first time that I'll be joining my dad. Well, maybe, maybe not. I think he's in heaven, but I'm not sure that's where I'll be.

It's still early, and I've only gone about a mile, but my lungs are working too hard. The charge at the bear seems to have taken a toll on me. My lungs have been going downhill ever since day one, and I know that I've not made the daily progress others would have been able to make. My lungs are the worst they've ever been. I'm going to have to do something soon. When a small point juts out nearby, I know I need to stop.

There is a shelf of rock with a cliff rising behind it. It's not a campsite shown on the map but looks like it could be. The shelf is about forty feet wide and forty feet deep in front of the cliff, which is solid rock, eighteen to twenty feet high. I think I must stop. As I ground the canoe on the rock, it lets me know it doesn't like rock, and this is not its favorite landing site. I pull it up on the rock and remove the backpack, and the first things to come out are the painkillers and the scotch. There aren't many pills left, but I need them now more than ever. I take a few, but they don't work very well, so I take them all. They are all gone now; even the antidepressant pills are gone. Without thinking, I throw the empty bottle into the lake. The realization that I'm out of pills hits me hard. Tomorrow will have to be my last day. My lungs are bursting, and my meds are gone. This will be an agonizing way to die.

There can be no more procrastinating. A bout of depression hits me as I think of what I must do tomorrow. The sun is warm on my face, and I lie down, looking up at the sky. Then, strangely, a calm comes over me. I think I can see the face of God. I'm at peace; I'm ready. I'll walk into the forest tomorrow. I'll save the rest of the scotch for the journey.

Checking the map for the last time, I see that this point is an ideal location. It is at the north end of Quetico Lake, and the northwest wind, along with the flow of the lake, will carry the canoe out into the middle of the lake. They'll never find me before winter comes. Tomorrow will be the day that I die. At least, I hope it doesn't last longer than one day.

The sun is still high. Looking up at the rock wall, I decide to scale it. I want to see the lay of the forest to the north behind the wall. The thicker the woods, the better the direction of my last walk on this earth. The wall has several outcroppings that look like they'll make good footholds and handholds, and it leans back about twenty degrees. I feel better now that the pills have worked, so I think I can climb the wall easily. I do climb easily until I reach the top. Then the rock under my right foot gives way. As I feel it giving out, I grab at a small bush growing out of the rock, but it does not hold.

CHAPTER TWENTY-TWO

Meet the Indian

As I fall, my right foot hits an outcropping and flips me backward. I land on the rocks below, hitting my head. Wave after wave of the brightest light washes over me. Then there is total darkness. My mind drifts and seems to float. I see myself from above. My eyes are open, but the side of my head is slightly misshapen. There is blood running from my nose down the side of my cheek. A fly hovers over the blood.

Damn it. I hate flies on my face. Brush it away.

I'm lying face down; my right arm is folded under my stomach. There's no movement except for one finger twitching back and forth. Blood rings my nostrils crimson in the bright sunlight. I'm going to have a hell of a headache when I wake up. Then I hear a voice above me.

"*Aanlin giin izhicigewin ji*?" (Why did you do that?)

"What?" I reply.

"*Aanlin giin izhicigewin ji*?" he repeats.

"Why did I do what?"

"*Aanlin giin nisidizo*?" (Why did you kill yourself?)

"I did not kill myself," I say.

"*En giin nisidizo*." (Yes, you killed yourself.)

"No, it was just a bad fall."

"*Aapijishin*?" he asks.

"Yes," I reply, "just a bad fall."

"*Gaawiin giin nisidizo*!" (No, you killed yourself!)

"Who are you?"

"*Ozaawi Wazhashk*," he replies.

"Brown Muskrat?"

"*En*," he replies. (Yes.)

"You are an Indian?" I ask.

"Ojibwe," he replies.

"Can you speak English? I don't think I can understand Ojibwe."

"Yes, you can. You even know the name of my language, *Anishinaabemowin*. I will speak in your language if it makes you more comfortable. After all, you are a new arrival."

"I'm not dead, and I didn't try to kill myself. It was an accident."

"Yes, you did," he insists.

"I tried to grab the plant when the rock broke, and my foot slipped."

"You knew that the rock was loose and the plant would not support you."

"No, I didn't."

"Why won't you admit it now? *You're dead!* What difference does it make now?"

"I'm not dead."

"Take another look," he says. "Look at your head, and look at the dent above your ear. Your arm is broken too. I am dead, and you are here with me. Admit it—you are dead."

I fall silent, and he doesn't speak as I study the body below me. I can no longer relate to the body, to my body, and I realize he's right. *I'm dead.* It was a good death, sudden and without pain. It wasn't according to plan, but it was just as good. "Crap, I'm dead. Now what? Who are you? Are you God?" I ask.

After a period of laughter, he replies, "You might say that."

"Am I in heaven?" I asked hopefully.

He laughs again, and I think I may be in hell.

"No," he says. "You have arrived at the Happy Hunting Grounds." He laughs again.

I am stunned and confused by his answers. Wazhashk is a comedian. I am dead, and I get a comedian.

"Is there a God?" I ask. "Are you God?"

There is a long pause, and then he says, "Yes and no. All of the dead are here, and together we are the Great Spirit. Your idea of a single being is only right in the aggregate. The gods of all the people are here as one. God is all the spirits together. When we move in unison, we are the power and the majesty."

"What do you mean, *move together?*"

"We are like a school of fish or a flock of geese that moves as one. We are all equal—there is no hierarchy. Like the herds on the Serengeti, we congregate and move as one. You have seen the ballet of schooling fish, how they move in synchrony, how they combine to make up a greater whole. Locusts fly in dense swarms without colliding; in the swarm, they are as one. So it is with us."

"So this is heaven?"

"Not exactly, but this is where you will find eternal peace. This is everything you ever wanted it to be."

"Where is hell?" I ask.

"There is no hell; everyone who ever walked the face of the earth is here."

"Hitler is here?"

"Yes, Hitler is here."

"Bin Laden is here?"

"Yes, bin Laden is here."

"How can that be? Is there no punishment for them?"

"Why should they be punished?"

"Because they were evil."

"Do you think they were born evil? Do you think they were evil babies?"

"I suppose not," I reply.

"Was it not others who made them evil?"

"Yes, I think the influence of their environment turned them to evil. Their friends and associates must have been evil too."

"So, you agree that their actions were not their fault, and if it had not been for others, they would not have turned out to be evil?"

"Not sure I agree, but you do make a point. What about the people who turned them into monsters?"

"They, in turn, were influenced by angry and evil people, and so it goes, on and on."

"So they are going unpunished?"

"Oh, no. They are punished."

"But you said that there is no punishment for them."

"There isn't; they punish themselves."

"What?"

"They punish themselves, and we weep for them. They are ashamed of themselves; they are ashamed of their lives on earth and cannot bear to face those who they have wronged. They do not join in when we are in unison, when we are as one together. They hide in their eternal shame. Those they have wronged forgive them, but it makes no difference."

"So when everyone here is as one, can you affect change on the living?"

"No, we do not concern ourselves with the living, but we do observe."

"Did you observe me?"

"Yes, I saw Mishipizhiw playing with you when your canoe dumped you into the water. You did not realize it, but he grabbed your paddle at the same time as the wind and current hit you, just to help you into the water. When they are successful, they shriek with glee."

"Who is Mishipizhiw?" I ask.

"He lives under the waters and rises up to make storms and swamp canoes."

"Is he real?"

"No," he laughs. "No one grabbed your paddle."

"Are you sure? Because I thought I heard a shriek when I went over."

"He is not real. You went over because you did not pay attention to the wind and your map. Your mind was someplace else. Maymaygishi is another spirit who plays tricks on us. Like blowing over our *babagiwayaanegamig* and stealing our dinner."

"Is he real?" I ask.

"No," he replies. "It is just the wind blowing our tents over or a bird swooping in on the fire and flying off with a piece of meat. Like when the jay tried to take your dinner. But I did believe in him when I was alive. Even today, some of my people leave tobacco and necklaces for these spirits, hoping for a safe journey."

"So you have been watching me all along?"

"Yes, your behaviors and progress were interesting to watch. I saw you attack the bear and was shocked but could not help but laugh."

"Tell me, what are we? How did I come to be here?"

"You are the essence of your life experience as recorded in your brain."

"But my brain lies dead."

"When your brain died, along with your body, your essence left and joined the spirit world."

"How is that possible?"

"When the brain dies, its network of electrical energy leaves the body and exists as an intact circuit. Now tell me, why did you kill yourself?"

"When you were watching me, could you tell I wasn't moving very fast and my progress was limited?"

"Yes, you were moving slowly for someone on a trip that long and at this time of year."

"My time was short. I smoked too much and developed lung cancer. Paddling along, my breathing was difficult, and I could only go so far. I came here to die."

"We also smoked too much, John, but I, like many of my people, never lived long enough to die from it."

"What did you die from?" I ask.

"I died at the hand of the Sioux. I am Ojibwe. We and the Sioux were mortal enemies. This land was Sioux land, until we pushed them out of the forest and onto the plains. The first inhabitants of the Quetico were the Sioux. They lived off the land for thousands of years until gradually, we pushed them to the west. We pushed them just as the white man pushed us from the east. The Sioux ended up on the Dakota plains and lived off the buffalo. When the French trappers arrived from the north, they befriended and traded with us. Many intermarried with us, but that was after I was gone."

"You said the Sioux killed you. How did it happen?"

"I was a *jiimaanike*."

"You built canoes?"

"Yes, I was a master canoe maker; my work was sought out by all my people. My canoes were built from the best birch trees. I would look at as many as one hundred trees before I'd find one with bark silky smooth, strong as deer leather, with no knots or branches. It had to be as round as a fat woman. When I skinned a birch tree, I always apologized for taking its skin. I whispered a *gaagilzom* to it. I built my canoes like the sturgeon's belly; that was the shape that I copied. We used the sturgeons for food and their hide for leather. Now, you white men have taken them all. I used spruce pitch to seal my canoes and jack pine roots to sew the seams and tie to the frame. They were the most well-made and fastest canoes in the Ojibwe nation.

"There were stories of a stand of birch to the west, many of which were so large that one could not get one's arms around them, and I decided to go there. The area was between the two nations, where we seldom traveled. As I made my way up the river, a party of three Sioux warriors and I met at a bend in the river, and the chase was on. I turned my canoe around and paddled as fast as I could to make my escape. The war whoops behind me gave me energy and my canoe was much faster than their dugout canoe. The Sioux made their canoes out of hollowed-out logs—no match for my birch canoe, which cut beautifully through the water. But then my canoe became entangled with a submerged tree, and the warriors were on me, with arrows flying through the air all around me. Just as I worked free of the tree, an arrow pierced my side. It was just a flesh wound. I knew that if I pulled the arrow out, I would just bleed more, so I broke the shaff off and left the head in my side and continued to paddle. I was getting away from them at first but was losing too much blood, and they were closing in. I decided to make a break for it through the woods, so I beached the canoe. Thinking I could lose them was a mistake. As I ran through the trees, I was easy to track. I lost a great amount of blood and fell to the ground. The first *ogichidaa* there hit me with his *bagamaagan*, and it was over. They scalped me and danced around my body. When they left, they took my canoe."

"That must have hurt too," I say.

"No, it was a compliment. Later, the wolves found me."

"That must have been terrible for you."

"No, the wolves are our spiritual brothers; we both hunt and live off the land together.

"I have never seen such forgiveness, Wazhashk. Is the Indian who scalped you here too?"

"Yes, he is here too."

"And you talk to him?"

"Oh, yes. We are friends."

"How can you be friends with the man who killed you?"

"I will explain it all to you again. We were enemies. We were all trained to fight and take scalps. This was our culture; this was the way we lived our lives. I would have done the same to him if I had caught him in our land. Not only that, we were the ones who drove them out of their land. We were more skilled as hunters than they were and so were better fighters in the woods."

"So you Indians really didn't like each other?"

"Your people are no better," he says. "I've seen how white men treat my people. They do not scalp the head, but they cheat and lie and steal our lands. The Indian does not tell lies. We told them to leave us alone, but they followed endlessly. Indians believe that the land is not ours to own. It belongs to all of us and to the animals. The white man came in and said he owns it and drove off my people. Your people have no respect for the land. That is why I stay here, John. Here, there are none of your cities, and few people go by. I know you white men well. You think we are all lazy, unreliable, and ignorant. You do not realize that we have different values. We love the natural; we do not love your big houses and fast cars. That is not our way. Our way is sharing and caring for each other. Your way leaves many behind. We think it is only a matter of time before you dig up our homeland for its iron and copper."

"I am sorry," I say.

"There is nothing to be sorry about. The cheaters are here, and they know who they are. Now you know, John. We take only what we need and nothing more."

I think back to when I was growing up in North Dakota. Everyone said how lazy and unreliable the Indians were. They would work until they got paid, and then they wouldn't show up for work again until they ran out of money. They were taking only what they needed.

I'm amazed we can communicate seamlessly; language is not a barrier. I can speak his language, and he can speak mine. "Wa-zhashk, how is it that I know your language, and you know mine?"

"John, when our circuits connect I can know everything that is in your mind, and you can also know what I know if you choose to. We are as one circuit; we are connected as one when we speak to each other."

I am dead now, and I think it was a successful trip after all. It was assuredly an accident, so there will be no need for an autopsy. The side of my head will be the obvious cause of death. It was an artful death.

CHAPTER TWENTY-THREE

Discover the Body

Wazhashk and I talk into the night and morning, but we fall silent when we see a canoe approaching. There are two people, a man and a woman, paddling from the east. They stop to look at the same pictographs I saw the day before. Then they paddle on toward us. When they approach, the woman says, "There's a canoe up ahead, Frank."

Frank says, "Yes, I see it."

They paddle past us and are almost gone when the woman says, "Frank, there is someone lying on the ground there." Frank keeps on paddling. "Wait!" she yells at him.

"What's wrong?" he asks. "They're probably just resting."

"Go back," she says, but he keeps on paddling until she yells at him again.

"Okay," he says. "I'll go back."

When they pull up alongside, she yells out, "Are you okay there?" Then she yells it out even louder. When she gets no response, she says, "Frank, pull up. We have to see if that person is all right.

Begrudgingly, he pulls the canoe up on the rocks. When it screeches on the rocks, he says, "Damn it. They're going to make us pay for the scratch."

She ignores him, bolts out of the canoe, races over to my body. "Oh, my God! Oh, my God, Frank! He's hurt bad. Take his pulse."

"No, I am not going to touch him. You take his pulse."

"Okay," she says and takes my wrist in her fingers.

"Well," he says, "is he alive?"

"I'm not sure. I don't feel anything, but I am not a nurse, I am not sure, but he's cold. If there is a pulse, it's very weak."

"Look, Sue. Look at his head; it is caved in above his ear. Look at the blood on his face. He must be dead."

"I think you're right, but what if he isn't? We have to get help. We have to notify the authorities."

"Try the cell phone," he says.

She runs back to the canoe and digs it out of a pack. "There's no signal," she yells back at him. "We'll have to go back to that spot where I called my mother."

"Damn it," he says. "That's a mile back."

"We have no choice; we can't just go by and leave him here, even if he *is* dead."

As they paddle back, she tries the phone repeatedly and finally connects. "Operator, we're in the Boundary Waters on a canoe, and we've found a man who has been seriously hurt. I need to speak to a ranger station on the Canadian side.... Okay, I'll hold.... Yes, we've found a man who is hurt, and we have no way to help him. You need to do something.... Yes, his injuries are serious; he has a bad head injury. We think he may be dead.... Yes, we have GPS, but no, we were so distressed that we didn't take a position. Frank, you talk; he wants to know where we are."

Frank gives the coordinates and then says, "Yes, we're on Quetico Lake. He's about three-quarters of a mile west of here on a rock shelf. . . . Well, the shelf is uneven, and there's a rock wall behind it. . . . No, I don't think it would be safe to bring a helicopter in there. . . . Yeah, the lake is at least a quarter mile wide there. . . . Okay, we'll go there and wait. Our names are Sue and Frank Corliss. . . . No, our cell phones didn't work there." He then turns to Sue and says, "They are going to come in with a pontoon plane, and they want us to wait until they arrive."

The silence is broken by the buzz of the plane as it circles overhead and then lands on the water. The men anchor the plane and inflate a rubber raft as Frank and Sue wait at the water's edge. They help pull the raft up on the shore, and the men rush up with a first-aid pack.

"Never mind the first-aid kit, Al. He's dead. No one could have survived that blow to the head."

"What do you suppose happened?" Sue asks as she watches the men hover over my body.

"I'm not sure. From his injuries, it looks like he fell. There's no one around here who could have hit him like that. He must have fallen from some height, and it looks like it would be the rock wall. Why he would be climbing that wall, I don't know. How long do you figure he has been dead, Jerry?"

"I'd say sometime yesterday. The blood is dry, and he's cold. Yesterday was a nice day; maybe he was climbing the wall for the view. We'll never know."

Al takes out a camera and photographs the area and my body from a few different angles. Sue and Frank stand silently off to the side, watching.

As Al comes in close for a photograph of my head, he yells out, "Look, Jerry! Look at these scratches on his neck and cheek. Do you see what I see?"

"What?" Jerry replies.

"They didn't come from any fall. That's bear. Those scratches were made by a bear. Come over and spread your fingers over these cuts."

Jerry looks closer and says, "Yes, five fairly deep, evenly spread scratches. That was probably a bear. I think you're right. Only a bear could do that out here. So now we have rogue bear problem too. Do you think we should get the gun out of the plane?"

"No," Al says. "He's long gone now. And why did he not chew on the body? They're storing up for the winter now. There's something we're not getting here. How did he get these different injuries?"

"I know what happened," Jerry says. "I'll bet he was climbing up the wall, and when he got to the top, he surprised a bear and was attacked and pushed back over the wall. What do you think?"

"Well, it all fits. How else would he have these different injuries? And it explains why his body is intact and why the bear wasn't down here to chew on him. Look at that twig in his hand."

"He must have tried to break his fall, poor guy."

"*Yes, yes, yes!*" I yell as Wazhashk and I look down.

"What's the matter with you?" Wazhashk asks.

"This is perfect," I say. "The perfect death that I was looking for."

"Well, not so perfect for some innocent bear that they will be looking to shoot."

"Maybe they will not look," I said.

"Al, get his backpack out of the canoe. I don't see a wallet on him. Let's see who he was."

"Here it is—his name is John Jacob Janne, and he's from the Twin Cities. Oh, for heaven's sake, yesterday was his birthday. He was fifty-six years old yesterday. He's six foot two and two hundred pounds. That's him, isn't it?"

"He doesn't look like two hundred pounds to me, but it has to be him."

"Turn his head and check his picture on the license. Yes," Al says. "That's him. There's not much food left in the pack, but there's a half-full bottle of scotch here. Do you think he was drunk?"

"No, I don't think he could have gotten all the way up that wall if he was drunk. It hardly makes any difference now anyway."

"He was saving his tin cans. He was a good camper. And he must have been a good canoeist to get this far along."

"*Yes, yes, yes!*" I yell again.

Wazhashk made no comment at first but now says, "You seem happy to be here, John."

"Yes, I am."

Al digs out my Popeil rod and starts laughing. "Look, Jerry. Look at what he was using to fish."

"What's the matter with that?" Jerry replies. "I have one of those too, and it works fine."

"I've never seen you use it."

"Actually, I'm too embarrassed to use it in front of anyone." They both have a good laugh.

"Al, look. There's hair here on this rock; this must be where he landed. Take a sample."

"Why?" Al replies.

"It must be his hair, and it would verify that he fell. If we don't, we'll hear about it from the boss."

Al takes out some rubber gloves and puts the hair into a plastic bag. "There is a small bit of scalp here too," he says. "I'll get the body bag out. Are you going to call it in?"

Frank and Sue have been sitting quietly as Al and Jerry go about their work. Now, Frank asks if they can leave.

"Where were you headed?" Jerry asks.

"We were going into Beaverhouse Lake."

"There's a short portage between Quetico and Beaverhouse. Then there's a campsite."

"Yes, I know of it," says Frank.

"There's a ranger station just down the shore from it. But it's late, so you won't make the portage before dark. Why don't you just stay here?"

"No!" Sue cries. "I'm not going to stay here tonight."

"Do you have a flashlight? You don't want to go through the portage in the dark."

"Yes, we have a small flashlight."

"There's a headlamp in his backpack. Take it—he won't mind. You've earned it."

Frank and Sue take off quickly.

"Al, I'm going to call it in. Can you get the satellite phone out of the pack?"

Al hands the phone to Jerry.

"Hi. We got here, and the man's dead. He is an American from Minneapolis. What do you want us to do? . . . Okay, we'll fly into Ely and wait for the coroner from Duluth to pick the body up. Looks to us like this guy was crawling up a rock wall for the view and surprised a bear. There are claw marks on him, but the bear didn't kill him. Apparently, the bear attacked, and he fell backward over the wall. The rocks below killed him. The cliff here is only about twenty feet high, but you know how unforgiving the rocks are. Call me back when you know when the coroner from the Duluth morgue will get here. What do you want to do about the canoe? . . . The ranger station on Beaverhouse is not that far away. Can they pick it up? . . . Okay, can you call around and see which outfitter it might belong to? His name is John Janne. He was alone. Will you notify the family? . . . Okay, we'll bring all his belonging with us and when the morgue confirms, you'll call them, right? . . . What do you want to do about the bear? I know you don't want rogue bears running around. . . . Okay, think about it and let me know what you want to do when you call me back." Jerry ends the call and then turns to Al. "Can you start packing up to go? I'll help you get him into the body bag."

As Al is loading the raft, the phone rings, and Jerry picks up. "You what? You want me to climb the wall and see what went on up there? Boss, it's getting dark, and the wall is twenty feet high. . . . Okay, okay, we'll go up the wall and look around." He calls out to Al again, "The boss says for you to climb the wall and look around."

Wazhashk and I howl with laughter.

Al says, "I 'm not going up there. For God's sake, he fell. I don't want to fall too. You go up. I'm not going up there and walk around, looking for a bear."

"The boss specifically said—and these are his exact words—'You go up.'" Wazhashk and I can't quit laughing. "Look, I will watch you, and if you fall, I can break the fall. You don't have to go all the way up. Just stick your head up and take a look around. That way, we can tell the boss we were up there. Would that make you feel better?"

"Not really. If I fall, then we'll both be hurt. But I'll try it." Al starts out climbing ever so slowly and makes it to the top.

"What do you see?" Jerry calls up.

"What do you think I see? Trees."

"Do you see any sign of a bear?"

"Yes, there's some scat up here. That's it; I'm coming down."

Wazhashk and I are still laughing, and I say to him, "You have a good funny bone, Wazhashk."

He dryly replies, "I have no bones."

When Al gets down, he has to rest and have a cigarette. "Let's finish his scotch," he says. "We've earned it, and he won't miss it. It wouldn't hurt if his wife doesn't find this bottle of scotch in his belongings."

I squeal and say to Wazhashk, "These guys are guys after my own heart."

Wazhashk dryly says, "Liquor never did my people any good."

Jerry raises a cup and says, "Here's to John Jacob Janne. May he rest in peace."

They load my body onto the raft and then onto the plane with great difficulty. Al exclaims, "This guy *does* weigh at least two hundred pounds."

The plane takes off, and as they fly into the dusk, I say goodbye to my remains.

Wazhashk muses, "Is it not good, John, to leave a sick body that's of no use to you anymore?"

"Yes," I reply. "I was going downhill fast."

My carefully planned adventure has come off to perfection. Well, okay, not exactly to perfection and not exactly as planned, but the Boundary Waters did not let me down. It was a beautiful place to die, and I am grateful. I am at peace.

CHAPTER TWENTY-FOUR

The Happy Hunting Grounds

"Wazhashk, how long have you been here?" I ask.

"I have been here many, many moons. In your years, it is over two centuries."

"You've been here a long time."

"We're in infinity, John. Time is meaningless here. Soon, your family will join you here also. They will mourn your death for a time and go about their lives, but in terms of infinity, they will be here with you shortly. You will all be together forever."

"So your family is here with you, Wazhashk?"

"Yes, they're all here. My *niwiidigemaagan idash abinoojiinh* are all here."

"So you had a wife and one child. Where are they now?"

"They stay where we lived, the camp where we lived over the cold winter. In the summer, we moved around looking for game. Would you like to visit our *gabeshi*?"

"Yes," I say. "Why not? I have the time."

"There is no time here."

"I'm a slow learner," I reply.

"There it is, on a bay off Surprise Lake by a small stream connecting to Bittern Lake. It's on the northwest side, sheltered from the northwest wind by a thick forest. There's an ample clearing on flat ground, and a few Indians are at the camp."

"Do they still camp there?" I ask.

"Yes, there are a few holdouts who won't accept the new life."

"How many were there when you lived here?"

"There were twenty times the number you see below. I could not make enough canoes to satisfy them all and the others who came from other camps."

He introduces me to his wife and child, but I don't have much to say, as we do not have anything in common. Wazhashk goes off to spend time with his family, and I simply observe.

When he returns, I ask, "Why don't you spend more time here with them?"

"I do," he says.

"How did you come to be where I died?"

"Because that is close to where I died. You will most likely stay there too. It is the place and time of your end and your beginning."

"It's certainly better than spending eternity in a hospital room."

"Would you like to see your father, John?"

The realization that my father is here stuns me. "Yes, I would, but how will we find him?"

"Where did he die?"

"He died in bed at his house in Edina."

Then we are there, and my father is there. We don't embrace, as there are no bodies, but it is as if our souls embrace.

"So, you are here now," my father says. "It's nice to be with you again. I've been watching you and my grandchildren. I wasn't happy that you spent so much time at work and not enough time with my great-grandchildren."

"Did I disappoint you?"

"No, all your life was a joy for everyone and for me. How did you die?" he asks.

"I was dying from lung cancer."

"I knew it; those things have sent many here before their time. Why didn't you quit smoking when everyone else did?"

"I don't know," I reply.

Then Wazhashk says, "John, do you want to see your body for the last time?"

"What do you mean?" I ask.

"It's at the coroner's. Do you want to be there?"

"Yes. Father, will you visit me in the Boundary Waters?"

"I will be there," he replies.

I'm in the autopsy room at the Duluth hospital. It's a terrible room—cold with stainless-steel body vaults, hard floors, and hard ceilings with glaring lights. My body is lying naked on an awful steel table. The coroner and the head ranger are in the room, looking over my body.

The ranger asks the corner, "What will be the official cause of death?"

"Well, there are several cuts and bruises on the body, but the blow to the head is what killed him." He rolls me over and says, "Look at these marks. There are multiple punctures on his leg here and what looks like a bite mark on his posterior. Also, when I removed his clothes, I saw these scratches on the fabric."

"Jerry and Al are convinced he had a run-in with a bear and the attack resulted in his fall onto the rocks. They say the cliff he fell over was around twenty feet high. They also found some hair on a rock close to the body."

"That swatch of scalp they gave me does match what's gone from his head."

"But what is it with those deep scratches on his face? Why isn't there more blood on his face?"

"There would not be much bleeding if his heart stopped upon hitting his head on the rock. That bite mark isn't from an adult bear, and those marks on his face aren't from a cub. He must have surprised a mother and her cub."

"Are you going to do an autopsy?"

"No, the cause of death is obvious. I won't do one unless the family wants one. I can't image they will. There's no point in it. What should I list as time of death? Do you know the time of death?"

"Jerry and Al think it happened in the afternoon two days ago, when the weather was so nice. They think he climbed the cliff for the view. It's all we've got to go on, so I'd go with it if you agree."

"I would place the time of death at two days ago."

Yes, yes, I think. *This is even better than my plan.*

Wazhashk is silent.

"Okay, I'm going to go with the fall on the rocks when I talk to the family. I think I have the right number." He dials the phone and waits for someone to answer.

"Hello, is this Mrs. John Janne? . . . Mrs. Janne, my name is Harold Munk. I'm the head ranger in Quetico Provincial Park. Was your husband John canoeing in our park? . . . Mrs. Janne, there's been an accident involving your husband. He has suffered a fall on the rocks. . . . Yes, Mrs. Janne. He is dead. We are sorry for your loss." After a long period of silence, he says, "Please, Mrs. Janne, call your minister and family. Can you write down my number? I'm sure you will want to contact me again for more details."

"What do you say now?" Wazhashk says to me.

I'm silent. There is no happiness for me, but it would have been no different in a few months if I'd died slowly in bed, dragging the agony out for weeks.

Then Harold says to the coroner, "You're not going to mention a bear in your report, are you?"

"Yes, why wouldn't I?"

"Because it's bad for our image up here and bad for the economy. People won't come if they're concerned about running into killer bears."

"Can't you hunt her down like you usually do?"

"I don't think so. It's too late in the year, and she would most likely hibernate before we could find her. I am not sure what to do."

"Well," the coroner replies, "I'm not bound to include the possibility that the scratches on his face are from a bear attack.

I'll just note that there are other injuries.But the family will surely see and wonder what caused those scratches and wonder if they are relevant to the cause of death. "When the paperwork is done, I'll send you a copy of what the family gets."

"That's fine." Replies the ranger.

"If they do question the marks, refer them to me, and I will tell them that there's the possibility a bear was involved. I'll be honest about it. If it does get into the papers, we can always say we are hunting for the attacker."

"See, Wazhashk?" I say."They are not going to kill an innocent bear." Then I have another thought. "Do the animals also come here when they die, Wazhashk? Many believe animals go to heaven, as they don't sin."

"When I was alive, John, I was sure I was no different from the animals. But when I crossed the great river to this land, I found that I was."

"But they have brains, too. Wouldn't they also rise like us?"

"Yes, John, they do. But their brains are not like ours. They are small and poorly developed. We are aware that they are all here, but there is no communication between the species."

"So the snake I killed is here?"

"Yes, but don't bother to apologize. He won't understand you, and he is happy to be here."

"What about babies? They are human."

"Yes, they are here, but their brains are not yet fully formed, and we can only communicate with them in a limited way."

"Are there other worlds?"

"We don't know. Remember, all we know is what our brains brought with us and what others here know. John, you ask too many questions. You will discover this for yourself."

"Wazhashk, one more question. What is infinity?"

"That, John, I do not know."

"Can you see into the future?"

"No. Again, John, we only know what our brains bring with us and what we observe of those who are still living."

"Tell me again how is it that I know your language."

"You know it because you are in infinity. When you died and we met, you took it from me."

"How is it that we can speak to each other when we have no bodies, no lips to speak with?"

"The circuits that form our networks connect, and it is seamless communication."

CHAPTER TWENTY-FIVE

The Funeral

"Wazhashk, will you come with me to my funeral?"

"Yes, if you would like me to be there."

Then we are above St. Francis by the Lake Catholic Church. The first to arrive is my son with his family. He opens the back of his station wagon and removes flowers, which he carries into the church and places on the altar with other flowers that are already there. Then, returning to the car, he removes an urn.

"I'm happy they cremated my body, Wazhashk. I wouldn't want people staring at my remains. I always hated going to funerals and telling the spouses how good their partners looked when they really did not. Dead bodies do not look good. It's better to remember the deceased as you last saw them."

After carrying the urn up to the altar, my son places it on a small table in front.

There I am in the urn. The Bible was right: dust to dust. I wonder if they'll remember that I wanted my ashes spread on the shore at our lake cabin. Some of my dog, Molly's, ashes flew up in my face when I poured them into the lake she loved so much. The lake is the place that my pooch and I loved above any other. When her ashes flew up and brushed my face, it was as if she wanted to give me one last kiss. Even though they've cremated me, I think it would be nice to have a small stone on the side of the lake. I would want it to read, "This is my lake," but they won't know to do this. I never communicated this thought to anyone, so it is not to be.

My daughter's family arrives with my wife, and they all congregate in the foyer. They set up photographs and mementos on a table by the door. There are tears and hugs for my wife. When Betty hugs my son and daughter, she tells them that when we had dinner just a few weeks ago, I told her how proud I was of my family. I'm so glad I said that. It's important to me that they know and remember that. My planning did not turn out perfectly, but most of the details did. It was an accident, not suicide—or maybe not, but I think it was artfully done.

My sister and brother arrive together with their families. They all look so nice, all dressed up. After another round of tears and hugs, they stand off to the side and greet people as they arrive.

"Wazhashk, if they knew how sick I was, maybe they wouldn't be taking it this hard. Hey, down there! Cut it out. I'm glad to be gone."

Wazhashk laughs softly and says, "It's not you they cry for, John. They cry for their loss."

The people keep coming. There are relatives, neighbors, friends of the family, and oh my goodness, there are a bunch of my partners. I had not figured they would be here, but of course, they would have to come. We all went to the funerals of the founders and partners when they died.

"Wazhashk, it will be interesting to hear what they have to say about me."

"John, are you sure you want to hear it?"

"Yes, I know it's not all going to be pretty. I wish I could go down and torment them."

"It's a good thing you can't, John," Wazhashk replies. "No one went down to torment you."

"Are you sure?"

"Yes," he replies. "You can't communicate with the living."

There's the accountant, Dick, talking to the managing partner. "Before he left, he wanted me to give his secretary, Anne, a substantial raise. Should I put it through or just throw it into the wastebasket?" Dick asks.

"Wazhashk," I say, "that Dick is a dick."

Wayne, the current managing partner, replies, "Let me think about it. Terry's going to have to take over John's clients, and he's going to need all the help he can get. If Anne's expecting a raise, she won't be a happy camper. She can help him a lot. Ask me again tomorrow. Right now, I think we should give them both a raise. He did bring in a nice chunk of the firm's revenue, and we want to keep his clients happy. I think Terry and I will visit them all and assure them that we'll continue to provide the level of service they expect. You know, the typical marketing visit."

Then the Dick says, "What about his equity position? We don't have the money on hand to cash him out."

I sigh heavily and say, "Wazhashk, I wish this guy would just go home. All he cares about is money. Just wait until he gets up here. I'm going to kick his ass. He's not mourning for me; he's just going to work his calculator in the back row."

Wazhashk laughs softly and says, "You still don't get it, do you, John?"

"Yes, yes, I do. He'll have to deal with himself up here, won't he?"

Wayne says, "The buy/sell agreement gives us thirty days to cash him out, so you'd better go to the bank and get a short-term loan for what we need."

Dick replies, "I could stall his widow for a while longer than that."

"No, get the money."

Then, that Dick *does* go to the back row, and he *does* pull out his calculator.

"Settle down, John," Wazhashk says. "No point in working yourself into a twig ball."

"Twig ball?"

"Just an old Indian expression, John."

Two partners are talking in the corner. "Did you read in the paper where they think he may have encountered a bear and fell off a cliff? There was no mention of a bear in his obituary."

"I doubt it. He was so ornery, he could probably have beat up a bear."

I smile. "See, Wazhashk? They're right. I did beat that bear."

"John, you may have chased off the mother, but the cub had your number." Wazhashk laughs and laughs and then says, "The cub was about to chew your leg off."

"I'm glad you're having such a good time at my funeral, Wazhashk."

Another group of three partners talks among themselves. "Well, we won't have to put up with him in the board meetings anymore."

"Yes, I was tired of being stared down whenever he didn't agree with me. It seemed that he always had to have his way. Remember when we had the long drawn-out board meeting where we agreed to merge with the Boyer and Goldman law firm? We all thought it was a done deal, and then he and Wayne went to lunch, and it just faded away as if we never even had a meeting."

"Yeah, and he seemed to always get his way. He was a hard-ass, but you have to agree that he was right most of the time."

"Maybe, but that sarcasm was hard to take. Remember how we would all snicker when he'd walk out of meetings for a smoke and then come back smelling terrible?"

"Yeah, we all thought that would kill him soon enough. How old was he?"

"I think the paper said he turned fifty-six on the day he died. Do you remember that board meeting when he raised the issue of our mandatory retirement policy? 'Why are we still at sixty-five years old?' he wanted to know. 'We need a complete review of our policy. Sixty-five is the new fifty. Why would we push experience out the door?' I think that son of a bitch just wanted to be here forever."

"Do you think Terry can pull in as much fee as he did?"

"We'll know within a year. If he can, we'll have to make him a full partner. If he can't, we'll just go outside and steal someone." Then they approach Betty and express their sympathies and say how very much they will miss me at work.

"John, you lawyers are much like the Sioux."

It's my turn to laugh.

"Are all lawyers like that, John?

"Yes, I guess so. I'm glad we came."

Then Judy, the firm's lone female partner, comes up to my wife and daughter. "You don't know me," she says, "but I must tell you how much I'll miss John. He was the most supportive person in the firm for women's issues. I don't even think I would have made partner without his pushing me and the firm along. He was my mentor. Whenever there was a personal problem or a legal question, I would go to John first. He never let me down and always offered encouragement."

My daughter smiles as Judy walks into the church. She turns to Betty and says, "Wow, he never let on about being a supporter of women's issues, did he?"

"That was nice, John. Not all lawyers are jerks."

"I never knew Judy felt that way, Wazhashk. It just goes to show, we don't take the time to tell others how we feel."

Then Anne arrives and talks to my son and daughter. "I was your father's secretary," she says. They just nod. When Betty is free, she gives Anne a hug. Anne cries so hard she cannot speak and just moves into the church.

Terry arrives with his wife and says to Betty, "I can't tell you how sorry we are," as he gives her a hug. Then his wife and

Betty hug. They know each other, as we took them out for dinner on several occasions. Terry says, "If there's anything we can do, don't hesitate to call. I was so shocked that I had to leave work. I just wandered around downtown for hours. I still don't believe it. I've spent the last few days answering calls from all his clients. They all express their sympathy and wanted me to convey that to you."

"Wazhashk, look. Those two are judges. I never would have expected judges to come to my funeral."

They introduce themselves to Betty. "We wanted to pay our respects to John," they say. "He was a nice man and a first-class lawyer—always prepared. He made our jobs easier. We're sorry for your loss and ours."

"John, your legacy is not nearly as bad as you feared."

"Yes, Wazhashk. I'm satisfied. My life was more successful than I thought. Too bad I can't come back from the dead."

All this time, my granddaughters have been standing off to the side, talking to each other. My grandson, Joey, however is bored and running around the vestibule, but they're soon instructed to go into the church and sit down. When everyone's seated, the priest starts with the Mass. It's sad to see all my family in the front row. My wife is crying, my daughter is crying, and my granddaughters are crying. I fall silent. My son has a stiff upper lip, and my grandson seems to not know that his grandfather is in the urn up front and won't be up at the lake to play with him anymore. My partners look as if they'd rather be racking up billable hours. One is actually tweeting.

Father Jake goes on with the Mass. While I have always gone to church every Sunday with my wife and have contributed at least a few grand every year, I was not a strong Catholic. I never much liked our priests. Father Jake has a beard and is at least eighty pounds overweight. He obviously never got the word that gluttony is a sin. He has a handshake grip that would make a wrestler jealous. He seemed to love mushing people's hands to juice. The other priest, Father Lynn, was small, with a squeaky voice. His mannerisms were very much like gays I had known. I often thought they might be getting along all too well together. After reading all that crap about the Catholic Church, I was convinced more than ever those two could very well be more than comrades for Christ.

"Do you want to find out, John?" Wazhashk asks.

"Oh, no. Wazhashk, no, it's none of my business."

After several songs, the priest approaches the lectern. "Today we are gathered together to celebrate the life of John Jacob Janne. John was a regular here at Mass, and we know his wife, Betty, well from her good deeds at the church."

"What he's saying, Wazhashk, is that he never really knew me."

The priest continues, "He was a generous man who gave willingly to all the St. Francis projects. John is survived by his loving wife of thirty-four years. Theirs was a good marriage and a model for all. John and Betty met in college and married upon graduation. Their two children were raised in a loving manner and are fine citizens today. I'm told by his partners and the judges here today that John's career as a lawyer was exemplary. We may mourn John's passing today, but he is in the hands of God now. John was still a young man. He's left us all much too early. To the young here today I say, our culture is preoccupied with your youth, beauty, and success, but you will also die. Do not ignore your mortality. Death will not be denied."

"Wazhashk, *that* is a commercial."

"John, he's speaking to your grandchildren."

"Okay, maybe it's a good thing to scare them a bit."

Then my son and brother take the lectern and begin to speak, but they break down. I can't bear it and do not listen.

Finally, Father Jake says, "I would like to read a poem found in John's wallet after he died.

> "Do not stand at my grave and weep
> I am not there, I do not sleep
> I am the thousand winds that blow
> I am the diamond's glints upon the snow
> I am the sunlight on ripened grain
> I am the gentle autumn rain
> When you awaken in the morning's hush
> I am the swift uplifting rush
> Of birds in circling flight
> I am the soft star that shines at night
> So do not stand at my grave and cry."

There is a murmur in the church after the poem is read.

"Crap, I know what they're thinking. I screwed up, Wazhashk. That wasn't supposed to be found. I forgot about it in my wallet. Why did I keep the poem? I knew it by heart; I didn't need to keep it in my wallet."

"John, no one's perfect. It will not matter. At worst, they'll think it was a premonition. John, no one has mentioned suicide. No one has mentioned cancer. You are home free."

Father Jake finishes by saying, "The poem has the essence of the place where John died. He was attracted to it by his vision of the Boundary Waters, where he was going."

"Wazhashk, I love Father Jake. He took some of the speculation out of it."

When the service is over, the attendants leave again, consoling my wife on the way out. Most of them go to the dining hall in the school for lunch. My partners leave, as they're not into hot dish and sandwiches with a thin slice of ham for lunch. When all the socializing is over, my family walks to their cars and leave. The scene of the empty church and parking lot is forlorn. As I look down, I know I've been scrubbed from the face of the earth.

"John, that went well, did it not?"

"Yes. Wazhashk, do you think there is a God?"

"What do you mean, John?"

"You know, a greater being above us . . . at a higher level."

"I don't think so, but I don't know either."

"I think, Wazhashk, that there is a God, and we may be in purgatory."

"Purga . . . what?"

"Wazhashk, if you can share the knowledge of everyone here, how do you not know about purgatory?"

"I have access to this knowledge, but that doesn't mean I have to take it on. It is better to not know some things."

"Purgatory is where you go to wash away your sins before you go to heaven."

"John, I have no sins to wash away."

"None of us is without sin, Wazhashk."

"Well, John, we'll just have to wait to find out who's right."

"Maybe on the last day, the end of times, we're all raised up into heaven and see God."

"You mean the Great Spirit."

"Okay, okay, the Great Spirit."

"Are you at peace now, John?"

"Yes, I know that death is nothing to fear. Leaving a sick old body is a relief. Yes, I'm at peace, but Wazhashk, there doesn't seem to be any happiness here."

"John, everything will be fine in the end. Can we go now?"

"Yes, Wazhashk. It is time to go."

The End

"But Wazhashk. Everything is not fine, so this cannot be the end."

ACKNOWLEDGMENTS

I wish to acknowledge and express my thanks to the following:

The *Minneapolis StarTribune* and *Newsweek* magazine, which provided tidbits of religious information that I have been collecting for over twenty years.

John Casey, author of *After Lives*, and Sigurd F. Olson, author of *Listening Point*, whose books provided inspiration for the story.

To the following authors whose works provided information for the story's technical accuracy:

Robert Beymer, author of *A Paddler's Guide to Quetico Provincial Park*

W. A. Fisher Co., for maps of Quetico Provincial Park

John D. Nichols and Earl Nyholm, for *A Concise Dictionary of Minnesota Ojibwe*

To Wikipedia for providing a measure of verification of my story's religious assertions.

I also wish to acknowledge quotations from:

Karl Menninger, sociologist
Friedrich Nietzsche, philosopher
Sigurd Olson, environmentalist
Mark Twain, humorist
Plato, Greek philosopher
Cicero, Roman philosopher
Socrates, Greek philosopher
John the Baptist, preacher
Lurenzo Snow, Mormon president
William Shakespeare, author
Harold Camping, Christian radio broadcaster
Jerry Falwell, Christian televangelist
Christopher Hitchens, atheist, author
Monsignor John Tracy Ellis, Catholic historian
General Douglas MacArthur, military leader
Hal Lindsey, Christian evangelist
Benjamin Franklin, Founding Father
Richard Holloway, bishop of Edinburgh
Mary Baker Eddy, founder, Christian Science
Dalai Lama, High Lama, Tibetan Buddhism
Thomas Jefferson, Founding Father
Oliver Thomas, author, minister, and lawyer
Krisnamurti Jiddu, Indian philosopher
Izaak Walton, angler
John Henry Newman, Catholic cardinal
William Faulkner, author